Also by Ann Brashares

Sisterhood Everlasting

Sisterhood **Everlasting**

A Novel

Ann Brashares

RANDOM HOUSE ⌂ NEW YORK

Published in the United States by Random House,
an imprint of The Random House Publishing Group,
a division of Random House, Inc., New York.

RANDOM HOUSE and colophon are
registered trademarks of Random House, Inc.

Grateful acknowledgment is made to Liveright Publishing Corporation for
permission to reprint three lines from "I like my body when it is with your" by
E. E. Cummings from *Complete Poems: 1904–1962* by E. E. Cummings, edited
by George J. Firmage, copyright © 1923, 1925, 1951, 1953, 1991 by the Trustees
for the E. E. Cummings Trust, copyright © 1976 by George James Firmage. Used
by permission of Liveright Publishing Corporation.

Library of Congress Cataloging-in-Publication Data
Brashares, Ann.
Sisterhood everlasting : a novel / Ann Brashares.
p.   cm.—(Sisterhood of the traveling pants ; 6)
ISBN 978-0-385-52122-2
eBookISBN 978-0-679-60509-6
1. Female friendship—Fiction. I. Title.
PS3602.R385S57 2011
813'.6—dc22   2010043106

Printed in the United States of America
on acid-free paper

www.atrandom.com

246897531

First Edition

Book design by Elizabeth A. D. Eno

For my three amazing brothers,
Beau Brashares, Justin Brashares, and Ben Brashares, with love.
The closest thing I have to a sisterhood is a brotherhood.

If you are not too long,

      I will wait here for you

all my life.

—Oscar Wilde

Prologue

Once upon a time there were four pregnant women who met in an aerobics gym. I'm not joking; that's how this story begins. These large, fit, sweatband-sporting women bore four daughters, all born in and around the month of September. These girls started out as babies together and grew to be girls and then women. A sisterhood, if you will.

As I look back on them—on us—I realize that though we aren't related by blood, we are like four siblings. The Septembers, as we called ourselves, are governed by the laws of birth order, even though we are all basically the same age.

Lena is the oldest. She is responsible, rule-abiding, selfless whenever required, steady as a metronome, and not always a thrill a minute, to tell you the truth. She knows how to take care of you. She knows how to be an adult, and she knows how to be serious. She doesn't always know how not to be serious.

I admit that I, Carmen, am a classic youngest child—compounded by the fact that I grew up as an only child. There's no end to my self-centeredness when I get going. I can be bratty and tempestuous, but I am loyal above all. I am loyal to who we are and what we have. I am worshipful of my sisters and worshipful of our sisterhood. I am not cool: you heard it here first. I feel like a mascot sometimes—the guy in the giant-headed fuzzy animal getup at football games, melting away inside his suit. When it comes to us, I'll throw anything in.

Bee is our true middle child—free as a butterfly. She loves you, but she doesn't care what you think. She's not afraid; she's got the rest of us holding that down. She's free to compete, free to kick ass, free to fail and laugh about it. She can be reckless. She's got less to lose; it's been a long time since she had a mother. She's such a force you forget she gets injured. You'll see her stagger and realize she needs help long before she does. Your heart goes out to her. She doesn't know how to feel her own pain, but she can feel yours.

Tibby is our younger middle child, our sly observer. She's the quiet kid in the big Irish family who only wears hand-me-downs. She can be cynical, instantly judgmental, and devastating in her cleverness. She can also, as an old friend memorably put it, "change her mind." She has a gift for exposing the lies—the lies we tell other people, the lies we tell ourselves. All of this is a casing around an exquisitely sensitive heart. She doesn't turn her wit against us, almost ever. She entertains us with it, and uses it in her scripts and short films. If only anybody would produce any of them. Sometimes Tibby's wit sweetens into wisdom. I think that's what she gives us.

There was a significant epoch in our lives when we organized our friendship around a pair of pants we shared. Really, pants. We called them the Traveling Pants, and according to our mythology, they had the power to keep us together when we were apart.

Our pants were lost in Greece almost exactly ten years ago. How have we fared at keeping together since we lost them, you ask? That is a question.

Growing up is hard on a friendship. There's no revelation in that. I remember my mom once told me that a good family is built for leaving, because that is what children must do. And I've wondered many times, is that also what a good friendship is supposed to be built for? Because ours isn't. We have no idea how to cope with the leaving. And I'm probably the worst of all. If you need a picture, picture this: me putting my hands over my eyes, pretending the leaving isn't happening, waiting for us all to be together again.

Sisterhood Everlasting

To make a prairie it takes
a clover and one bee,
One clover, and a bee,
And revery.
The revery alone will do
If bees are few.

—Emily Dickinson

Once, when she was thirteen, Carmen remembered turning to Tibby with her *CosmoGirl* magazine in one hand and her eye pencil in the other and declaring that she could never, ever get sick of doing makeovers.

Well, it turned out she could. Sitting in the makeup chair in early October in a trailer parked on the corner of Bleecker Street and the Bowery in the East Village of Manhattan, getting her hair blown out for the seven millionth time by a girl named Rita and the foundation sponged onto her face for the eight millionth time by a girl named Genevieve, Carmen knew it was just another mile on the hedonic treadmill. You could get sick of anything.

It was true. She'd read an article in *Time* magazine about it. "You could even get sick of chocolate," she'd told her mother on the phone the night before.

Her mother had made a doubting sound.

"That's what I read anyway."

Being an actress on a TV show, even a moderately good and successful TV show, involved a few minutes of acting for every few hours you spent in the makeup chair. And even when you were done with the makeup—temporarily, of course; you were never done with the makeup—there was still a whole lot of sitting around drinking lattes. That was the dirty secret of the entertainment industry: it was boring.

Granted, Carmen didn't have the biggest part in the show. She was Special Investigator Lara Brennan on *Criminal Court*. She showed up at least briefly at a crime scene in almost every episode and sometimes got to appear as a witness on the stand.

"Eyes up," Genevieve said, coming in with a mascara wand. It was rare that Carmen needed a prompt. She knew exactly which way to turn her eyes for each portion of the mascara application. If she didn't stay ahead of it, Carmen feared she'd end up like one of the many dolls she'd mangled as a child with her constant brutal efforts at grooming.

Carmen studied her hair in the mirror. She'd never thought she'd get sick of that either. She squinted down the highlights. They were a little brassy, a little bright this time. She would have liked to go darker, but the director wanted her light. Probably because her character's surname was Brennan and not Garcia.

Carmen jiggled her phone in her hand and thought of who to call. She'd already spoken to Lena once and her agent twice. Her mind summoned a glimpse of Tibby's face, more out of loyalty than an expectation of actually talking to her. Since Tibby had moved to Australia with Brian almost two years before, Carmen had almost given up hope of reaching her in real time. Tibby's move had been hasty, somewhat disorganized, and just . . . far. The sixteen-hour time difference was a constant impediment. Tibby had gone from place to place at first and didn't get a landline until long after Carmen had given up on the idea. International calls between their cellphones were plagued by stupid complications, mostly on Tibby's side. In a couple of weeks. In a month. By next spring. Those were the times when Carmen told herself they'd resume regular contact. Carmen often thought of hauling over there for a visit. This past June she'd staked out a date on the calendar, and Bee and Lena had instantly agreed to the scheme. When she'd emailed Tibby about it, Tibby's return had come more quickly than usual. "Now's not a good time."

Carmen took it personally for once. "Did I do something?" she'd asked in her next message.

"Oh, Carma, no. You did nothing wrong. *Nothing.* Just busy and unsettled here. It'll be soon. I promise. I want to see you and Len and Bee more than anything else in the world."

And there was Bee. Carmen hadn't seen her since Bridget's last swing through New York over the Christmas holidays, but there were long periods when Bridget and Carmen talked every day—that is, as long as Bee hadn't lost her phone or neglected to pay her bill for too long. Bee was the best possible distraction from an hour in the makeup chair. But Carmen hesitated to call her now. It had been awkward between them for the last few weeks, since Bee had effectively called Jones an asshole.

Well, to be fair, Bee hadn't just come out and said "Your fiancé is an asshole." In fact, to be fair, it was Carmen who'd called him an asshole and Bee who'd lost no time in agreeing with her. But Carmen was *allowed* to say Jones was an asshole. She was the one marrying the asshole.

Carmen's phone rang, saving her the trouble of dialing anyone, and she snapped it up. The earphones were already stuck in her ears. She was one of the few people she knew who answered the phone *as* she checked the caller ID, not after.

"Hey, babe."

"Hey, Jones."

"In the chair still?"

"Yep." Jones was in the business, so he knew how it went. Besides, he'd called her half an hour before.

"How late are you shooting tonight?"

"Till around seven, Steven said."

"If you can, cut out a little early and come directly to the Mandarin, all right? It's the pre-party before the big Haiti benefit. It's important for you to at least show."

"It won't make a difference to Haiti if I don't get there in time for the pre-party." It was one of three benefits they had on the calendar that week.

"It's not about Haiti," Jones said, as though she were being dense. "It's about the Shaws. They invited us, and I don't want to stiff them. She's probably going to be head of production by next year. We'll be out of there by eight. Nobody's going to stay for the whole thing."

"Oh. Of course." Cynical though she was, Carmen never remembered to be quite cynical enough. Why would she think the Haiti benefit was about Haiti and not about the Shaws? Why would she think the gala was about the gala and not about the party before the gala? If not for Jones, she could have been one of the boobs who thought it was about Haiti and stayed for the whole thing.

It was endlessly tricky being in the know. It was a state Carmen had achieved with a certain bravado, but she found it difficult to maintain. Without Jones, she could easily slip out of the know, relapse into her natural eagerness, and probably never get hired for another part in her life.

"It's a game and you play it," he often told her when she felt discouraged or repulsed. "If you want to succeed in this business, it's what you do. Otherwise, you gotta pick a different business." He was thirty-nine years old to her twenty-nine. He'd been doing it for sixteen years, he always reminded her. But he didn't need to tell her. Whether or not she liked it, she was perfectly good at playing the game when she chose to.

"I'll try to be there before seven," she said.

Carmen felt vaguely dissatisfied as she ended the call. It wasn't that Jones didn't care about charities. He did. Every month he put five percent of his earnings into a charitable fund. You couldn't fault him for that.

"Was that your boyfriend again?" Rita asked.

Carmen nodded distractedly. Sometimes it was hard to know what you could fault him for.

"He's an executive at ABC, isn't he?"

She nodded again. Everybody in this business was looking for another contact.

"Lucky you," Rita said.

"Yes," she said. And not just because he was her boyfriend, but because he was her fiancé. If she was lucky, then she was extra lucky.

And what if she wasn't lucky? Then what was she?

Lena put her feet up on her desk. The pink polish her sister, Effie, had applied to her toenails during her last visit had long since started to chip. Lena balanced a sketchbook on her knees and began to flip through it.

She'd promised herself she'd clear out her apartment today. She was committed to filling a couple of trash bags with stuff—her place was too tiny to store anything extra—but of her twenty-seven sketchbooks, she hadn't yet been able to throw away even one. This one, for instance, was an old one. On the first page was a pencil sketch of Mimi, Tibby's old guinea pig, fat and asleep in her shavings. As long ago as it was, Lena vividly remembered the joyful chaos of pencil lines that had gone into sketching those shavings. There was a drawing of Bridget at sixteen, knees up on the couch, watching TV with a tipping sombrero on her head. It must have been a week or two after she'd gotten back from her soccer camp in Mexico. It was a loose pencil sketch, and Lena smiled at the hatching lines she'd used to represent the suntan on Bee's cheeks. Every few pages was one of the inescapable drawings of Lena's feet. There was a half-finished sketch of grumpy morning Effie at fifteen, too grumpy to let Lena finish it. There were three studies of Carmen's hand from when she still wore a mood ring and bit her fingernails. How could you throw this away?

The later sketchbooks would be easier, Lena decided. They were mainly just feet and dated from about two years earlier, when Lena had mostly petered out on drawing. Instead, these last couple of years she had been putting her energies into her paintings, which were composed, formal, and largely abstract. You weren't going to build a career out of making messy little sketches of your friends and family and your feet.

Why all the drawings of her feet? They were not her best feature, probably her worst. They were size nine and a half, ten in some shoes, and prone to sweating when she was excited or nervous. Her toes were kind of long, especially the second and third—the Home and the Roast Beef, as Tibby's mother would call them. The only advantages her feet had going for them as subjects was that they were attached to the bottoms of her legs and at enough distance that she could look at them from different angles. They were living and stayed still when she told them to, and they didn't charge modeling fees. She imagined the far future if anybody ever cared enough to look back at her drawings. *This girl really had a thing for her feet,* they would think. Maybe she would throw those last two sketchbooks away.

The phone on her desk rang. She plucked it from its cradle without moving her sketchbook. She didn't have caller ID (it added $6.80 a month to her plan), but she knew it was almost certainly one of three people: her mother, her sister, or Carmen. Whichever one it was, she was on her cellphone, she was in a hurry, and she was calling to "check in."

Lena cleared her throat before she hit the talk button. It wasn't a teaching day, so she hadn't spoken to anyone yet, and it was already three o'clock. She hated getting busted for that.

"Hey, Lenny, it's me. Were you sleeping?"

Damn. "No. Just . . ." Lena heard an ambulance and a lot of honking through the phone. "Where are you?"

"On Greenwich Ave. I just got a facial. I look scary."

It was either Carmen or Effie; still too noisy to tell which. Lena held the phone between her shoulder and her ear and went back to flipping pages. "What are you doing tonight?"

Three of many words were intelligible: "theater" and "benefit" and "Jones." It was Carmen.

"Great." Lena couldn't pick which of those words summoned the worst thing.

"Jones bought a table."

Yes, she could pick. The worst was "Jones."

"I would have invited you, but you wouldn't have come."

"That's true."

"And you are . . . staying home and watching a movie with Drew."

"Yes." Sometimes Carmen made it easy for her.

"That's just sad."

But never that easy.

"No, it's not sad. It's what I like to do. Anyway, we can't all be rich and glamorous."

"Len, I'm not demanding glamour. You're just not allowed to be that boring."

Lena laughed. "Hey, did you do the kissing scene yet with the renegade cop?"

"No, that's Friday. He has terrible breath." Carmen's voice was swallowed by what Lena guessed was a bus plowing by.

"Can you come to New York next weekend?" Carmen's voice was asking when it came back.

"So you and Effie can take turns biting at my flesh until I'm dead?"

"Oh, please. Len. It wasn't that bad last time."

"How about the drunk DA who asked if he could give me a sponge bath?"

"Okay. I promise I won't drag you to any dinner parties or introduce you to any men this time."

"Anyway, I can't. I'm teaching Saturday morning and I've got a painting to finish." Lena was genuinely looking forward to a quiet weekend in the studio.

"You haven't been here since Labor Day. You used to come all the time. What happened?"

What happened? That was a good question. And it wasn't just the slobbering DA to blame. She'd gone all the time when Bee, Carmen, and Tibby all lived in a pile on Avenue C. She had gone every weekend. But that was a long time ago—more than three and a half years ago. Before they'd lost the lease, before Tibby had moved in with Brian and subsequently moved to the other side of the world, before Bee had moved to California, before Carmen had gotten semi-famous and taken up with the infernal Jones. Before her little sister, Effie, had moved to New York in a blur of open bars, pedicures, and sample sales, chewing up Manhattan from one end to the other. New York felt different now.

"I won't make you do anything," Carmen promised. "You don't have to buy, wear, or say anything. I can't speak for Effie, star journalist, but I will leave you to wander around the Met for two days if that's what you want. Anyway, Jones is gonna be out of town."

That made it slightly more tempting.

"You'll let me know," Carmen said, stealing the words from her mouth.

Lena thought of something. "Hey, Carma?"

"Uh-huh?"

"Did Tibby text you about something coming in the mail?"

Carmen must have ducked into a store or a lobby, because it was suddenly quiet. "Yes. Weird, huh. You didn't get anything yet, did you?"

"No." Lena hadn't checked her mail slot yet today. She made a note to do that, with some combination of excitement and speculative concern. They heard from Tibby little enough that they circulated the news quickly when they did.

"Nothing good ever comes in the mail," Carmen opined.

Carmen was so attached to her iPhone she might have had it sewn into her skin if iSurgery were offered at the Apple store. She didn't trust information that came any other way. But Lena liked the mail. She was talented at waiting.

Carmen's phone started beeping. It always did that eventually. "My manager," Carmen said. Her voice was once again immersed in street noise. "Talk to you. Love you."

"Bye."

Lena had less than ten minutes of peace before her phone rang again. This time it was her mother from the car. She could always tell that particular connection.

"Hi, sweet. Just checking in."

"Okay." At least her voice was broken in now.

"How are things?" Her mom sounded relaxed, which meant she probably hadn't talked to Effie yet. She usually called her two daughters in a row, and Lena and Effie agreed, it was always better to get the first call. Her mom was a worrier. After she talked to Effie, she was tight with concern about all the parties and the credit card debt and the crazy goings-on. After she talked to Lena, she was tight with concern about the absence of parties and credit card debt and crazy goings-on. Lena insisted that her mom worried about Effie more, but Effie insisted that no, it was definitely Lena.

"She'll die in her bed alone or with cats" was Effie's cheerful summary when anyone asked about Lena. But then, Effie's idea of a quiet night was getting home from the clubs at three instead of five.

"How'd you sleep?"

Her mom always asked that, however near or far from sleep Lena might have been. "Fine." That was how she always answered, however well or unwell she'd slept.

"Did you have lunch?"

Lena glanced up at the clock. Should she have? "Yes."

"What did you eat?"

"Mom. Why do you need to know that?" It was as though her mother believed if she stopped asking, Lena would stop eating. If she stopped calling, Lena would stop talking. If she stopped bothering her, Lena would cease to be. It wasn't enough she had given Lena life at the beginning. Her mom seemed to feel the need to do it every day.

"I don't. I was just asking."

She loved her mother and depended on her mother, and yet every single word her mother said annoyed her.

"A turkey sandwich. How's Dad?"

"Fine. I talked to Ariadne about the painting. She says forty by forty-eight would work, but do you have anything with more blue?"

"With more blue?"

"She's redecorating. She bought a new couch."

"Seriously, Mom. More blue?"

"I'm just passing along what she said."

"I don't have any other landscapes that size. I have figures, but they aren't blue."

"Lena, don't sound mad. She wants to support you."

Lena knew that. And she could have used the sale. If she didn't want her mom pimping her paintings to suburban friends with blue sofas, she'd have to submit to showing her paintings in the normal way. Two times she'd been given spots in group shows, once in Providence and once in Boston. Both times she'd sold her paintings and gotten unambiguously positive write-ups in the local press, and both times she'd gotten an outbreak of cold sores so bad she could barely eat for days. When the dealer called to read her the review in the *Herald,* her feet sweated straight through her socks. Even good things could be traumas to her.

"Well, who knows. Maybe the muse will come." Her mom wanted to wrap it up without an argument. Lena heard her turn off the car.

"The muse doesn't get to pick the color."

"I've got to go, darling. I'll call you tomorrow."

Lena hung up and glared at her feet. The next time the phone rang, she wouldn't answer. She would let it ring itself out. She would be like Bee and lose her phone, maybe even stop paying the bills until the phone company turned off her service. Then she could enjoy a little quiet and not have to invent turkey sandwiches or defend her way of being.

But the phone began to ring less than an hour later and she didn't let it go. *What if it's Tibby?* She knew it wasn't, but she couldn't suppress the thought. When was the last time Tibby had called her? When was the last time Tibby had even responded to an email? But she thought of Tibby's recent text and she couldn't let the phone go past the second ring, even though it was obviously not Tibby, but rather Effie, or possibly Carmen telling her what movie she should rent tonight.

In some way she didn't like to admit, Lena was always waiting for a call. Not from the people who were always calling, but from the ones who never did.

"Bridget, what are you doing?"

Bridget looked up. Eric was mostly blotted out by the setting sun as he strode up the walk, pulling his tie loose and his collar apart as he always did in the final stretch of his way home from work.

She stood and kissed him on the lips. "We don't really need this anymore."

"That's my nightstand."

"You can just pile the books on the floor, can't you?"

Bridget was carefully laying clothes on top of the nightstand before she carried the whole setup from the front steps to the sidewalk.

"But I like having a nightstand."

"I need to move the plants in from the kitchen, because they aren't getting near enough light in there. The leaves are turning yellow. Our bedroom has the best light. It's like the plant ICU."

"I can't rest my coffee cup on a plant."

"You can rest it on the floor," Bridget said reasonably as she hobbled to the sidewalk with the nightstand. "It's not like we have a real bed. The nightstand looks weird with just the mattress on the floor."

Eric was shaking his head, but he didn't look mad. Not really. "Bridget, I'll be lucky if you don't leave me on the sidewalk to be carried away."

"You won't be carried away," she assured him.

The truth was she was always looking for things to put out on the curb. There was a large community of homeless people who convened in Dolores Park, and she'd gotten to be kind of friendly with them. She didn't like to give handouts, but she was happy to leave things that might be useful, or things they could sell at the Mission flea market. Twice she'd actually bought her own possessions back by accident.

Eric jokingly accused her of wanting to be homeless herself, and she did frankly romanticize a life of sleeping under the stars. "I'd probably rather be a cowboy or an explorer," she told him. Maybe she'd been born in the wrong era.

"What's for dinner?" he asked her cheerfully, following her up the stairs to their second-floor apartment.

"I don't know. What do you feel like? Maybe Pancho's?" She could tell he was hoping she'd made something, or shopped for something to make. She should've. She hadn't worked today. She was still temping and she hadn't gotten called in a week.

What had she done? She'd spent the first part of the day searching the apartment for things to give away or throw away. She'd spent the middle part of the day waiting in the express mail line at the post office to send Lena and Carmen each a package of authentic corn tortillas she'd bought from a Mexican lady with a cart on Sixteenth Street, spending five times as much on the postage as she'd spent on the tortillas. (She'd gotten some for Tibby too, even knowing that she didn't have Tibby's current address and that Australia was too far to send something that would spoil.) She'd spent the last part of the day realizing she'd been a bit too zealous in throwing stuff out and searching for her cellphone in the garbage cans out back. She'd called herself from her neighbor's landline about ten times, listening for the trash to ring.

"We had Pancho's last night."

"We did? That was last night?"

"Yes, it was. Do we have any eggs? I could make an omelet," he offered.

She checked the refrigerator. "We have five."

"That'll do."

"And I got some handmade corn tortillas."

"Perfect."

"We could eat outside," she suggested as she began assembling ingredients. They shared a tiny backyard with the two other tenants. It consisted of recycling bins, a plastic table, two chairs, and a gorgeous Meyer lemon tree.

He went into their tiny bedroom to change into jeans and a T-shirt.

"How was work?" she asked through the open door.

"Good. I got a new case."

"Immigration?"

"Yes. Has to do with a second grader named Javier. A great kid."

Eric always had a huge load of cases, and half the time he ended up doing it for almost no pay. His mother was from Mulegé, so Eric spoke Spanish like a proper Mexican. Half the cases came with stories that could break your heart, and Eric never turned down any of them. People from his graduating class at NYU Law worked at fancy firms making twice the money, pushing paper for big corporations, but Eric never wanted that. "My heart wouldn't be in it," he said.

She looked up as he came out of the bedroom in his oldest jeans and an Amnesty International T-shirt. It was the same thing almost every time Eric came home from someplace or even just walked back into the room where she was. She felt something, some little clap inside her head like a distant echo of the thunderous knock she had felt when she'd seen him the first time at soccer camp just before she turned sixteen. It wasn't always entirely comfortable.

"What you two have, that's called *chemistry*," a nutty drunk in the park named Burnt Sienna had told her once.

"I tried to call you a bunch of times today," Eric said. "Did you get any of my messages?"

"I . . . um . . . no. I didn't have my phone with me." She didn't want to say her phone was likely in one of the garbage cans out back.

Eric got a certain look, somewhere between impatience and amusement, when she misplaced her phone again, or gave away large portions of their belongings, or spent the afternoon fishing in the bay with a homeless man named Nemo, as she had done the day before. "Nobody could accuse you of being boring" was what he often said when he got that look. And frankly, having somebody like Bridget around was what Eric needed, because he was prone to habits and ruts and he knew it. Who else got him out to street festivals, free concerts, bike-a-thons, and community gardening projects? Who else got him to try surfing and jujitsu and the leggy, oily creatures they served at the restaurants in deepest Chinatown?

"You didn't lose your phone again, did you?"

"Uh. I don't think so." She started flipping through the free newspaper she'd picked up at the BART station.

He gave her that look. "Bridget, if you don't want the phone, it would be cheaper just to cancel the service. That way Carmen and Greta and Perry and your dad and I and whoever else wouldn't have to leave all those messages for you that you never pick up. You'd save us the trouble."

"That's true. Hey, look," she said, pointing to an ad in the paper. "There's a one-bedroom on Guerrero for $1,850 a month. That's pretty good."

"I like this place. I don't want to move again. We've moved four times in the last year and a half."

"I like Guerrero. I bet it's a fifth-floor walk-up, but I don't really mind that if it's high enough to get a lot of sun. I wonder what cross street."

She spent her life following the sun, seeking the brightest apartment in San Francisco. She didn't really care about any other feature. There was always a sunnier place than the one she had, a better spot for the plants, which accounted for a lot of the moving. When she'd found this place, she'd actually pounced on it while Eric was at work, and he'd come home to an empty apartment because she'd forgotten to tell him they'd moved. "We don't live here anymore," she'd told him when she'd finally discovered him, bewildered, in the bare bedroom.

She'd thought this place would be the answer. But it turned out the kitchen wasn't really very sunny at all.

Eric started cracking eggs. He got egg white on his jeans. *He is very handsome,* Bridget thought. He loved her in spite of herself, and that seemed like a lucky thing.

"I was calling you because I had an hour free at lunch and I wanted to take you to that little shop behind Union Square to get you a dress for Anna's wedding."

"Oh, right." His cousin Anna was getting married in Petaluma the following weekend, and he was excited about it. Eric thought weddings were romantic, and they gave him the opportunity to bring up the topic of marriage. Bridget got a certain look, somewhere between anticipation and fear, when Eric started talking about getting engaged. "I don't need a new dress. I can get Carmen to send me one of her leftovers."

"Carmen is four inches shorter than you are and her clothes are totally wrong for you. Remember that weird black stretchy thing with the feathers?"

Bridget laughed. "That didn't look great on me. I admit."

He came over and put his arms around her and kissed the side of her neck. "You are going to be the most beautiful woman at that thing. I want you to wear your hair down. I want to show you off. Let me be shallow once in a while, will you?"

Bridget wasn't so sure she wanted to be the most beautiful woman at that thing. There was the bride to consider, first of all. And besides, she didn't have much to prove in that way. She knew she was put together well. She had always known that. She had the attributes that people thought they wanted: blue eyes, long legs, a graceful neck, genuine yellow hair. She'd thought her hair would fade a bit as she got older, but it hadn't. It was her mother's hair, her grandmother's hair, her bittersweet birthright; she wouldn't get rid of it that easily.

Bridget didn't suffer from those ailments that picked at you over a lifetime, like allergies or acne, dandruff or a sore back, floaters in your eyes or lust for food that made you fat. She went straight to the hard-core stuff, the rough waves in the gene pool, like the depression so severe it had taken her mother's life. Sometimes she felt that the outside of her gave a very incomplete account of the inside of her.

She knew she should do a better job of strutting her stuff once in a while for Eric's sake. She certainly did take pleasure in the way he looked. But she hadn't accumulated much in the way of clothes and makeup. She couldn't really afford it. Eric thought her disinterest resulted from a puzzling lack of confidence, but it wasn't that. She knew how she was.

Eric cocked his head and walked to the back window. "Do you hear that?"

"No. What?" Eric had weirdly good ears.

"It sounds like a phone ringing. It sounds like your ring."

Bridget went over and craned her neck out the window. It sounded like her phone, all right. "I had a feeling it might be down there," she said.

With his weirdly good ears, Eric followed the sound down the stairs and out the back door to the large square plastic trash bin. She heard his laughter rising to the back window. "God, Bee, have I been calling the garbage all day?"

A whole stack of memories
never equals
one little hope.

—Charles M. Schulz

"Big surprise," Jones told Carmen when she walked into their loft two nights later. "I got your dad a room—a nice room, an upgrade—at the SoHo Grand for this weekend."

Jones still had his jacket and tie on, which indicated to her he'd made a reservation at either a good or a trendy restaurant, where she would be able to eat barely anything, because she'd eaten a sandwich for lunch and hadn't had time to go to the gym. You didn't stay a size 0 by eating lunch *and* dinner, not if you had an ass like hers.

Carmen hung up her jacket and checked the mail. Jones was talking to her from his seat in front of the giant glow of their living room computer.

"But I told him he could stay here," she said.

"Of course he can stay here. But you gotta admit it's a lot cooler to stay there."

Her dad came to visit her in New York from his home in Charleston every few months since his wife, Lydia, had died, whereas Jones's parents tended to stay put in Fresno, where he liked them. Her and Jones's loft wasn't the SoHo Grand, maybe, but it was pretty nice. A lot nicer than any of her friends had.

"I'll ask him," she said.

"I already asked him. He's into it."

"You talked to him?"

"Yeah, he called here about an hour ago."

Carmen sighed. Would her father never learn to call her on her cellphone? "All right."

"You gotta love that bar. Maybe he'll meet a girl."

"Jones."

He smiled and she couldn't help smiling back. His conciliatory smile was always pretty winning.

She watched him clickety-clacking on the keyboard. She considered how the light gathered on his bald head, which he shaved as assiduously as she followed any of her beauty regimens. He said it was the only way he liked it. Jones was all about choosing, but she also knew that certain patches of his scalp were going to stay bald whether he liked them to or not. It was amazing, really, the effort that went into the absence of things.

"Is this all the mail?" she asked.

"I think so. Why?"

"Tibby said she was sending something."

"Tibby?"

"Tibby."

"You hardly ever talk about Tibby anymore."

"That's not true. I talk about her. I just don't talk *to* her." That was why Carmen had been ecstatic to see a text come in under Tibby's name and why she was impatient to get home to the mail.

Jones finished whatever he was doing at the computer and came over to her and kissed her shoulder. "Put on something gorgeous, gorgeous. I'm taking you out."

"Where?"

"Minetta Tavern."

"No way." She loved that place. Damn. How could she not eat?

She started thinking her way through her large closet. The new Gucci? The pink Stella McCartney from last year? She wouldn't need to spend much time on her hair and makeup, having already spent most of the day on it. Maybe the little Catherine Malandrino dress that Jones loved? She'd definitely end up having sex tonight if she wore that one. "What's the occasion?" she asked.

He kissed her ear. "I've got a gorgeous woman, who's going to be my bride."

She laughed. "You have that every night."

"That's why I want to celebrate."

"I guess turkey would be good."

Lena leaned her elbows on the counter and watched Drew's back as he sliced the turkey, slowly transforming the edge of poultry-blob into a fringed and delicate pile. He kept going until the pile was absurdly tall and then flipped it onto a piece of whole wheat bread. One of the good things you could say about his job was that he got free sandwiches.

"Lettuce, tomato, peppers, mustard, no mayo," he recited, turning his head to check with her.

"Yes, please." She considered his brown shirt with the hood. It seemed like everything he wore had a hood. Sometimes he had on as many as three hoods, when he wore a hooded shirt with a hooded sweatshirt and his hooded parka.

He expertly cut her sandwich in two, placed it on a deli paper plate with a ruffled edge, and put it on the counter in front of her. He added half a pickle.

"Thanks," she said.

She stood and ate at the counter to keep him company, as she usually did. She was used to their conversations being punctuated by customers ordering sandwiches and she didn't mind. If anything, it facilitated them.

She watched him as he made a complicated wrap involving some kind of cheese she'd never heard of. She watched him and chewed her sandwich and wondered whether he was the sort of person—or even the actual person—she might marry. Maybe it was because of Tibby, whom she had not seen in almost two years, and the mysterious thing coming in the mail, which got her thinking about time and the changes it brought or was supposed to bring. She would be thirty years old on her next birthday. All four of them would turn thirty in and around next September. Somehow the fact of their doing it together made her feel less accountable to it.

Though Carmen claimed she was engaged (maybe it was Lena's wishful self, but she didn't totally believe it), none of them was married. When Lena had mentioned this fact to her mother's friend Maria Cantos, Maria had said, "Well, who are you waiting for?"

Thinking about it after, Lena wasn't sure whether Maria meant were they waiting for the guy to come along? Or were the four of them waiting for one another?

Drew was growing a beard. Lena could tell it was important to him by how often he touched it. It was kind of patchy, and fairer than the light brown hair on his head, so that even the parts that did grow blended into his face. He'd been growing it since the beginning of the semester and hadn't made much progress. It seemed hopeless to her, but she tried not to judge. She'd grown up mostly among Greek men who could grow a full beard by bedtime but never did—who in fact shaved twice a day.

"Do you want to watch something after you close up here?" she asked between bites.

"Sure." He wiped the counter down.

"A movie? Or an episode of *The Wire*?"

"Either one." He wasn't just saying that; he meant it. He was possibly the only person in her life who wasn't opinionated or stubborn.

"Maybe *The Wire*," she said.

He liked her to pick, because he said he could never tell, even while they were watching, which ones she hated and which ones she loved. And it was true she experienced even the strongest pleasures and poignancies down pretty deep. They tended not to make it all the way up to her face.

Lena finished her sandwich and sat at a table to wait while the rest of the customers made their way out. She rested her chin in her hand as she watched Drew put away the food, lock up the kitchen, turn off the lights.

"Ready?" he asked.

She followed him out of the shop and watched him pull down the noisy metal gate and lock it with a key. As they walked he didn't reach out to put his arm around her shoulder or grab her hand, and she didn't expect him to. They walked side by side along the dark sidewalk. Companionable as they were, she felt as though the night air encapsulated each of them separately.

A few months before, Effie had declared, having already broken two engagements (and sold two rings on eBay), that if you were almost thirty years old you should *not* be in a relationship with a guy you didn't at least *think* you could marry. Lena wasn't sure Drew met that qualification. No, if she was honest, she did know. Drew was considerate and smart. His eyes were a lovely pale blue and he liked most of the things she liked. But she wasn't going to marry him. She knew that, and it didn't put her in any hurry to break up with him. Truthfully, it was kind of a relief not to have to be spinning into the marriage vortex.

Lena was content walking beside him, but she knew there was more. Drew might not know that, but she did.

She'd fallen in love with a Greek boy the summer she'd turned sixteen, when she'd gone to stay with her grandparents on the island of Santorini. Kostos was the pride of the village, grandson of her grandparents' dearest friends. He'd broken Lena's heart by mail at seventeen, and later she discovered he'd gotten married to a girl he'd knocked up from his village. Two summers later he'd come to the United States to find her, and she'd angrily sent him away.

The last time Lena had seen him was at nineteen, when she and Tibby and Carmen and Bee had returned to Santorini together in search of their lost pair of pants. Kostos had explained a few important things that last night: there wasn't a baby, there had never been a baby, the girl had manipulated him, his marriage had been annulled. He hadn't stopped loving Lena, he said. He said they'd be together, not now but *someday*. He said the word in Greek, whispered it in her ear, where it had stuck.

When Lena was almost twenty-two, the day after she graduated from RISD, Kostos had sent her a long letter, seemingly out of the blue, asking her to come back to Santorini to spend the summer with him. No pressure, he'd said.

He might as well have sent her the Ebola virus tucked in with the letter. She'd been racked with desire, misery, uncertainty. She said yes. Her agitation grew. She bought a plane ticket to Fira, set to arrive on July 4. She called her grandmother and made arrangements to stay.

As the days passed she became too nervous to sleep. Her stomach and intestines teamed up against her and stopped digesting properly. Once, in the middle of the night, she went to the emergency room with terrible pains in her chest, fearing her heart had turned against her too.

On July 3 of that year, the morning of the night she was supposed to fly to meet him, she'd canceled the trip. By email. "Now isn't the right time," she'd said, and made some excuses that felt cowardly to her even as she typed them. Kostos didn't write back for two long days. He didn't try to talk her out of it. He was disappointed, he said, but he'd figure out a way to get over it. Instead of flying off to Greece, she spent another summer in the studio in Providence.

She didn't see him or talk to him after that. Six years passed without a word between them. But while her life ambled along quietly, his did not. She first became aware of this by means of a newspaper clipping stuck to her easel by a so-called friend from her first year in graduate school. It was from *The Wall Street Journal,* and it declared Kostos Dounas to be the youngest managing partner in the history of his bank. At the top there was a line drawing of Kostos looking groomed and serious. The article went on to trumpet the multibillion-dollar deal he'd negotiated between one gigantic conglomerate and another. Lena had stared at that sketch, but she couldn't see her old Kostos anywhere in it. Because the portrait was stiff and artless, for one thing, but also because she had the strange sense that he was rocketing irrevocably from her world into a different one.

That sense only increased over the next few years. She didn't make a habit of reading business journals, but his name and picture found her anyway. She couldn't avoid it. He'd been named one of *Time* magazine's most influential people under thirty-five. Nobody from Santorini could help bragging about him, including her grandmother. Even her father rhapsodized about him occasionally, failing to pick up on the sharp looks from his wife. Once Lena saw Kostos's face on the cover of *The Economist* as she passed a newsstand at the train station.

I doubt he's thought of me, she found herself musing with uncharacteristic self-pity as Kostos stared at her from the magazine cover as if she were any other passerby.

Kostos had said "Someday" to her, but the notion seemed preposterous to her now. He was so far beyond the scope of her small, quiet life; he occupied an alternate universe that intersected nowhere with hers. He no longer represented *someday*, a possibility. He represented a road not taken, a road that suddenly shot so far into the distance she couldn't see where it went anymore.

Did she regret her decision? She asked herself that question once in a while. What if she'd gotten on that plane? What if she'd gone to Greece that summer, as he'd wanted her to? Would a life with him have suited her?

Probably not, she decided. The force of her feelings, the fear for her heart, might have overwhelmed her. She liked the life she had. She loved habits. She craved a day with nothing in it, a long, quiet stretch of hours in the studio.

And in that quiet, her life as a painter had flourished. Her gifts as a teacher had blossomed. She was the only graduate student who'd been offered a salaried teaching job at RISD upon finishing her master's degree. Now there was a waiting list among undergraduates to get into her class. She was proud of that. Could she have achieved any of it standing by the side of the mighty, world-conquering Kostos?

When her grandmother Valia had died the January before last at the age of ninety-two, Kostos had sent her a beautiful letter of condolence. Regardless of how alien the Kostos of the magazines appeared, those words came from the person she had loved. To say that the letter touched her didn't come close to capturing the ache of it.

She'd carried Kostos's letter around with her for two weeks. It had taken her four drafts to write him back. She'd lavished hours on the response. She'd written and crossed out and written and crossed out, done and undone, so that by the end it hadn't said much of anything at all. The intensity of feeling summoned by that letter exhausted her.

And yet. A life spent with Kostos would have been something, wouldn't it? She'd never felt about anyone the way she'd felt about him. Not even close. She knew that when she got old it would be more fun to look back on a life of romance and adventure than a life of quiet habits. But looking back was easy. It was the doing that was painful. There were plenty of things she would like to look back on but wasn't willing to risk: hang gliding, cave diving, ecstasy.

She and Drew stopped to pick up a pint of Ben & Jerry's from the Foodmart on the way back to her apartment. She liked the kind with the cookie dough in it, and so did he.

Lena and Drew were waiting for the elevator in the lobby of her building twenty minutes later when she thought of something. "I'm going to check my mailbox," she said. He let the elevator come and go without complaint as she fished around for her key and opened the slot. There was the regular junk and a thick yellow envelope from Tibby. She ripped it open with a tingle of excitement, both welcome and not.

She drifted back toward the elevator as she pulled out the contents. The first page was so unexpected it took her a long time to figure out what it was. Tibby's handwriting, messier than usual, was scrawled along the bottom. "Here's an insane idea," she'd written. "Please say you can do it."

It seemed to be a receipt for an eticket in Lena's name, for a round-trip flight from New York. It had cost $603 and had been paid for with Tibby's credit card. The departure date was October 28, less than four weeks away, and the return date was six days later.

The page behind was a similar ticket for Carmen and the one behind that for Bee, in her case departing from and returning to San Francisco.

"I'll be there a day early and will be waiting for you at the airport," Tibby had written at the bottom of the last page. Under that: "Lena, email me when you get this!" And under that: "Please, you three, say you will come!"

The most shocking thing was the destination: Fira, the principal city of Santorini.

If there was one thing Bridget was good at, it was riding her bike uphill. That was what she was thinking as she conquered the hill at Duboce and Divisadero by the late-afternoon light.

Besides some pictures and a few keepsakes from her friends, the one possession that really meant something to Bridget was her bike. It was sturdy, old-fashioned in style but modern in function. Eric had gotten it for her twenty-fifth birthday, and she'd spent the next four years tricking it out. She wasn't very artistic, but she'd decorated it with bright enamel paints and silk flowers. It was the one thing, besides a duffel bag of clothes, she'd brought with her to California.

She was known throughout the Mission and the Castro as the blond girl with flowers on her bike. She felt some pride when she overheard neighbors or shopkeepers talking about her. "There is no hill in this town that girl can't bike to the top of."

In the old days, in high school and college, her physical accomplishments had been obvious and easily recognized. She scored the most goals, had the most assists, ran the fastest dash, did the most push-ups. She operated in the safe and structured universe of a high-level soccer team, where even when you did badly it was still a game. That was what she was thinking about as she glided down alongside Dolores Park and turned in to her street without using her brakes.

The problem with that universe was that it ended, and then it extruded you into the chaos of a post-team existence. That chaos appeared to be ruled by people who were good at talking and liked to stay inside. Bridget found herself seeking little ways to measure herself that gave her even a faint feeling of how it used to be. Like the hills.

As she coasted down her street she saw Eric waiting on the front steps. It was unusual for him to get home before her.

He stood up to kiss her and held out a letter.

"For me?" she said, kissing him an extra time.

"Yes," he said. "It's from Tibby."

"Really? No way." She flipped it over excitedly and looked at the return address.

"When was the last time you heard from Tibby?"

Bridget shook her head. "A while." She considered. "On her birthday I emailed her a picture I found of her in her Wallman's smock and she wrote back a few lines." She turned the envelope over again. "Why did she send it to me care of you at your office?"

"Maybe because she knows we have no fixed address."

"Yes, we do," Bridget said, suddenly nervous as she tore it open. "It just changes a lot." She scanned the pages. "Whoa."

"What is it?"

"It's a plane ticket."

"For who?"

"For me. Hold on." She slowed down, taking in each of the parts, and Tibby's scribbled message at the bottom. "Oh, my God. She bought each of us a ticket to Greece. She planned a trip for us." Bridget felt tears fill her eyes and bend the words on the paper. "Can you believe that?"

"Wow. That's a big deal. To Lena's family's place? When?"

"Twenty-eighth of October. I can't believe this." She felt herself bouncing on her feet.

"For how long?"

"Just about a week. I guess it's a reunion."

Eric saw her tears and her uncensored joy. "That's great, Bee. I'm happy for you. I'll miss you, but I'm happy."

She nodded. God, how unexpected this was. The answer to a wish she hadn't let herself articulate in a long time. "I think this is what we really, really need."

Suddenly her legs took root,
and her arms grew into
long and slender branches.
Apollo reached the laurel tree,
and,
still enamored with Daphne,
held the tree in
a special place in his heart.

—*Encyclopedia Mythica*

On Friday night, after she finished work, Carmen went directly to the SoHo Grand to meet her father. It was a forbidding lobby, all right angles, muted surfaces, and minimal cheer. She was a successful actress in New York with a big loft in Nolita, a closetful of enviable clothes, a boyfriend—make that fiancé—who was a network executive. This was her world, and even she felt constrained by the coolness.

"Albert Lowell," she said to the brittle, long-nailed woman at the front desk. "Can you tell him Carmen is here?"

The woman conducted her brief conversation with Carmen's father in hushed, proprietary tones, as if he belonged to her and not Carmen.

"He'll be down," the woman informed her.

"Thanks," she said.

She settled into a chair with a view of the elevators. She quickly checked her three different email accounts on her phone.

She realized she had an idea of the man who would emerge from the elevator, and though the one who appeared in the blue Izod shirt was certainly recognizable, it wasn't him. Her father was tall, and this person was sort of bent over. Her dad had light brown hair, whereas this man was mostly gray. Her father was confident, where this man looked slightly bewildered. When her dad was in her apartment, she didn't need to see these things. Leave it to an eleva-tor in the SoHo Grand to make you change everything you thought.

She stood. "Hi, Dad."

He came over to hug her. "Hi, bun."

She held on to him for longer than usual. She felt sad. "How's the room?" she asked when she let him go.

"Great. Great. It's got everything. In the minibar there are these fantastic nuts. Kind of spicy nuts."

She was glad Jones wasn't there to hear her father talk so eagerly about the nuts. Her dad seemed sophisticated to her in places other than here. And then she wondered why she let Jones judge her dad when Jones wasn't even around.

But it wasn't Jones, really; it was her, wasn't it? She could blame Jones because she didn't want to be the one questioning or judging her dad. She preferred to stay innocent.

"That's great," she said. "So do you want to go somewhere and get a cup of tea? Or a drink? Or we could just sit here in the bar. Jones is meeting us at eight at a restaurant on Bond Street."

"Is that nearby?"

"Pretty near, yeah. Maybe a ten-minute walk."

"What do you want to do?"

"I know a place around the corner. Let's go there." She didn't like what the SoHo Grand was doing to either of them.

She realized as they crossed the lobby that her dad was wearing jeans. He almost never wore jeans. It broke her heart to think of him choosing his outfit, thinking this would be good for the chic hotel in SoHo.

They settled into an Irish bar on Grand Street. She waited for her dad to grow back into himself.

He ordered a whiskey sour, which came with a maraschino cherry, and she ordered a glass of white wine. She still felt a little weird ordering a drink in front of him.

"How's Paul?" she asked. She actually knew how Paul was, be-cause she exchanged emails with him almost every week, but Paul was such a hero to them all he seemed like a safe subject to talk about.

"It's good to have him back from Afghanistan. He's doing well. He always asks about you. What a life, you know?"

"Yeah," Carmen said. She thought of Paul as her stepbrother, but was he still her stepbrother, since his mom had died? He was the only one in the family Jones hadn't met yet.

"He sent me a video of F16s taking off from the aircraft carrier. One of them was his. Pretty incredible."

In the old days, Carmen might have felt threatened by her father's obvious pride, but a year and a half ago Lydia had died of breast cancer and all she felt was sad. And anyway, Carmen was an actress on TV. She knew her dad was proud of her too.

"How's Krista?"

This was a little more complicated, and her dad was smart enough to know it. Krista, Lydia's daughter, was the one whose house he went to for dinner every Sunday night. "Good. The baby is . . . almost one, I guess."

"Is that Tommy?"

"No, I think the middle one is Tommy."

She wasn't sure whether this confusion was for her benefit. "The baby is . . . Joey?"

"Yes. And the oldest is . . . he's gotta be five."

"Jack."

"Right, Jack."

Krista was younger than Carmen, and yet she'd already managed to produce three children. Sometimes that seemed kind of thrilling to Carmen and other times grotesque. But it was good, really, that Krista was stocking the family with grandchildren, because Jones was adamant about not having any.

"Have you babysat recently?" He and Lydia used to do it together every Friday night, and now he sometimes volunteered to go it alone. He was brave that way.

He nodded and raised his eyebrows high. "There's a handful for you."

Carmen nodded too. She was glad Krista was still in Charleston, living in a house with a proper dining room just a few miles away, giving her father grandchildren and keeping an eye on him. Carmen was grateful for that. Whatever else she might feel, gratitude was the main thing.

There was pathos in the way it all fit together. When Carmen was growing up, her dad had been more of an idea than a father to her. Now she was more of an idea than a daughter to him.

"How's your mom?"

Her dad always felt the need to ask that question at some point. It used to seem dutiful, but now it had a different cast.

It was amazing, the reversals you could see if you only kept track. It used to be that her dad was in the middle of a happy marriage and a boisterous family and her mom was single and uncertain. It had been her mom who would ask in that wistful way, "How's your dad?" Now her mother was happily married to a successful lawyer, living in a big fancy house in Chevy Chase with Carmen's eleven-year-old half brother, Ryan, and her dad's face was the one that betrayed longing when he asked about her.

"So, I have something exciting to tell you," Carmen announced. She couldn't hold it in any longer. Her father, of all people, was the right person for this news.

"What?"

"Tibby sent me a plane ticket yesterday. To Greece. To Santorini."

His eyebrows lifted. "Santorini? Where Lena's grandparents lived? Where you all went when you were in college?"

"Yes, exactly." Her dad was always good for remembering the facts. "She sent tickets to Lena and Bee too. We're going to have a reunion." She felt the tears spring to her eyes as she said it. Nobody could want this, need this, more than she did. She hadn't known how much until it was presented to her, and now she felt she would perish without it.

"That's wonderful news." Her dad was nodding. "Tibby must be doing well for herself."

"I think Brian's doing well for the two of them. That's the impression I get. He's got his software company going. He's kind of a genius."

"Well, good for them. When do you go?"

"October twenty-eighth," she said, savoring the date. "I'm so excited we'll be back together." She breathed in the bar smells and felt the white wine melting all that was left of her reserve. "I really cannot wait."

Her dad took a sip of his whiskey sour and gazed at her thoughtfully. "I picture you four girls back when you were small. I hardly knew where you ended and the other ones started."

Carmen nodded. "Me either."

For the last four years, Lena had sharpened her Greek by means of weekly hour-long conversations with Eudoxia. She had first been referred to Eudoxia through her online Greek course, and had paid sixteen dollars to talk to her for an hour on the phone. Lena could have easily talked to any number of people fluent in Greek, including her parents, but they all had in common that they knew her, and when they were talking they wanted to talk about her. Eudoxia had the benefit of being a stranger at first, and somewhat old and hard of hearing and kind of loopy.

After the first year, Eudoxia had advised that they move their conversations from the telephone to the (Greek) coffee shop equidistant from their two apartments. Initially Lena had paid the sixteen dollars plus the price of coffee and the occasional pastry, but about a year in, Eudoxia started refusing her money. And for the past year Eudoxia had insisted on picking up the tab every week because her husband, a police officer, had retired with his full pension and gotten a job as a security guard at a shoe store. Lena had offered to help Eudoxia practice her English part of the time to make things fair, but Eudoxia wouldn't hear of it.

Wednesday at four o'clock, Lena walked into the coffee shop as she always did and spotted Eudoxia, perched in their regular booth. No matter how early Lena got there, Eudoxia always got there first. Eudoxia jumped up and hugged Lena. She was fat and soft and droopy where Lena was tucked in tight.

"You are excited about something," Eudoxia declared in Greek.

Lena kissed her cheek and replied in Greek. "How do you know everything?"

The waitress appeared, another Greek transplant with dark

teased hair. Lena saw her more often than she saw her dearest friends. "Just coffee for me today," Lena said in Greek, exactly the way Eudoxia always said it. Lena was a fairly gifted and subtle mimic. She was so used to copying Eudoxia's expressions and rhythms that she had begun to suspect she spoke Greek like a sixty-four-year-old lady from Salonika.

After Lena got her coffee she unleashed the big news. "I am going to Greece."

Eudoxia bowed her head and whacked her palm on the table, as she did when she was excited. When she lifted her head her curly hair was still bouncing and the coffee cups were still quivering in their saucers. "That is *wonderful*. When?"

"Twenty-eighth of October. Tibby planned it. She bought the tickets for all four of us so we could be together."

"Tibby?" Eudoxia knew about all of them. She talked about Lena's friends as though they were hers.

"Yes, Tibby."

Lena secured her cup while Eudoxia whacked the table again. "In Greece! How wonderful. How wonderful."

"I can't quite believe it."

"Nor can I."

"I didn't know if I should accept. It's a lot of money and everything. But I emailed Tibby and she said I had to. She said I was doing my part offering the house."

"You'll all stay in your grandparents' house in Oia?"

"Yes. It's still empty. My father keeps pledging to go over there and sell it, but he hasn't found the time. And with the economic climate over there the way it is . . ."

"Maybe he likes to keep it."

"No, I think he likes to sell it. You should hear him complain about the taxes and the upkeep." Lena touched her saucer and considered for a moment. "But I don't think he wants to have to confront all their old stuff and not know what to do with it. He hates not knowing what to do."

"That will fall to you, then."

Lena nodded. "Maybe so."

One of the good things about Eudoxia was that her life overlapped with Lena's in no way other than these lessons. She was like a therapist or a bartender. Lena got to represent her world exactly the way she chose without needing to balance it for fairness or fearing that her words would make their way around in some distorted or uncomfortable way.

Eudoxia sipped her coffee. Her face was thoughtful.

"Has something happened to Tibby?"

"What do you mean?"

"You haven't seen her. You barely talk to her. You say it wasn't always like this. Why do you think she has planned this?"

Lena prodded her backpack under the table with the toe of her boot. "I think she just misses us and wants to be together."

"You think that's all it is?"

"What else could it be?"

"I don't know her. I couldn't guess," Eudoxia said honestly. She called the waitress over and ordered a cheese Danish with her customary look of relief and surrender. When it arrived she cut it into careful shapes with her knife. "Maybe you will see your young man there," she said with a note of mischief.

Eudoxia always referred to Kostos as "your young man." Drew she referred to as "the sandwich maker."

Lena was tempted to act like she didn't know what Eudoxia was talking about, but she didn't bother. "Probably not. Imagine how busy he is. He works in London now."

"He goes back and forth. That's what he said in his letter."

Lena pressed her fingers to her warm face. It was her own fault. She'd spent a lot of hours stumbling around in Greek trying to describe that letter. In fact, her fervency had ushered in a series of conversational breakthroughs, and Eudoxia had noticed it. She started calling Lena "my Daphne," and when Lena asked why, she said, "Don't you read your myths?" After that she always liked getting Lena to talk about Kostos.

As for the subject of Drew, it did not yield any breakthroughs.

"You should write to him and tell him you are coming," Eudoxia declared. "You could write it in Greek! I could help you! Wouldn't that be a surprise?" She whacked her hand on the table again.

Lena hesitated. She could imagine how many people from Kostos's old life were clamoring for his attention. She didn't want to do that to him.

In the silence Eudoxia seemed to recognize this was not something she could reasonably hope for. "But promise me this, my Daphne," she said, leaning forward. "Promise me that at least you will call him. You will call him before you leave that island."

Lena just laughed. *Not bloody likely.* "Maybe," she said aloud in Greek. "You never know what will happen."

When you jump for joy,

       beware that no one moves the ground

              from beneath your feet.

—Stanislaw J. Lec

Carmen was a terrible one for bargaining with God. She knew it was wrong, but she found herself doing it anyway. When she was nine, the night before she was flying to Orlando for a holiday weekend in Disney World with Lena's family, she flopped around in her bed for hours, so excited she couldn't stand it. As the hours passed, excitement grew so big it transformed into terror that she would die before morning. Her desire turned monstrous, and she was suddenly sure it would swallow the happiest day of her life. She begged God to please just keep her alive through tomorrow, please, and then he could do whatever he wanted with her.

Two decades had passed since then, yet she lay in her bed on the night of October 27 with the exact same feeling. She wriggled and turned and stuck various limbs outside the covers to cool down, asking God to please just look after her until she was reunited with her friends in Santorini the following day. If she could just get to that, she would be happy. He could do whatever he wanted with her after that.

What could she offer in return? She'd be a better person. She'd spend less money on shoes. She'd play in the network's charity softball game. She'd mentor a high school student. She would call her father twice a week absolutely and without fail. She would read the editorial page of *The New York Times* every day. She would no longer search the Internet for cellulite photos of actresses who got the roles she was rejected for.

Though Carmen felt foolish, she also felt lucky that she was bargaining with God, who was all-forgiving, as opposed to somebody who would surely come back to collect on her wager.

Lena prided herself on her capability as an abstract thinker, but sometimes her brain was as concrete as a lizard's. It took the actual sight of Bridget and Carmen, flesh and warmth and flying hair, racing toward her through the international terminal at JFK in New York City, to make her understand how terribly much she had missed them.

Bridget reached her first and grabbed her without entirely braking. Lena felt herself pulled into the familiar momentum.

Carmen in her tall cork sandals got there a few seconds after. She squeezed Lena's forearm so hard it would make a bruise. She screamed so loudly in Lena's ear she left it ringing. She stepped on Lena's toes without thinking. Lena felt tears pricking in her eyes and she laughed. It was so good to feel these things, even the ones that stung.

Bee made it a huddle. She tried to pick the two of them up off the ground, and Lena drew in the familiar stimuli: Bridget's peppermint shampoo, the delicate sponge-cake texture of her skin against Lena's cheek, Carmen's grapefruit-scented hair junk and sticky lips. The smells on them were deeper, the colors brighter, than on other people.

Lena liked them to stay the same, and they were awfully obliging about it. In recent years her joy at seeing them was always mixed with anxiety that there would be some telltale change. She wasn't sure what it would be: a supercilious brow, the forgetting of some little ritual, a set of crow's-feet, a this or a that, that would separate one of them from the rest, or from their bond or from their past.

Bee was especially accommodating. She was practically a Bee museum. Her faded lavender T-shirt had been gathering snags and extra stitches since ninth grade. Her yellow hair was long and messy as ever, the flow of it interrupted by skinny braids here and there that reminded Lena of Bee's cornrow phase in sixth grade. She dragged along the shiny airport floor the same worn-out Israeli clogs she'd bought with Lena on a jaunt along Eighth Street the summer after college. Lena amply forgave her for the drooping blue socks, which she'd shamelessly stolen from Lena on the last trip to Greece.

Well, Carmen did show some signs of change, even in the two months since Lena had seen her: her highlights were slightly lighter, her jeans slightly tighter, her eyebrows slightly thinner. But she was the makeover queen, so what would you expect? With Carmen they were always the same category of cosmetic changes that did nothing to mask the eager animation of her face. Change was the weather with Carmen. It would be weird if she stayed the same.

Tibby would be waiting for them at the airport in Fira. "She texted me that she got there yesterday morning. She opened up the house," Lena told them excitedly, though they already knew, because she'd texted them too.

Lena settled into a bouncing stride between Carmen and Bridget, unabashedly clutching their hands through the long terminal. She had a magazine under her arm, candy in her bag, and an unaccustomed feeling of robust hunger in her stomach. She was looking forward to her life with brazen joy, and that was a gift she almost never gave herself. She looked forward to every single piece of it, from the airplane food to flying through the night under shared blankets, to Carmen's sleep-sputtering (God help you if you called it snoring) in her ear, to the first sight of the Caldera from the air.

Most of all she looked forward to seeing Tibby when they landed. With an ache she pictured Tibby's freckled, heart-shaped face, lost to her for almost two years. The last time she'd seen it, it was framed in the door of their old neighborhood bar on East Fifth Street, where the four of them had met to celebrate Carmen's first getting cast on *Criminal Court*. Tibby had been looking over her shoulder, a final glimpse as she said goodbye. Lena hadn't known it was goodbye at the time, but maybe Tibby had. Tibby had always been awkward about showy rituals. And she wouldn't have wanted to take anything away from Carmen's big night. But within a week Brian had gotten some tremendous opportunity and the two of them were rushing off to Australia. Just for a few months, Tibby had thought at the time. But it had been two long years, and even Lena's lizard brain could sense that expanse, now that their reunion was so close. Seeing Tibby would make her joy complete.

Lena was good at convincing herself of things, and dangerously good at thinking she could be herself without these friends of hers. As the three of them yapped contentedly all the way to the gate, through the lengthy boarding process, onto the plane with its blankets and pillows that gave it the atmosphere of an international slumber party, she felt her face opening into expressions she'd forgotten how to make. Lena remembered herself in all the old familiar things they said. She existed in her friends; there she was. All the parts of herself she'd forgotten. She knew herself best when she was with them.

Blinking in the artificial morning light with her weary, late-night eyes, Carmen could read the same tired bewilderment on her friends' faces. Their plane had carried a big bellyful of America, which had dissipated the moment they stepped into this bustling, overheated little airport.

"Are we late, do you think?" Lena asked.

Bee squinted at the board showing arrivals. "Are we early?"

"I'm not sure my phone has the right time," Carmen said, studying it.

Carmen had geared herself up for seeing Tibby first thing off the plane. They had all calibrated their patience to that moment and no further. So after ten minutes of swinging heads and darting eyes and thudding under ribs, Carmen was fairly sure that Tibby had not yet arrived at the gate, and the excitement started to wear on them.

"Maybe she's at the baggage claim."

"Yeah. Probably."

"These things are always confusing."

"Maybe that's Tibby." Bridget pointed to a corpulent middle-aged woman in a blue head scarf.

Carmen laughed. "Well, it *has* been a while."

Carmen's eyes were still darting. She studied every face through the glass wall of the arrivals area. She wished she had not been so vain as to pack away her distance glasses.

"Let's go to baggage claim."

"She'll be there."

They moved as a tired six-legged creature toward the sign that said Baggage Claim, all of them scanning the crowd for a freckled, wiry, much-missed American.

The smell of cigarette smoke was strong, and the amount of sunshine in the airport felt out of step with the notion of nighttime still lagging in their bodies. It had seemed a lot more important to talk through the flight than sleep. At the time it had. Carmen felt a slight sick feeling of exhaustion starting in the bottom of her stomach.

They stood in the baggage claim. They were so busy scanning for Tibby they kept forgetting about their bags. Bee's army-surplus duffel went around the belt multiple times unclaimed.

They could barely pass a sentence between them, so eager were they to catch sight of her. She was just . . . there. Just behind that pillar. Just walking through those double doors. She was so close, Carmen could practically bring her to life with the effort of her mind. Any second. Every face was, for a flash, Tibby's face.

Finally they retrieved the bags and sat on them in the middle of the room. To Carmen it felt like they were stalled out ten feet from the finish line of a marathon. Everything had gone smoothly until now. They'd accepted their medals. They'd bathed in the congratulations. They'd donned those silly tinfoil blankets. You weren't allowed to stop here.

"Something got messed up," Bridget said. "The time, the date, something."

"She might have gotten lost on the way to the airport," Carmen offered.

"It's not easy getting around this island," Lena said. "Just getting down from Oia is a challenge. She probably didn't leave enough time. She's probably getting taken to the cleaners by some crooked cabbie as we speak."

"Did you check your phone?" Bridget asked. Carmen had never expected Bee to say those words.

"It doesn't work here. I told you that."

"She's probably trying to call us," Lena said.

Bridget nodded. "We'll just wait here."

"Until she comes," Lena said.

The three of them might have stayed there sitting on their suit-cases until darkness fell, had not a porter respectfully ushered them out of the airport and to the curb around midday. The baggage handlers and airport officials were eager to get a meal. People went home for lunch here. There wasn't another flight coming in for two hours.

"If we go back to Lena's, though, I'm worried we'll pass her on the way," Carmen said to the porter, who gave no sign that he understood English.

Lena tried to translate, but that just made Carmen feel stupid. It wasn't a thing you said to be heard or understood. It was a thing you said to say.

In disarray they packed all their stuff and themselves into a taxi. Lena said a few words in Greek. Carmen felt misgivings about leaving. This was where they were supposed to meet. She remembered the direction always given to them as children: "Just stay in one place; we'll find you."

Bridget seemed to understand Carmen's mind. "Don't worry. She's probably at your grandparents' house wondering where the hell we are. She couldn't get to the airport for whatever reason. She'd figure we'd come to the house. She'll be there. Where else would she be?"

Lena nodded and then Carmen joined in the nodding, but for the long, expensive taxi ride they remained mostly silent.

They walked and dragged the last uphill stretch to the house. The road was too narrow and too steep for a full-size vehicle. By the time they were halfway up the hill, Bridget was carrying all three bags.

"Who needs a mule," Carmen said.

Lena tried the handle on the weathered egg-yolk-colored door, in case Tibby was inside, but it was locked.

"Hello?" Lena called, unlocking and pushing open the door. The three of them stood sun-drunk and huffing in the dark of the shuttered house. "Hello?"

"Tibby?" Carmen shouted in such a loud voice it made Lena wince.

Lena opened a shutter and Bridget put down the bags. Slowly Carmen's eyes took in the familiar contours. "Anybody home?" she called.

"I don't think she's here."

"We should've stayed in the airport," Carmen bleated wearily. "What if she's there?" The more tired she felt, the worse she was at keeping her moods to herself.

"She may be stuck somewhere in between," Lena pointed out in a reasonable voice, "but she'll find her way back here eventually." She waded deeper into the house. "And look, she was definitely here earlier. Look at these flowers!" She opened another couple of shutters. The girls had all been trained by her voluble grandmother not to open them willy-nilly, that a house here was essentially a fortress against the sun.

There were pink roses on the dining room table and white ones on the coffee table and in the small kitchen. A large bowl on the counter was piled with fruits and vegetables.

"She went shopping," Carmen said. There were two loaves of bread atop the short fridge, and milk, cheese, butter, eggs, and bottles of water inside of it. She peered into a white bakery box and found a fancy cake.

Carmen felt her tired eyes welling at all the little offerings. The hand of Tibby so close and yet not here.

"I bet she'll be back any minute," she heard Lena saying as she headed up the stairs.

In the bedrooms Carmen found more pink and white roses in teacups and jam jars. They'd already decided it would be Bridget and Tibby in one room and Lena and Carmen in the other and no one in Valia and Bapi's old room, because that would be creepy. Tibby knew Lena loved the front room with the views of the Caldera, and so she had left her two bags in the back bedroom. Also out of deference to Lena, Tibby had left her stuff pretty tidy, though she was a known slob.

Carmen heard Lena calling Tibby's cellphone from the house line downstairs. "She's not picking up. I'm just getting her message," Lena called out in a general way. "I wonder if her phone works here."

Carmen wandered in a circle around the little room. Seeing Tibby's familiar things made her presence so acute, she half expected her to jump out from under the bed. The angle of Tibby's discarded shoes instantly bridged two lost years. You could build a whole Tibby from that alone. Nothing had changed, really.

The rest of them had big feet, from Lena's nine and a halfs to Carmen's eight and a halfs to Bridget's somewhere in between. Three of them could always share shoes in a pinch. But Tibby's sixes looked like child shoes in comparison. They could never share shoes with Tibby. She wore these chunky, grommety, attitudinal shoes all the time, but they were too small to really make the point.

The particular scent of Tibby brought more tears to her eyes. Neither a sweet, perfumy smell nor a bad foot odor–ish smell, just a smell that conveyed Tibby about as uniquely as anything could. With the tears came a rushing feeling of missing her, the helpless sadness of not seeing her. Carmen hadn't realized she'd been forcibly holding the sadness in. Now she let it overcome her.

Lena always described how she dreaded and mourned things before they even happened. Carmen was beginning to suspect that she was permitting herself to mourn this long separation only now that it was over.

Fate is not an eagle, it creeps like a rat.

—Elizabeth Bowen

Bridget pictured them as the three ants trapped in an amber bead of a necklace Tibby's great-grandma Felicia had worn. It was odd the things that stuck with you. Bridget couldn't remember most of her birthdays, her mother's last day, her father's current address, her college graduation, but how frequently she thought of those three damned insects stuck in a necklace belonging to Tibby's ancient ancestor who happened to have been bananas.

It was dark. It was dinnertime and Tibby still hadn't turned up. They didn't want to eat anything or do anything or even say anything until Tibby got there. The three of them sat paralyzed in the living room. Bridget had the eerie sensation that their state of suspension was the culmination of nearly two years spent like that.

There were four of them. There were always four of them. It seemed, as it had always seemed, disloyal to allow any aspect of their friendship to progress without all of them present. No way could they start their magical week before Tibby appeared.

Lena was looking agitated. "Could she have gotten lost? The roads are really treacherous. I hope she wasn't driving."

"Lenny, she's twenty-nine years old. She can handle herself. She's the second-best driver of us, and even if she did get into some mishap it couldn't be serious."

Lena was nodding.

"She's dependable with the seat belt, and you can barely go ten miles an hour on these roads."

Lena, still nodding, wandered back to the kitchen to check again that there was a dial tone on the phone. It was a quirk of her father's that he left the phone on in an empty house. Indeed, there was a dial tone, just as there had been a dial tone half an hour before. "She might not have this number," Lena murmured.

"Probably not," Carmen said from her stiff perch on the couch. Bridget could read Carmen's anxiety by the way her collarbones stuck out.

Bridget cocked an ear. "Len, do not call her again. When she sees the number of times you called, she's going to think you are psychotic."

"I'm not. I mean I wasn't," Lena said, floating back to the living room. "I was just checking."

Carmen picked at her fingernails. "Judging from the stuff in the kitchen, it seems like she made plans for dinner. Whatever happened, she's going to figure out a way to get back here in time for dinner, right?"

By nine o'clock the wind had come up, and the mystery was turning rancid.

"They eat dinner really late here," Carmen noted.

"Maybe she ran off with a handsome Greek." Bridget was trying to be funny, but not even she found herself to be.

Between nine and ten, they barely moved. Bridget got up twice, once to look out the window into darkness and once to open the door. She looked up and down the windy, empty street, hoping this would be the moment that Tibby would come around the bend.

"I wish there was someone we could call," Lena said.

"Do you think her parents might know anything?" Carmen asked.

Lena shook her head. "Anyway, it's around four in the morning there."

"What about Brian?" Bridget asked.

Carmen looked up. "Do you have a number for him?"

Bridget shook her head, as did Lena. They only had Tibby's cell-phone number, no landline in Australia where they might find him. "I wonder where he is?"

"Australia, I assume. He's not here."

Lena looked thoughtful. "What do we even know about them anymore? Do we know they're together? I know they moved to Australia together, but do we know for sure what's happened since? She hasn't mentioned him in a long time."

Bridget shrugged. Her legs were aching from holding them in one position for too long. "Tibby would have told us if they broke up."

"She hasn't mentioned much of anything in a long time."

Bridget nodded. This was a conversation they'd had many versions of before. "I wish I knew why all the mystery." In the light of the present, unsettling mystery, it seemed especially strange—unacceptable, really—not to know these things. How could they have gone around knowing so little? How could they have let that stand?

"This doesn't happen by accident. There's got to be some reason for her being out of touch," Lena said.

Carmen crossed and uncrossed her legs. "She sent out emails. We've all gotten a few. What do you expect when she lives halfway around the world? Anyway, she obviously wants to be together now."

Bridget shook her head, annoyed at herself for letting this go, for not spending enough time badgering Tibby. For not just getting on a plane and going to Australia if that was what it took. "When she turns up here, we're going to sit the poor girl down and get some answers before we let her out of our sight."

Carmen's arms were crossed and her bones stuck out. "She's just been busy, like all of us. Brian has been utterly, totally in love with Tibby since she was fifteen, and she's the same way about him. There's no way they broke up. Who besides us would she talk to about it? There's no way she could go through something that big without us knowing."

"Something is wrong," Bridget said. They'd waited implicitly until midnight to say so. They'd waited for Bee to be the one to say it.

Lena's hands were on her neck. "What should we do? Call the police? The consulate?" She'd been thinking of it since the sky turned dark. Her mind flashed back to the hundreds of signs they'd made when they were looking for their lost pants ten years before, and she felt like she was choking.

This island was a fucking sinkhole. It had lost most of itself under the ocean, for God's sake. It was a terrible place for losing things.

Bridget got up and started to pace. "I feel like going out and looking for her," she said.

"I think call the consulate first," Carmen said to Lena.

Lena found the number in one of her grandparents' ancient directories but couldn't get a live voice on the phone.

Carmen's face was serious. "The police?"

Lena found the number of the local precinct number and called it. Her heart was mashing around and her head was grasping for the way to say anything in Greek. The phone rang many times before a man picked it up.

"English?" was the first thing she asked him, disappointingly.

"A little. No. You want to call back?" he asked her in Greek.

"No. I need to talk to someone now," she said, also in Greek. She didn't realize she wasn't speaking English until she'd spoken. She explained, in Greek apparently, about Tibby. She talked and listened for several minutes, noticing Bee's and Carmen's surprised eyes on her face. They hovered as she hung up the phone.

"How did you do that?" Carmen asked her breathlessly.

"I've been practicing."

"What did they say?" Bridget asked.

"He said to call back if she's missing for twenty-four hours. She's not technically missing until then. But he took down all the information. He has her name and age and description and our number and address and everything." She pressed her lips together. She felt suddenly tired, though nowhere near sleep. "I don't know what else to do."

"We'll wait," Bee said.

Nobody tried to suggest eating or sleeping. Talking was the only comfort they had.

———

By the time dawn made its way through the slats of the shutters, they couldn't think of any more stories to tell themselves about what could have happened. It had been two nights now without sleep, and the whole world had taken on an alien aspect. Carmen had long since searched the back bedroom for any note or clue as to where Tibby might have gone, though it felt wrong to open Tibby's duffel bag.

"There is some logical explanation," Carmen told them. "There always is."

The knock at the door came around two hours past dawn.

Though they had sat seemingly inert, two on the couch, Lena in the chair, for the last hour, they were all three on their feet and at the door almost instantly.

It wasn't Tibby. It was the opposite of her. It was two men in uniform, one young and one middle-aged. The older one took a step forward. "Lena Kaligaris?" he said.

Lena raised her hand like an elementary school student. "Me," she said.

"You called the precinct last night," he said to her in Greek.

"Do you speak English?" Whatever he had to say she didn't want to hear alone.

"Yes. Okay." He looked at his partner. Lena was searching for some reassuring casualness in their manner, but she didn't see it. "You called about your friend. Tibby." The way he said it sounded like "Teeeby." "She did not come home?" Lena felt Bee's hand wrap around hers.

"No. Not yet. Is everything okay?" Her words made a faint whisper in a howl of a windstorm in her head. People like this didn't come to your house if everything was okay.

He glanced again at his partner. "Early this morning a fishing boat passing Finikia . . . they called the guard. Well. They found a body. A girl. A swimmer. A bather, you say? She must have drowned many hours before. We regret to say we think this could be your friend."

There was a sound that came from somewhere. Maybe Carmen. Maybe her. Lena shook her head hard. There were these thoughts, these ideas, climbing, scraping, shouting to be let in, but she wouldn't let them. She felt Bee's arm shaking at the end of her hand. "I don't think so. No. I don't think she would go swimming. I think that must be somebody else." Her voice didn't sound like hers, it sounded strangely like Valia's, impermeable, stubborn, and sure. No, that drowned swimmer must belong to somebody else's tragedy. It didn't feel like theirs.

"Are you, any of you, her family? What you call next of kin? If someone could come to"—the police officer took out his handkerchief and wiped his face—"to identify the body, if it is your . . ."

"The body fits the description you gave on the phone," the younger partner offered solemnly in Greek. "If this is a mistake we are very, very sorry."

And if it wasn't? Lena couldn't help choking on the thought. What was he then?

But it was a mistake. "She wouldn't be swimming. It's late October. Nobody goes swimming now," Valia's voice insisted, coming out of Lena's mouth.

The older one shook his head. "The beaches are full with bathers all day. This month is very warm. The water is still not so cold but the currents are dangerous." The perspiration dripping down his temples seemed to make the point.

There was that scratching wriggling somewhere under Lena's skull, like mice that couldn't escape, and how long could she continue to ignore them?

"We are her friends," Bridget said. It hurt Lena's heart to see Bee's mouth quiver like that.

"All just friends? Not her family?"

Bridget shook her head slowly. It felt like a heavy penance to be wrested from her at such a time. "Just friends. Not her family."

Lena needed only to glance at Carmen's face to see the childlike rebellion going on in there. *Just* friends? More than family! *Do you have any idea who we are?*

"Do you know where is her family? She is not married? We found some clothes and a mobile phone left overnight at the beach at Ammoudi. We think they could be hers. The phone is registered to a number in Australia. We tried to call it but we spoke only to a message machine."

"She lives in Australia now. Her family is in the United States. She is not married," Bridget said.

"We are like her family," Carmen couldn't keep herself from adding. Lena heard the sob at the end of it. It just hung there.

Lena shook her head hard to try to relieve the scritch-scritch-scratching at the base of her skull. "We can call her parents," Lena said. "If that's what you need."

"You want that I call?" the older officer asked deferentially.

Lena tried to breathe. "No, I don't want you to call. I will call."

This is the way the world ends
Not with a bang
but a whimper.

—T. S. Eliot

It seemed to Bridget when she thought of it later that there had been two systems operating in her mind through that long day and that they had never matched up, like two wildly spinning gears not quite close enough to fit together.

There was the small gear spinning the minute-by-minute things— *Tibby is uncomfortable, why are they making her lie on that hard table? Her head hurts. Tibby, get off there.* Her orange toenail polish, the familiar freckles along her shinbones, the glint of a tiny gold stud in her nose, the wrong color of her skin. Why was she stuck in a bag? How could she stand it? Tibby was the one who'd scream when you covered her with the blanket in hide-and-seek. *Do not zip that up. No, please don't. It is so cold in here. She could get sick.* Regular colds went right to pneumonia with Tibby.

The second gear spun with the big, abstract, unfathomable things. *Tibby is not really here anymore. Tibby is gone. She won't be coming back. That is forever.*

All the places where the two gears might have fit together and pushed her understanding forward, they didn't. They just spun apart, getting her nowhere.

You are my friend. You are here and I need you. That was living and true. *You are gone. You are not coming back.* That was also true.

Between alive and dead there was no common ground.

Even long after, Lena wasn't sure her mind was working that day. She did things and said things and saw things, but they bounced off her head like so many Ping-Pong balls. She knew they were terrible things, destroying her happiness by the minute, but she forgot each thing as soon as it happened. How she got to the police station, the hospital, where she sat, who drove them, what the basement of the hospital looked like, what the detective told them, and later, what Lena said to Tibby's mother, Alice Rollins, on the phone from the precinct. And what Alice said to her.

She forgot everything instantly, as though she had no memory apparatus at all. But in a sick-feeling way, she also knew her eyes and her ears were taking these things in and keeping them. These images and words would be there waiting for her, settling into some deeper layer that would someday resurface—maybe that night, maybe tomorrow, maybe months or years from now—and make her feel crazy and scared. They would sneak into her dreams and fracture in weird ways that would make her dislike a certain kind of car she couldn't remember having ridden in, or the particular perfume on a person she didn't remember speaking to, or the taste of a certain cup of tea she didn't remember drinking.

Oh, you'll remember them.

She knew that memory divided into terms short and long. In the short term Lena was only aware that she was standing. Long term, she was scared that she was full of cracks and soon to fold.

Late that night, without food or discussion, they returned to Valia's house and trod upstairs one by one. Bridget went into the bedroom she was sharing with Tibby and tipped onto the bed like a tree cut at the base. She waited to hear the others using the bathroom, but she didn't. There was no talking. There was no noise at all. She understood it. In midst of all the big traumas there were the small ones to avoid too. Like having to look at yourself in the mirror over the sink while you brushed your teeth, knowing what you knew.

After a while, Bridget changed beds. She got into the one on which rested Tibby's soft duffel bag. She got under the covers and put her arms around the bag. She could smell Tibby. It used to be she couldn't smell Tibby's smell in the way you couldn't smell your own; it was too familiar. But tonight she could. This was some living part of Tibby still here, and she held on to it. There was more of Tibby with her here and now than in what she had seen in the cold basement room that day.

Each time her mind flashed on that image for a second, a fraction of a second, it blinded her like a flashbulb, burning out the center of her mind's eye to blackness. Already she could feel the image dividing her life into two halves. Her life leading up to today was innocence and unrealized joy for not yet having seen that image. The rest of her life would unfold as the part after she had.

And what if the second part blotted out the first? What if the second part was all she was left with? The thousand precious images of their lives together she suddenly imagined curling up and melting in the basement furnace at the end of *Citizen Kane*. She knew that movie because Tibby had made her watch it the whole way through, fearing Bridget would spend her life as a film imbecile, knowing nothing but *Napoleon Dynamite* and *The Princess Bride*.

I'm sorry, Tib. I think I did end up a film imbecile, and there's no help for me now.

Carmen lay in the quiet dark imagining where Tibby was, wondering how it felt to be there. It was the worst thing to think of, but she wanted to try to be brave, as it seemed horrifically brave of Tibby to be dead.

She couldn't fathom how Tibby could have gone to this place where they couldn't follow her. She tried to imagine the moment it had happened and whether Tibby was scared. It was the worst thought, but she tried to follow it, no matter how much it hurt, because she didn't want Tibby to have to be all alone. It was the only way Carmen could think of to be with her.

Later in the night it struck Carmen as all out of order. She felt that Tibby's leaving this life ought to have more parallels with how she had come into it. The four of them did these things together. They were born together. They grew up together. They should get married at the same time, at least roughly. They should have children together. They should complain about menopause together and judge people who got face-lifts together and be grandmothers together and all die within seventeen days together. That was how it ought to happen. Carmen felt that a mistake had been made, that an oversight had been so specifically mishandled that if it were brought to the attention of the right person, maybe it could be recalled, like a batch of bad ground beef. It was a mistake.

But if it couldn't be rectified, then what? They weren't on the map anymore; they were living some other kind of life, unfamiliar and deeply inferior, for which they were unfit.

But Carmen didn't really believe it. She didn't really believe Tibby belonged to death, to that big idea, to the careless world.

She belongs to us.

Sitting on the top stair, alone in the night, Lena realized that a fundamental layer of their happiness depended on the four of them being close to one another. Their lives were independent and full. Their friendship was only one aspect of their lives, but it seemed to give meaning to all the others.

The most perfect bedrock of happiness was the four of them at nineteen, gathered on the ledge and staring at the place where the ocean blended into the sky on their last day in Santorini. Or the summer night when they were twenty-four and the power went out in New York City and they lay on blankets on the floor, surrounded by candles, talking all night, eating everything perishable in the fridge and freezer, including two and a half pints of ice cream. Even that last night, at Teller's Bar on East Fifth Street, the goodbye she hadn't known was goodbye, Lena had looked around the table with a sense of security and a feeling of joy about the future she hadn't felt since.

That happiness eroded when they were apart, out of sync and out of touch. It quaked the night Lena discovered Tibby had moved to Australia without even explaining it to her and she couldn't get either Bee or Carmen on the phone to ask them what they knew.

And now what? If happiness depended on their being together, then what could you possibly say about this day?

And for all our inventions.

In matters of love loss,

we've no recourse at all.

—The Shins

Lena had tried to make Tibby's parents feel welcome when they arrived in Santorini. They did what they could. She, Bridget, and Carmen, the three of them, silent and dark, like shadows without bodies to cast them, managed to rent a car and get to the airport and wait for the plane to come down. It was an airport they had learned to loathe.

Lena had tried to air out her grandparents' old bedroom and had made it up with clean sheets, but the Rollinses insisted on a hotel, and that was fine. They needed to grieve alone, was what Tibby's dad said. Lena wondered if, really, there was any choice in that. Everyone grieved alone.

During the three black days of that trip, Alice Rollins came to the house in Oia exactly once. Once Lena met Tibby's parents at the morgue, where she attempted to translate their desire to waive the full autopsy. The cause of death had been determined to be accidental drowning, and they wanted to get the body home to the United States as soon as possible. During the same three days, Carmen dragged Lena and Bridget to see Tibby's hollowed-out parents at their hotel in Fira exactly once. The Rollinses had managed to find the only grim, gray-office-building hotel in a spangled holiday town that mocked them day and night with blasting cruise boats and endless vacationers getting drunk on open terraces.

In the dreary lobby five of them drooped over cups of bitter tea.

Alice's skin looked as thin and colorless as skim milk. Tibby's father bit at his lips savagely.

Of the many topics they did not discuss, one was Brian. A detective at the precinct mentioned at some point after they'd claimed her body that he'd received a call from a distraught man responding to the message the detective had left at Tibby's home phone number in Australia. He didn't recall the man's name—he'd written it in the file. "Not her husband. Her boyfriend," he'd said dismissively in Greek. "But did you tell him?" Lena had asked. "Yes, I told him," he'd responded. Between the detective's tone and his lack of English, Lena doubted the conversation had gone easily. She felt incipient compassion for this boyfriend, who she felt sure was Brian, but she didn't have the stamina to think it through, let alone make contact with Brian herself. She was too scared of her own feelings to take any part in his. She didn't know whether Tibby's parents had spoken to him. She doubted they had.

As she watched them all, Lena felt heartless and detached—detached from herself as well as from them. They'd all fallen down the same hole and were staring at one another in a mixture of unassigned blame and disbelief that the tragedy that had sent them down here could never be undone. They were here all at once, but not together. Survival took self-absorption, and it made them strangers with nothing to do and no way to relate. Emergencies gave you a shape and a plot to take part in, while death was no story at all. It left you nothing.

Lena felt cold on the surface. Cold and eerily electrified in a way that made the hair on her arms stand on end. She felt a dry snap in the air that touched the outside of her skin, and a roiling, stewing punishment waiting underneath.

None of them really knew how to comfort one another. She guessed that every one of them felt privately like the most bereaved.

The one time Alice came to Lena's house was to collect Tibby's belongings. It had to be done. Bridget had offered to bring the bags to the hotel, even to go through them with her, but Alice said no.

Alice spent a long time in the back bedroom with the door closed while the three of them sat in a row on the couch. Now and then they heard a choke or a sob come from Alice that wasn't much different from sounds they had made and heard among themselves.

At last Alice came down and dumped a suitcase on the floor in the middle of the living room. "I think this is all stuff for you girls," Alice said. Her face was splotchy. "Okay."

The four of them looked at it. None of them moved.

"Okay," Alice said again, staring at them as though they were supposed to do something. Nobody knew what it was.

Bridget wondered at how little of Alice seemed to touch the ground by this point. She was all gaze and no traction.

I'm sorry we're still alive, Bridget thought. She didn't begrudge Alice the feeling she was almost certainly having as she looked at her daughter's friends. Plenty of times Bridget had wished every other mother dead if she could have kept hers. *You love us, I know, but when it comes down to it, we are other people's daughters.*

That was the tone of Bridget's brain now. A diseased, philosophical lassitude she could barely recognize.

It didn't dawn on Carmen until they were gathered around Tibby's duffel bag and the bag was open and they were surrounded by the boxes of frosted strawberry Pop-Tarts, bags of Cheetos, and Ziplocs of sour gummy worms and unlit candles what thing this was meant to be and what perverse thing it actually was.

It was the last night—Carmen and Bridget were leaving the next day. They couldn't have left it any longer. The suitcase was in the middle of them. How else could they have looked at it all at once? These were the things in the suitcase. There wasn't much choice about taking them out. Carmen took out the CD, a relic of sorts, and it was all she could do to look at the names of the songs in Tibby's boyish handwriting. The terrible, ritual-sweet, late-eighties dance stylings of Paula Abdul, Janet Jackson, and George Michael.

It must have taken some doing to get real American Pop-Tarts all the way to Australia and then here.

Tibby, who had smirked, mugged, and grimaced her way through the Traveling Pants ritual, had come here to stage a Traveling Pants ritual, even with no pants. Under the first layer of snacks and atmospherics, Carmen's hand came upon a stratum of papers, envelopes, and packages. The first was a true artifact. "Oh, my God," Carmen murmured, her heart trying to beat its way out of a thick sludge. "I didn't know Tibby had this." She could hear the same kind of wetness at the bottom of Bridget's breathing. For a moment they were tricked out of their stupor.

There it was. Lena's careful fifteen-year-old handwriting on Gilda's Aerobics Studio letterhead.

We, the Sisterhood, hereby instate the following rules to govern the use of the Traveling Pants.

It was not right. It was a cruel trick to have to see this and remember. Carmen wanted to scrabble back into the stupor as fast as she could. They couldn't look at one another. She anchored the piece of paper under a box of Pop-Tarts. She couldn't stand to see it any longer.

There was a second sheet of paper. It was covered in Tibby's writing, looser and messier than it had once been. Carmen saw all of their names written at the top. She handed it directly to Lena without reading anything else.

Lena read for a moment. Her face turned a deeper red and then went to no color at all. She looked up. "I don't know what this means." Something about the way she said it made Carmen feel scared.

Bridget got to her feet and started pacing in a tight loop behind the sofa. "What does it say?"

Lena glanced away. She put the paper down and her hands were shaking.

"Can you tell us what it says?" Carmen pressed, not wanting to know but needing to know.

"I can't. I don't understand it." Lena's hands looked like skeleton hands grasping at her own face.

"Then just read it." Carmen felt panicked. She needed to get this over with.

Lena turned to her with a glare she'd never seen. *"I don't want to."* Her voice was biting and cold, as Carmen had never heard it.

Bridget stuck her arm in and took it. She walked back behind the sofa, jiggling on the balls of her feet as she looked at the paper. She began reading aloud in a deliberate way, as though she weren't even listening to what she was saying.

> *"I'm writing this down, because it is going to be hard for me to say it. Because this is probably our last time just us. See, I can write that down, but I don't think I can say it. I'm not doing this to say goodbye, though I know that has to be part of it. I'm doing it to say thank you for all we have had and done and been for one another, to say I love you for making this life of mine what it is. Leaving you is the hardest thing I have to do. But the thing is, the best parts of me are in you, all three of you. You are who I am, and what I cherish in myself stays on in you."*

Bridget's voice shook and broke and then stopped. She put the paper down on the coffee table. Carmen watched her walk up the stairs. She watched Lena grimly put the contents of the suitcase back inside and close it. Carmen put her head on the table. No one made a sound.

After that, as far as Bridget was concerned, Lena had disappeared. Even as she stood in the middle of the room, holding the phone to call the cab to take them from the bottom of the hill to the airport, she was gone. She had become a black hole of a person, but not the kind that pulled you in.

In a completely unfair way, Bridget wanted Lena to drop all that and help her. She'd gotten used to Lena's coming to her when she was in distress. Fate had been kind to them before this, doling out traumas not all at once but one at a time, so that whenever something awful was happening to one, the others were there to help.

The explosions came at them from the outside while they huddled together for protection.

This explosion came from the middle of the huddle. This was an inside job.

After the letter, Bridget saw Carmen as a stranger. Her voice a little too loud, her teeth a little too white, her collarbones jutting out too far. Was this what she really looked like now? How powerfully memories could soften a face. How beautiful love could make a friend's face. You could recognize its power when it was gone.

For some reason Bridget thought numbly of the old apartment on Avenue C. For two and a half years they had paid rent below the market rate. It had crept up only slowly, by tiny increments, thanks to three decades of rent stabilization enjoyed by dozens of impoverished hipster tenants before them.

And one day the landlord sent in two Nicaraguans in weightlifting belts to tear out their perfectly shabby little kitchen. For three weeks they were left with a dank cavity and a bunch of chopped-off pipes and wires stumped like snakes looking for their heads. Eventually the grumpy superintendent sealed up the hole with cheap new appliances and cupboards, all plastic and composite board. For that honor, they got their rent doubled all at once, a so-called fair market rent.

The next month they'd moved out. It was the end of an era. Tibby had moved in with Brian in Long Island City. Bridget spent an itinerant year on couches or floors or house-sitting or sub-subletting before she began her slow trek to San Francisco. Carmen roomed with the bulimic paralegal uptown. Lena got a better teaching job and mostly stayed in Providence. The thing you had had and loved and taken for granted caught up with you all at once and for no sensible reason suddenly cost more than you could afford.

Bridget paced the living room of Lena's grandparents' house, waiting for it to be time to pace somewhere else. She couldn't stand the hurt and disappointment she would see on Carmen's face if she looked at her. She'd rather jump into the cauldron after Tibby than have to look at the things Carmen needed from her. *Please let's all love one another. Please let us act like it's the same. Please let's act like we still believe in us.*

There was one time at the end of that terrible last day when Bridget's eyes did drag across Carmen's, but she didn't see what she was expecting to see. It was a different blow. Carmen's eyes were as dead as Bridget's; they weren't asking for anything at all. And maybe not seeing Carmen's neediness was even worse than seeing it and disappointing it. Maybe Carmen didn't believe in them anymore either.

Tibby, who was not fond of change, had once told Bridget that the present, no matter what it brought, couldn't change the past. The past was set and sealed.

But that wasn't true. Now every time Bridget glanced behind her, the past, whether near or distant, opened and morphed and reset into images and uncertainties she'd never even thought of. If this could happen to Tibby, then nothing about their friendship, about their past, could be trusted. It seemed ironic to disagree with Tibby at such a time, but she didn't believe their past anymore and was extra sorry that Tibby herself had been the one to prove its frailty.

Carmen stared out the window of the taxicab, chewing through an expensive manicure and absently spitting out bits of fingernail as she hadn't done since middle school. The taxi took them along the coast road, delivering them to the plane that would take them away from here. For the first day she could remember on this island, the sun wasn't shining. The clouds came down low and the wind blew hard and erratically. She tried to orient herself with a glimpse of the Caldera—she knew it should be just outside her window—but she couldn't see it.

Instead she pictured the heavy envelope now sitting in her bag with her name written across the front in Tibby's scrawl. It had been in Tibby's duffel bag. There had been one for each of them, with a few words of instruction written on the backs, including dates on which the envelopes were supposed to be opened. Lena had distributed them before she'd closed up the suitcase for good, as mystified as Carmen and Bridget were. She said she was going to take the bag back to her parents' house and leave it in the basement unless anybody had another idea, which no one did.

As she thought of the suitcase, Carmen's inner eye turned to another paper in there; the famous rules of the pants—the Manifesto, they had grandly called it. How splendid they thought they were. With an uncharacteristic feeling of scorn, she couldn't help but consider now: how many of those rules had she broken? They had never enumerated the consequences of breaking the rules, but maybe they should have.

Were four fifteen-year-old girls so powerful that they got to make the rules? Was it because of the broken rules that the pants had been lost, and the sisterhood along with them? Was it because Carmen had taken a wet washcloth to the pants several times in defiance of rule #1? Was it because she'd thought *I am fat* in the pants many, many times, in defiance of rule #3? She'd certainly picked her nose in them, who was she kidding, and a couple of times at least, she had worn them with a tucked-in shirt and a belt. So much for rules #5 and #9.

But it was rule #10 that genuinely burned in front of her eyes as she imagined it. It was #10 where she had truly failed. They had all failed. And that was the one that actually mattered, the unforgivable, unthinkable root of their loss.

10. Remember: Pants = love. Love your pals. Love yourself.

But why would you wanna break

a perfectly good heart?

—Taylor Swift

After Carmen and Bridget left in the taxi, Lena sat at the little white Formica table in the kitchen of her grandparents' house. This was where she'd sat eating cereal with Bapi the summer she'd turned sixteen. He'd sat in the chair across from this one, day after day, and quietly eaten his Cheerios.

It didn't look the same as it had back then. Not this room or any other part of the house. It was faded and indistinct. She could barely make herself think of it as the same house. But everything was like that now. Even her own wrists and feet seemed strangely foreign to her. Maybe it was her eyes where the problem lodged.

Sometimes she would sink so deeply into her mind—no particular thoughts, no particular narrative, just mud and murk—that it would take her a bewilderingly long time to remember where she was and why. It was almost like she was falling asleep and waking up so many times a day, forgetting and remembering, that she was starting to live in between.

The phone rang and she picked it up. It was the woman from the coroner's office again. The woman talked rapidly about paperwork and signatures and schedules, and though Lena listened as carefully as she could, she kept getting lost. She heard the words and knew the words and forgot them and tried to remember them, and by then the woman had already leapt ahead by dozens more words.

Over the past few days, Lena had tried, she really had. She knew the Rollinses, Bridget, and Carmen were counting on her. It was her place where this had happened. But her Greek wasn't up to it. She wasn't up to it. It was possible her brain wouldn't process what had happened in any language.

"Do you understand? Do you understand?" the woman kept saying.

Lena held the phone with both hands. "I really don't," she said.

Lena found the number through the operator and called it that afternoon. Once she thought of it, she didn't hesitate. It was a local number, picked up by voice mail after a few rings.

She listened to his voice, his outgoing message, which was in Greek. "Kostos, this is Lena Kaligaris," she said in English, in a voice she hardly recognized. "I am in Santorini and I'm sorry to bother you, but if you are in town I need your help. Please call me at my grandparents' house if you get this message." She left the number in case he had forgotten it.

She hung up the phone. Her heart kept on with its same heavy thud. She listened for the sounds of Carmen's and Bee's footsteps even though they were gone and had been since that morning.

They hadn't been able to look at one another to say goodbye. Between them was a seething, putrid mess of blame and fear and recrimination: *What have we done? How did we let this happen? What did you know? What did I know? What didn't you tell me? What didn't I tell myself?*

They had let Tibby slip away from them into complete darkness and *not even known.*

What does this mean about us? Who are we now? Who have we become?

When Bridget called Eric from the airport in Athens to let him know when she was getting in, he told her he'd take the afternoon off work to pick her up from the airport and to spend some time with her. She landed at SFO and saw his anxious face the moment she passed through the doors from the terminal into the baggage claim.

He took her in his arms right away. "I'm so sorry," he murmured in her ear. He rocked her, saying it over and over.

But no matter how many times he said it, no matter how much she knew he meant it, the words stirred around in her ear but didn't get into her brain. Sometimes he could comfort her. Sometimes he said what she needed, but today he couldn't reach her. Nothing could.

She stared out the car window on the way home. She watched the brown hills, wondering when they would be green again. Eric didn't try to make her talk.

As they headed into the Mission she experienced a stretch of time when she couldn't remember where she lived. She kept picturing the place they'd had when Eric had first moved out here, when they'd first moved in together, the little place on Oak Street. She couldn't remember anything of what her life was after that.

When she stepped into the apartment, it didn't seem to belong to her, though she'd picked it—even forced Eric into it. She saw that Eric had laid the table with things she loved: a black bean burrito from Pancho's, a sliced ripe avocado, a bowl of cubed mango, a plate of oatmeal cookies, and a pitcher of lemonade made with seltzer. She turned to him and thanked him by putting her arms around him. She was grateful, she really was. Even if none of it seemed to relate to her anymore. Even if she couldn't eat any of it.

"Okay, here's the big surprise," he announced, throwing open the bedroom door.

Bridget stared into the little room in disbelief. There was a bed. A big wooden four-poster job riding high with its box spring and mattress, its fluffy comforter and pile of pillows.

"Brand-new sheets and everything," Eric declared proudly. He walked toward it and she followed, slowly.

"I realized we've never had a bed," he said, admiring it, patting it with his open hand. "We always sleep on a mattress on the floor or a futon or something. I feel like it's time for us to have a real bed, you know? I took a while picking it out. There were a lot of different kinds. I hope you like it."

He turned to look at her. She couldn't say anything. She sat on the floor in the doorway and burst into tears.

"Bee, what?" Eric asked, kneeling down next to her. "What is it?"

She couldn't catch her breath. He put his arms around her, but she couldn't settle her gasping.

"Please. Tell me what's wrong."

"I—I don't want that b-bed," she sobbed.

"Why not? What's wrong with it? I thought you'd like it."

She looked up at it. "It's n-not a b-bad bed. B-but do you have any i-idea—" She stopped and again she tried to catch her breath. "H-how hard it will be to m-move?"

"I don't want to move. I want to stay here. I want to settle down with you. I can take care of you, Bee."

She felt like her lungs had turned inside out. They wouldn't fill with air. It was urgent, what she felt, but she couldn't explain it. She could never make him understand.

Lena believed it was the afternoon after the day Carmen and Bridget had left for the airport. She calculated it was the day after she'd spoken to the coroner and left a message for Kostos. She'd sat for a long time at the kitchen table and then she lay on the couch in the dark while some amount of time passed. It was probably the next day, but an extra day could have slouched away and a new day could have slipped under the door, and she might not have noticed it.

She believed, though, it was the day after they'd left that Kostos arrived.

She heard the knock on the door, and she gathered herself up off the couch and opened it. She didn't expect it would be him. She didn't expect it would be anybody. It used to be that a knock on the door indicated someone was almost definitely there, but just as time had gone haywire, her mind had shrunken away from most matters of cause and effect. Occurrences just kind of bubbled up in front of her eyes and either stayed there for a while or disappeared again. The occurrence, in this case, was Kostos.

He opened his arms to her, and she walked into them. He wrapped her tightly and she felt her face pressing into his cotton shirt. The smell in his collar was very familiar. He'd somehow fallen back down into the world where she lived. She sensed the emotions, the surprise and strangeness of this, but she couldn't quite feel them.

"Come in," she said, and she led the way to the couch. She'd forgotten how dark it was, that all the shutters were closed, until he was sitting next to her and she couldn't see his face.

"I guess it's dark in here," she said wanly, walking to a front window and unlatching it. The sunshine crashed through, more of it than had been invited.

His face was sad, she realized. He picked up her hand and held it. She thought to ask him what was wrong. She was confused, forgetting where she was again. And then she remembered. On the whole, forgetting was easier, but it never stayed away long.

"Tibby's gone," she said. She had no idea there were tears leaking out, but there they were. Her face was wet; they had to be hers.

He nodded. Somehow he knew about it already. That was a relief in a way, because she wasn't sure she could put enough words in a row to explain it.

"She drowned."

He nodded again.

"Here."

"That's what I heard."

"I thought you would probably be in London."

"I was."

"How did you get here?"

"On a plane."

She nodded in spite of her confusion. Did that mean he'd come here because she'd called him? Did that make sense? This and other possibilities hovered in the air, but she couldn't consolidate them. "I felt like I should be able to handle the police and the coroner and the embassy and everything else, but I haven't done very well at it."

"I hope I can help."

She nodded. "They've all gone back. Tibby's parents and Carmen and Bridget. They were all gone by yesterday morning. I think." She paused. She was going to say something about Tibby going with them. Tibby's body going with them. But she couldn't figure out the way you said it. There was a way you said things like that. "I think it was yesterday morning."

"I see," he said.

"At first we thought it was an accident, but now it seems like she knew she was going to drown."

He tipped his head; his eyes registered confusion. "What do you mean?" He looked not just sad but surprised now.

"It seems like she brought us here to say goodbye." These were things Lena had not dared say out loud to anyone or even fully think, and here she was saying them to him. She who usually did so much thinking and considering for every word that left her mouth, she didn't think at all. She just opened her mouth and these were the words that came out.

"Why do you think that?" His face was tender. He was still holding her hand.

"Because she left things for us. To say goodbye."

Kostos nodded. He was quiet for some time. "Are you sure?"

She shook her head. "Not of anything anymore. But she wrote to us about getting along without her. She left us envelopes of things to be opened later, when she said she knew she couldn't be with us."

"Could she have been planning to go somewhere? To move away?"

Lena considered. "She wrote to us about how she wanted us to remember her."

With the hand that wasn't holding hers, Kostos rubbed his eyes. "It does seem like she knew something was going to happen."

"Yes."

"And you are afraid that if she did, then maybe she meant for it to happen."

That was the step Lena couldn't follow. You would think that, but she couldn't have meant for it to happen.

"Did anyone talk to the police or the coroner about that?"

She shook her head, stricken. "Because I just can't imagine it." She didn't remember crying, but her face was wet again. She hoped he wouldn't notice.

"But that's how it seems."

"That's how it seems."

———

Bridget sat down at the laden kitchen table and stood up again. She paced the sunless room. She ate half a slice of avocado and felt it curdling her stomach.

She couldn't seem to focus on Eric's face, or really on anything. Her eyeballs seemed to vibrate in their sockets. She tried to sit down again, but she couldn't. Her legs would not be still. She felt Eric's concerned eyes on her and tried not to let the panic show. He was expecting her to tell him about Tibby, but she couldn't do it.

"I'm going to walk," she announced. "I need to get something at the drugstore."

He stood. "I can get it. I don't mind."

"No, thanks. I need to move around a little. I was on a plane for a lot of hours."

"But you didn't eat yet."

She grabbed half the burrito in its foil to eat on the way. "It's a girl thing I need. Can't really wait." She was halfway to the door before he could stop her.

"Do you want company?" he asked, following her.

"No, no. I'll be back soon." She didn't even look behind her. She stumbled down the stairs and let the big door close after her with a bang.

She walked. She walked quickly without thinking of where to go. She paused long enough to drop the half burrito into a garbage can. She would have liked to have her bike, but she didn't want to go back for it. She didn't walk to the drugstore. She didn't get or need girl things. She needed to keep moving.

She walked up Divisadero Street and saw the sunset. It was a beautiful pink, orange, and deep gray sky, but the beauty of it didn't enter her eyes. It stayed on their surface, a reflection.

She would have kept walking down into the Marina and into the sea, but the thought buzzed and nagged every few minutes like a clock-radio alarm set to snooze that just would not leave you alone: Eric was waiting for her. Eric was sitting with a table of her favorite food. Eric was worried about her, and the thought of him wouldn't leave her alone.

At last that alarm nagged so loudly she stopped and turned

around and walked straight back down Divisadero. She walked all the way home, harnessing her panic to propel some kind of plan. A bad plan, a wrong plan, but the only plan she could tolerate.

"I was starting to worry about you," Eric said as soon as she walked in the door.

She went directly to the bathroom and closed the door. She hadn't been sensible enough to bring home a bag. "You shouldn't worry," she called through the door.

She sat on the closed toilet and put her head in her hands.

This is the man you love, some part of her felt the need to say.

I don't even know what that means, the rest of her responded. *I don't know how to do that now.*

She thought of the bed. The four posters. She came out of the bathroom when she could.

Eric was reading legal papers at the kitchen table. He'd put away the food.

She stood sheepishly in the doorway. She touched her fingers to the messy part in her hair. She hadn't washed it in days. "Hey," she said quietly.

He smiled at her, but his smile was uncertain. "Do you want to watch something? A movie?"

She nodded. It seemed easier than talking. He spent a lot of time perusing their small library. She knew he wanted to be careful. Nothing with death. Nothing dark or challenging. At last he put on *The Princess Bride.* He knew she loved it. It would be distracting if not captivating.

He sat on the couch and she sat between his knees on the floor, trying to figure out some way to settle her restless legs short of chopping them off.

The movie was neither captivating nor distracting. By the time they got to the fire swamp, Eric was yawning and Bridget could no longer pretend to sit still. She reached for the remote and turned it off.

"You go to bed," she suggested. "I know you're tired. I'll unpack for a few minutes and then I'll join you."

"I wish you'd come now," he said, but with a look of resignation.

"I need to unpack a few things. I'm on Greek time." She stopped herself before she added a third poor excuse.

He went into the bedroom and she went through the motions of opening her suitcase in the living room and pulling things out of it. Soon enough she heard the rhythmic sound of his breathing.

Eric always fell asleep quickly, in the way of a good person. He slept deeply, the reward for innocence and hard work.

Bridget stood in agitation by the kitchen window. She moved in agitation to the doorway of the bedroom and watched him sleep. She couldn't get in the bed. It looked like a prison cell to her. She retrieved her hiking pack from her closet. She brought it into the living room and transferred about half of the things from her suitcase into her pack. The apartment felt like a prison to her.

She tied her sleeping bag to the pack and left it by the front door. She grabbed her cellphone from the front table and stuck it in her pocket. She went to the side of the new bed and leaned down to kiss Eric on the temple.

"I can't do it. I'm sorry," she said, too quietly for him to hear.

She jotted a note and left it on the table.

I can't stay. I have to keep moving. I'm sorry to go.
I love you.

With her pack on her back and an ache in her chest, Bridget walked across the city. She walked down through Cole Valley and up into the Haight, through the disaffected late-night hordes. She walked all the way down Fulton Street to the ocean and stood on the dark beach. She took off her shoes and socks and walked to the edge of the surf. The Pacific was mighty. It could swallow anything. She took her cellphone out of her pocket and threw it as far as she could into the waves. She'd offer that for starters.

She laid her sleeping bag out on the sand and crawled into it, trying to stop her body from shaking. She lay on her back, staring at the quiet stars, wondering when the fog would roll over her.

Her body was a prison, her mind was a prison. Her memories were a prison. The people she loved. She couldn't get away from the hurt of them. She could leave Eric, walk out of her apartment, walk forever if she liked, but she couldn't escape what really hurt. Tonight even the sky felt like a prison.

———————

Kostos walked out the door of her grandparents' house, explaining about needing to pick up a few things. Lena closed the door behind him and promptly presumed she had hallucinated the entire episode.

But a short time later he returned, carrying a leather satchel and two bags of groceries. Within minutes he was fielding phone calls, one from somebody connected to the U.S. consulate and one from the local police precinct. He seemed to know everything and everyone without her having to say a word. She wondered if she was still hallucinating.

He hung up the phone, unpacked his groceries, and made her a plate of scrambled eggs and toast with sweet tea. She sat across the little kitchen table from him and ate. It had been so long since she'd put food in her mouth it felt strange, as though her tongue had forgotten how to taste and her teeth how to chew. She took a break in the middle and rested her chin on her hand. It was oddly exhausting, eating.

She considered his face, more in pieces than as a whole. She couldn't take it all together. There were those emotions down there, and though she couldn't quite feel them, they were strong and she feared them. It was like watching a thunderhead from high up in a plane, and though you weren't under it, you knew how it would feel if you were. You knew you'd have to land eventually.

His cheekbones, his nose, and his jaw were more prominent than she remembered. His principal expressions had become etched into his face—the eye crinkles from laughter, concern, and maybe nearsightedness, the subtle lines around his mouth. She watched the lines shift and move when he talked.

He had yesterday's whiskers, lightened by sparkles of silver. *You are older,* she thought. But this was her Kostos, the man she remembered, not the man from the magazines. Could there be two of him? She had the remote idea of looking at his hand for a ring. He didn't have one on the marriage finger, but he did have a silver one on the middle finger. She didn't know what signified what in Greece or in London, and she couldn't follow her own thoughts.

"How strange this is," she said quietly, to him, her eggs, herself.

I figure I basically am a
ghost.

I think we all are.

—John Astin

Dear Dad,

I appreciate you calling all those times and I'm sorry I haven't called back. That was a really nice note you sent. I know you want to be there for the burial, but Alice says please wait and come to the memorial service in the spring. I know you want to help, and I really appreciate it. I'll call you when I get back to New York, or maybe I can come down to Charleston for a visit sometime. So, anyway, thanks a lot, Dad, and I'll talk to you soon.

Love,
Carmen

Carmen stared at the email for a long time without pressing send. She lay in her old bed, her old bed in her mother's big new house, and in a strange way she felt like she and her dad were slowly switching places.

She remembered how frustrated she used to be with him for avoiding her sadness, blandly saying things like suffering made you stronger and hard knocks were for the best. In the old days she'd wanted most of all to share something important with him, to be brought closer to him by it. Now he was ready to acknowledge her grief, to show her the way, and she didn't want any of it. Who was the avoider now? She couldn't take his grief and she couldn't take her own.

She glanced down at the email icon on her phone. It showed there were five new messages, and she saw in them a couple of minutes of salvation. She recognized in herself the familiar old maneuvers: the dodge, the stall, the float-above-it-all. She recognized them from having watched him. And in his plaintive offerings she recognized an old self of hers who tried harder to be brave.

"Do you want to sleep?" Kostos asked Lena as she yawned over her tea.

"If I could, I would," she said.

He had an open and sympathetic face. He always had—even when he was crushing her hopes most brutally. "You lie down on the couch and I'll answer the phone or the door. I'll watch over everything."

I'll watch over the sadness for you, he seemed to be saying. *I'll watch over the worry and the big, dark questions so you can get a little rest.*

"Thank you. I'll try," she said. She lay down, her hands under her head, and he gave her a wool blanket. He spread it over her as though it were his house, not hers. And it was his more than hers. He'd been spending time in this house his whole life, and she had only come four times, always to lose things—her heart, her grandfather, her pants, Tibby, and along with Tibby her sense of comfort that she understood anything about the world or ever had. He touched her anklebone by mistake.

He sat in the green upholstered chair across from her. She watched him carefully, openly, as he got up and retrieved his bag from the other side of the room and took out his newspaper. She forgot that she was supposed to be sleeping and that it was a weird thing to do.

He put his feet up on the coffee table and glanced at her. She closed her eyes, but they didn't want to stay shut. Her lids felt not heavy but rubbery and light, and perhaps too short to even cover her eyeballs. Strange.

She turned over to face the couch instead. Maybe her eyelids had become short because she wanted to look at him. She gazed at the pattern of the couch for a while—green, blue, yellow, ochre, garnet-red hydrangea puffs that didn't really look at all like hydrangea puffs but like a fantastically druggy impression of them. This was a couch that wouldn't go with any painting.

And then she started to wonder what would happen to this couch. This would be one of the things her father wouldn't know what to do with. She pictured it sitting out on the winding street, waiting for someone to claim it, the harsh island sun picking out every sign of wear.

She pictured her grandparents buying it. She imagined the boxy furniture store in Fira in about 1972, her grandmother effusive over the colors and her grandfather with his sweet face and nothing to say. She pictured how the couch would look in her studio apartment in Providence. It wouldn't fit. She'd have to get rid of her bed. It was a thought.

When she flipped back over she discovered that Kostos's newspaper had drifted to his lap, his head had drifted backward, and his eyelids had closed. With wide-open eyes she watched him sleep. *I guess I can watch over you,* she thought. The sight of his sleeping self seemed almost like a feast offered to her eyes, both inviting and overwhelming. She had hungry eyes, even now. The thing that always held her back was that she hated being caught looking. And now she could look all she wanted. For a time, his face belonged not to the important world, but to her.

She did a strange thing, which was she got a sketchbook and charcoal from her bag. Those two items lived permanently in her bag, but she hadn't gotten them out and used them in a long time. Kostos slept quietly and she drew his face, full as it was of dramas she could barely remember right now. Even if your brain didn't understand anything, your eyes could still see. Even if you were high above, looking down on the thunderhead and not yet getting pummeled by it, you could still draw. That felt like a saving grace.

When he opened his eyes it took him a few seconds to come back to her. A look of apology materialized on his face. He had wanted to watch over her. He really had meant to, but the sadness and the worry were like unruly children, very difficult to babysit.

Kostos talked on the phone in her grandparents' kitchen and Lena sat by the window and looked out at a small segment of the street and the house a few yards across it. She could have gone upstairs and given herself the whole magnificent expanse of the Caldera, but sometimes a close view was all a person could handle.

She listened to his voice. It had been electrifying in the past, but it lulled her now. For some reason her mind strayed to an image of her hyperactive cousin who needed a stimulant to calm down.

Kostos was, as she'd known he would be, the perfect person for this burden. He was already the trusted friend of the guy at the consulate, the go-to man for the last loose ends at the precinct. At some point she realized he'd switched from English to Greek, but she hadn't noticed right away because she hadn't stopped understanding.

Lena thought for a moment of Eudoxia. *I did call him after all,* she thought sadly.

Kostos was quiet for a while, and when she went to check on him, he'd taken apart the kitchen faucet to fix the drip. She watched him for a few minutes from the doorway, forgetting to be self-conscious and that he might be.

"Nobody's taken care of this house for a long time," she said.

"What's going to happen to it?"

"My father says he's going to sell it. But that will require him coming here and putting it in order and sorting through all the old things."

He nodded. "I hate to think of this house belonging to anyone else." When he'd finished reassembling the faucet he looked up. "You could do it."

"Do what?"

"Get the house fixed up."

"*I* could?"

He nodded. "I could help you."

The storm cloud crackled below her. She blinked away tears. "But I have to go back."

"Why?"

It wasn't even that she was scared. Maybe she would have stayed. She looked at him in the eyes. "The burial."

His face was pained. "Oh." He nodded slowly. "Of course. When?"

"Tomorrow. I go back tomorrow. The burial is the next day. Thursday." She was still of no mind to keep track of the days, but she remembered how Alice Rollins kept saying Thursday. In her mind Thursday had nothing to do with Tibby, but it was one of the few fixed points on her horizon.

He opened his mouth as though he was going to say something, but he didn't. He wrung out the sponge in the sink and began wiping down the counters.

She went to the bathroom to wash her face and blow her nose, and when she came back, Kostos, star financier, was taking apart the hinges of the back door that would no longer open.

Bridget's body was in pure revolt and her mind had nothing further to say about it. It had nothing to say about anything. She thought nothing, had nothing, belonged to nothing, owned nothing. Except her bike.

She went back the second day to retrieve it, when she was sure Eric would be at work. She wondered for the miles she walked back to the apartment how she would get it without the key to unlock the door to the garage. That was where she'd stored her bike the day she'd left for Greece.

She felt a pang. She'd been so happy at that moment right before Greece, imagining that her life would be coming together, not falling apart. She pushed the memory away.

Eric kept the garage key on his key chain. Bridget barely ever used it. She never used the car and preferred to lock her bike on the front porch for quick access. Could she jimmy the lock? Could she climb through a window? She was remarkably good at both of those things.

But when she got there, she found the garage door swung open, almost as if Eric had left it that way for her. There was her bike in the corner.

Her mind stayed mostly quiet, and it was better that way. She wheeled her bike out and all the way to Sixteenth Street before she got on. She wasn't as glad to see it as she'd thought she would be. It didn't feel so much like it was hers. The silk flowers looked stupid. She didn't know why she had ever liked them.

She rode up through Pacific Heights, punishing her restless muscles on the most precipitous hills, and then down to the Presidio. She turned north and stopped at Fort Point long enough to unwind the flowers from her bars and basket. She stood on a wall and threw the silk flowers into the greedy water. It could have those too.

Kostos thought maybe a walk would help, and Lena thought maybe he was right. Maybe she would be better at moving than staying still.

When she stepped out the front door the sunshine was so strong her shoulders stooped under the force of it. She squinted and blinked, trying to adjust her eyes and her pores to the onslaught.

She glanced down the road to Kostos's grandparents' house. She was still slightly afraid of them from the time she'd made a spectacle of herself the first summer. It was many years ago, granted, but she had an acute memory for her mistakes. She'd imagined she would at least stop by and say hello. She'd imagined she would talk with Rena a little about her grandmother. She'd even packed a little gift for them, and a note from her mother. But then, early that first morning, all previous notions had been scattered or obliterated.

"Are you staying with them?" she asked, gesturing to the house. It was so close, she remembered thinking that first summer, that if she'd tripped and rolled, and the Dounases' door happened to be open, she would have rolled right into the living room of Kostos's house.

"No. I always see them when I come, but I have my own place."

She tried to picture it. "You still have the apartment in Fira?" she asked. She remembered that when he'd been married to Mariana, that was where they had lived.

He looked puzzled at first, and then seemed to realize what place she meant. "No, no." His expression told her it would have been impossible for her to be more wrong. "A few years ago I bought a place opposite Oia, overlooking the Caldera."

"Your own house?"

He looked vaguely uncomfortable. "A weekend house. A vacation house."

"Can you go on vacation at home?"

That didn't assuage his discomfort. She backed off. She hadn't meant to ask him any of those stupid questions.

They walked up the hill instead of down. It didn't matter; either way was fraught.

As they climbed she talked to herself rather than to him. She chastised herself for her dim-witted confusion—thinking he still lived with his grandparents, forgetting who he actually was now. It was because she couldn't contemplate having the will or the means to buy a house for yourself—especially not in a place you weren't even living. Lena barely had the courage or cash to buy a toaster oven. What small amount of money she had she spent on rent and food. Even when she managed to stash away some savings, she tended not to acquire or accumulate anything besides photos, keepsakes, and sketchbooks. That was normal for college students, especially art students, and for people who refused to let time move forward.

But Kostos was long past that. He was over thirty years old. He had a hugely powerful job. He'd been on the cover of a magazine, for God's sake. Lena had trapped herself in time, but only in her delicate delusions was he trapped there too.

Going uphill was fraught because at the top of the hill, on the plateau, was the little grove they'd shared in a variety of moods, including shame, lust, betrayal, and forgiveness. If he led her there, she was worried she might find herself down in the heart of the storm.

But he didn't. Instead he led her to a parched stretch of rock, and they sat on a precipice overlooking the water.

This was the view she'd been avoiding, and as her eyes blurred into the blue horizon she understood why. Something moved in her brain, maybe something opened or something shut. The horizon wobbled and spread and the tears rolled over her cheeks. Her breath caught and her shoulders shook.

She found her head tipping against his shoulder and vaguely she felt his arm come around her. The water seemed to dissolve her. Maybe it was the salt in her tears melting her, turning her inside out like a slug. She didn't fight it. She couldn't have anyway.

She remembered crying like this in Bee's arms, and it had been over Kostos. She remembered crying like this in her mother's arms a different time, and it was also over Kostos. And now here were Kostos's arms around her as she cried over Tibby and their whole lost life.

Who would have imagined that he, the source of all fret, would turn out to be a source of comfort? She'd built him up so far and high, it was hard to imagine he was right here with her at such a time. It seemed like a hallucination, but not one to be poked at or questioned, so she let it be.

She cried for a long time. Or so she guessed by the changing of the light. Kostos was a patient man. It was his nature, as true to him as his polite manners, his guilt, his oversized accountability. The guilt was for her.

She'd cried over a broken heart before. She knew what that felt like, and it didn't feel like this. Her heart felt not so much broken as just . . . empty. It felt like she was an outline, empty in the middle. The outline cried senselessly for the absent middle. The past cried for the present that was nothing. Tibby was too deeply incorporated within her for Lena to go on without her.

"I lose everything here," she said.

He couldn't really know what she meant, but he thought it over carefully nonetheless.

"Maybe you gain things too," he said.

"Maybe I do," she said. She considered that and shook her head. "Nothing I get to keep."

Bridget indulged one of her old desires. Sometime around mid-night—she wasn't sure what time it was anymore—she locked her bike to a lamppost and unrolled her sleeping bag on a bench in Dolores Park. She stretched out on her back, her head resting on her pack, and looked up through the branches of a familiar tree to the disjointed pieces of the sky.

She tried to lie low, not to alert her friends, because they might tell Eric—the Tall Mexican in the Suit, as they referred to him—and he would worry about her descending immediately into homeless-ness. But she discovered as it got later and colder that though this group talked up sleeping outside, most of them seemed to get ab-sorbed into nearby churches and shelters long before dawn. In the darkest hours it got very quiet.

She was nearly asleep when she felt something nearby. She opened her eyes and saw nothing, so she closed them again. A few more minutes passed and her breathing evened out. And then sud-denly there was a shadow over her face and she felt her pack pulled from under her head.

There was one benefit to having a body so charged with agony and adrenaline. She got her hands on her pack almost instanta-neously and yanked it back.

Her eyes took a little longer to adjust. It was a man with a knit hat and a beard.

"Get off my pack," she growled at him.

"I've got a knife," he said menacingly.

She pulled on her pack even harder. She didn't care if he had a knife. Let him have a knife. Let him kill her with his knife. That would be fine, but he wasn't taking her stuff.

She was up on her feet, towering. She was taller than he was and a lot angrier. She'd given nearly everything she had to the people in this park, but she'd done it on her own terms. She wouldn't do it on his.

With more strength than she knew she possessed she wrenched the pack out of his hands. He came at her, trying to tackle her, but she was balanced and strong. She clutched her pack in one arm and with the other punched him as hard as she could in the jaw. It hurt her hand, but it hurt his jaw too, she knew. In surprise he put his hand to his face and she punched him again in the ear.

If he had a knife, she never saw it. He turned and walked away. He seemed to know she was crazier than he was. She was tempted to follow him and hit him again. He might have been a felon or a junkie, but he had more to live for than she did.

"Fuck off," she spat at him.

Her hand hurt. She hugged her pack. She didn't want to give anything away anymore.

Lena and Kostos sat on the couch that night. First they were sitting up on opposite ends, then they turned to each other, she cross-legged. His nice shoes came off, and eventually, as it got late, they each leaned back, symmetrically resting on pillows propped against the arms of the couch, their knees bent and feet not quite touching. The conversation flowed and stopped and started as it would, a third thing in the room, not quite controlled by either of them, but mostly benevolent.

She began to doze off, and when she woke she realized she'd stretched out her legs and he'd taken her large feet on his lap. They were not her best part.

"Do you have any idea how much that letter meant?" she found herself asking him. It must have tied in with a dream she'd been having. She wondered why she said it, unguarded as it was, and not connected to anything. But why not say it? What was there to hold on to anymore? This was her hallucination and she could say what she wanted in it.

He held her feet. He was puzzled. "What letter?"

What letter. Was there any other letter? God, how small her life had become. It was probably one of five he had written that week. She took a breath. "The letter you wrote to me after Valia died."

He nodded. "I loved her like she was my own grandmother. I walk up this street and I miss her every time."

"She loved you too. You know that. She was so proud of you. She felt like everybody abandoned this place. We all made homes in other places, and you, the hero of Oia, always came back."

He shrugged and shook his head. There was almost no blaming with him. "Everybody leaves here. Except the tourists. The Germans. They stay."

She smiled. It was probably a smile. "I couldn't understand my own feelings about Valia until I read your letter, and then I could."

"That makes me glad to know," he said. He considered, his eyes down. "I disappointed her, though."

"Valia?"

"Yes."

"Impossible."

"I did."

"In what way?"

His face had turned inward and complicated, and she found herself unsure about wanting to follow him in. He rarely paused to search for words as he was doing now. He glanced down and then looked up at her. He smiled, but not easily. "I didn't marry her granddaughter."

Lena's caution seemed to slow her thoughts—she could almost watch them going by like words on a very slow ticker tape. Kostos didn't marry Valia's granddaughter. Lena was Valia's granddaughter— one of her granddaughters, most likely the one he meant. Kostos didn't marry her, was what he meant. Kostos was supposed to marry her, Lena, and he hadn't.

Lena looked up at him in alarm. She hadn't thought he would ever say that out loud. She was too far gone to process the impact of these words and also too far gone to make any attempt to hide from them.

No, he hadn't married her, had he? He had married somebody else. He had divorced somebody else. He had gone on with his life, clearly not held back by any of it. You couldn't let a grumpy grandmother—somebody else's grumpy grandmother—tell you whom to marry.

Kostos's eyes were cast slightly down, but not focused on anything. She sensed he was looking at Valia in his mind's eye. "Before she died she asked me why. And I couldn't explain it to her satisfaction, but I told her I loved you, and she said, 'What good does that do me?'"

Kostos looked up, refocusing his eyes on Lena.

He smiled, trying to lighten the mood, but her face was stricken, she knew. She didn't have the wherewithal to compose it in another way.

He looked regretful, sorry for her. "It was all a long time ago."

She didn't know what to say. She gaped at him like a gutted fish.

"So much has changed since then," he added quickly. He didn't want her dangling on the hook.

She nodded. She couldn't seem to speak. She sat up and withdrew her feet.

"I'm sorry I brought it up," he said.

Lena wanted to say so many things. She wanted to close this abyss, to cover it graciously, to make him feel okay, cross over it carefully, to get to the other side and keep on walking.

She also wanted to dive into it and ask him whether his love was only in the past tense anymore. A part of her wanted to tell him she still loved him, and that even though this love was hopeless and long over, it still consumed her year after year. It was a tangled hairball of feelings and she couldn't pull forth any one strand.

"I'm sorry," he said again. "You don't have to say anything."

He got up off the couch and went into the kitchen. Lena hugged her knees. She wondered if she was having a stroke, if the entire speaking apparatus of her brain had flooded and shut down.

He came back with a loaf of bread and cheese, two apples, and a bottle of red wine. He carefully sliced the bread, cut into an apple. He poured the wine, letting the strange air in the room begin to settle back toward normal.

She held the glass and balanced a plate on her knees. "Thank you," she choked out.

He lifted his glass. "To friendship," he said.

She nodded and lifted her glass in return. She worked on a smile. Even that would help.

They chewed and sipped in silence for a few minutes.

"You know what I'd like to do?" he said.

She shook her head.

"I'd like to write you a letter about Tibby. I'd like to write something that could help, I really would." He looked almost tearful. "But I don't know what it would say."

She was moved by the sympathy in his face. It took her a while to pick her words. "I don't know what it would say either.".

He nodded. His face expressed something like defeat, and she hated for him to feel that way. He'd spoken to three local bureaucrats on her behalf. He'd fixed her eggs and tea, bread and wine. He'd repaired the kitchen faucet and the back door, and had even cleaned out the cabinets when she wasn't looking. He'd lain with her for hours on the couch. He'd held her feet.

Who knew why? Who knew what—other than guilt and a sense of responsibility toward Valia—made him do it? But strange as it was, Kostos, her customary causer of sadness, had given her enormous comfort.

She swallowed the bread she was chewing and cleared her throat. "Your being here is kind of like the letter," she said.

Lena could hear the wind outside late that night. It sounded like the beginnings of a storm. She could almost feel the anticipation of it on her skin.

It was well after midnight, and she had expected that at some point Kostos would go back to his alleged vacation house, which she knew had to offer accommodations more comfortable than her grandparents' old couch. But he didn't. He lay with her, or mostly with her feet, sipping wine, occasionally talking, and eventually dozing.

Tonight we make strange bedfellows, she thought. Her loss, his guilt. Her insecurity, his good manners. Usually these things kept them apart, but tonight they brought them together.

Was there an attraction anymore? There had been, fiercely, before. But she was too distant from herself, too sad and empty and confused to know anymore. What, besides sympathy, did he feel for her now? He was large and dashing and glamorous, moving through time with ease, where she felt stunted and small and stuck, a stick figure of pity with large feet.

She could imagine how it seemed to him. If you couldn't bring yourself to marry the sad granddaughter, you could at least take pity on her.

He didn't touch her in any romantic way. The set of his body—even crimped with hers on this couch—was not suggestive or in any way demanding.

And if it had been otherwise?

Then it would have been all wrong. It might have momentarily flattered or reassured her, but at such a moment in her life, it would have felt desperate and sad. She wouldn't have been lifted up by an expression of his attraction right now, she would have been diminished by it. Over time, she would have resented him for it.

So why be disappointed by wishes you would not want to come true? That was the road to unhappiness if ever there was one, and she had traveled it extensively.

Whether or not he had ever wanted to marry her, he seemed to know the right way to care for her at a deeply fragile time, and that in itself was something like love. The love of a near-relative, the love of an old friend. Whatever it was, she was too depleted not to take what was offered.

She'd been certain she wouldn't and couldn't fall asleep in such a configuration of limbs—his limbs, of all limbs!—and yet she opened her eyes and there was light poking in at the bottom of the shutters. She had slept, really slept, for the first time in days.

Kostos was opposite her, still sleeping peacefully with his arms crossed around her ankles. She wanted to imprint this on her brain, to scratch it in deep so she could have it for later, when she could feel things again.

God often gives nuts to toothless people.

—Matt Groening

The following morning Bridget's hand was still pounding and swollen. She wondered if she'd just bruised it or broken a bone. She ripped one of her old T-shirts into strips and tied it up. It didn't help anything, but it made her feel a little more protected.

She ducked into Pancho Villa for a late-morning burrito and was happy to see the familiar ladies in their hairnets smiling at her. She wished she could speak Spanish. She wished she were like Eric, who dreamed in Spanish. In fact, she wished she thought and dreamed in a language she couldn't understand.

She wasn't hungry, exactly, but she needed to eat. She ate two-thirds of the burrito and drank a Mexican lime soda before she felt sick and dumped the rest in the garbage. She hated to waste it. She would have eaten it if she could have.

As she unlocked her bike, she had an idea. She pedaled up Guerrero until she came to a gas station. She spent a portion of the little cash she had on a foldout map of California. She was getting good at riding with her pack on her back. So she set out eastward into the Great Central Valley with a hat on her head and her aching hand and three bottles of water.

Davis was seventy miles away, a lot of it hot and relentlessly dry. Even on the smaller roads there were hours without shade. *You want sun?* the sky seemed to be taunting her. *I'll give you sun.*

It was nearly five o'clock when she arrived at the little gray bungalow. She locked her bike up on the porch. She knocked and peered in the windows, but nobody was home. She could probably find her way into the house if she wanted to, but she decided against it. She didn't want to be overwhelming right away.

She sat in a wicker chair on the front porch, grateful for the shade. She must have fallen asleep. She opened her eyes and saw Perry coming up the walk. She stood and hugged him. She pulled back and could see he was genuinely happy to see her and also awkward about what to say.

"I heard about— I'm so sorry about Tibby—"

"I know," she said quickly. She didn't know how to finish his sentence either.

"Are you all right?"

"Yeah," she said, too quickly to convince anybody. She pulled her pack up onto her shoulder. "Do you mind if I stay with you and Violet for a couple of days?"

"No. You can stay as long as you want. Where's Eric?"

"Home." She said it in a way that didn't welcome more questions.

"What did you do to your hand?"

She hesitated and then shrugged. "I hit it on something. It's fine."

Her brother was relatively easy to put off, and she was grateful for it. He turned to put his key in the door. His hair was blond again from living in California. He was much stronger and sturdier than he had been when he'd lived back East. Even though she'd seen him every few months since he'd moved here, she still somehow expected to see the old Perry every time.

"How's school?" she asked.

"Good. Almost done. I start my residency in July."

"Amazing. Do I get to call you Doctor?"

Perry laughed. "All you want. But I can't offer you much medical care."

"Unless I were a bird," she said, following him into the cool house.

"Yes. Or a dog or a horse or a swordfish."

"A swordfish?"

"Okay, maybe not a swordfish. A dolphin. Then I could help you."

"Are you still doing the oily bird network?"

He smiled. "Oiled wildlife. Yes."

Perry spent what seemed to her a million hours a week in school and doing schoolwork, and in his nonexistent free time he was part of a rescue network for injured animals. She knew that was the most important thing to him.

By the time Perry had made lemonade and changed his shoes, Violet had come home. She was surprised to see Bridget, but not unwelcoming. She gave Bridget a hug. "I'm sorry for what you've been through," she said.

Violet had a pointy chin, black eyes, freckles, and serious-girl glasses. She worked in a lab at the vet school, doing research on infectious animal diseases. She and Perry had gotten married on the beach at Monterey among the elephant seals two years before. Violet was thirty-three. She told Bridget they were going to try to get pregnant as soon as Perry got his DVM.

Perry made pasta with pesto sauce and Violet made a salad. Bridget ate voraciously and then fell asleep on the couch without even brushing her teeth. She woke a while later, to the sound of them cleaning the kitchen. They must have thought she was asleep.

"Do you think she's okay?" she heard Violet asking in a quiet voice.

Perry's response was muffled.

"Do you think Eric knows she's here? Should we call him?"

Bridget couldn't fall back asleep, but she couldn't get up off the couch either. What a reversal had taken place over the last decade. It used to be she who was the functional one. She had the best friends, went to a good college, played on a team, while Perry stayed in his room, so lost in his obscure role-playing games on the computer that he barely ate. It was Perry people whispered about, Perry they worried about. Not her.

Now Perry had a wife, a house, friends, a purpose, a graduate degree coming in May. And what did she have? The college didn't matter, the team didn't even really matter. But the friends. The friendship. Without it, she didn't know who she was. Without them, without the idea of them, she had nothing.

Kostos made Lena coffee in the morning and hustled her to the ferry dock. She was relieved to be taking a boat before the plane. She felt tremulous at the thought of leaving the surface of the earth just yet. She didn't trust anything to stay where she wanted it.

He carried her heavy bag and Tibby's duffel. He pulled her by the hand when it looked like she was in danger of missing her boat. He promised to close up the house, to make sure everything was left in order. He said it with such a sense of purpose she half expected he'd spackle the walls and refinish the floors before he considered himself done.

It was a rushed goodbye that would have to last for a long while, she guessed. Maybe forever. She hugged him zealously, her body able to express more than her brain. She pressed her face into his chest. He must have had the same feeling. He hugged her in return like she was someone he might not see again.

He kissed her hard, not on the face but above her ear. She wondered about the nature of this kiss.

They let go of each other. How to leave it? *I'll call you? Don't forget to write? See you next time!* None of that seemed to fit.

Because why say these words? When was next time going to be? Bapi was gone. Valia was gone. The house would soon be gone. They were two people who had never come together of their own volition. They'd come their weary way always by circumstances, usually bad ones. These few days had been like a cozy foxhole dug out of time—a big, prosperous life in his case, a tragedy in hers. It was time to go back to those things.

"Thank you," she said tearfully. Those were the parting words that fit.

She lugged the two bags the last few yards onto the boat. She weaved through the other passengers and parked at the first empty stretch of rail. Quickly she turned again to catch his face. She felt a sense of desperation as the engines began to churn and pull her away from the dock. She wanted to keep him in her mind as he was now. She didn't want to lose him.

What if this was her life? What if his was the face she was coming home to rather than leaving? What if she had arrived here on Independence Day all those summers ago? She pictured Kostos standing just where he was now, but the engines churning in the opposite direction, bringing her to him maybe forever. Was that the brave life through which she would have earned the right to keep Tibby?

He didn't move from his spot on the dock. The crowd drifted and dissipated and he stood there as the distance between them grew. And yet the wind was so oddly calm and the water so glassy she could imagine it was he who was drawing away and she who was staying still.

She hadn't chosen the brave life. She'd chosen the small, fearful one. She hadn't gotten to keep Tibby.

Finally she stopped waving, dropped her hands to her sides, and just looked at him as he got small. It gave her the feeling that her memory was already closing in on him. The distance between them stretched and finally broke. She never got to keep anything.

She turned to face the horizon, the blurring line of water and sky, the great vacuum, the place where things went when they left her.

But this morning it wasn't empty. This time she could barely open her eyes enough to see it because there was something large and fierce right in the middle of it and it was the sun.

She was not one

who expected to get away

with much in life.

—Larry McMurtry

Carmen lay on her mother's bed after the burial and let her mother rub her back, the way she'd done through all the many tragedies of Carmen's childhood. Carmen found herself longing for those tragedies, when a back rub and a long cry on her mother's pillow would do the trick, instead of this one, when nothing seemed to help.

At least the burial was over and she didn't have to dread it anymore. It had been small and grim, just a handful of shattered people standing in the gray November air: Tibby's family, Carmen and her mother, Lena and her parents. Vaguely Carmen wondered about Brian, what he knew and where he was. She wondered many things, but she didn't pursue the information. She was terrified by what little she knew; she didn't want to find out any more. That was wrong of her, maybe, but she didn't have the energy to make it right.

They muttered prayers standing on hard grass, but nobody tried to do any real eulogizing. Only the minister spoke of Tibby, and he kept calling her Tabitha. They'd plan a proper memorial service for the spring, Alice said. It was too shocking, too soon, too rushed, too confusing to attempt more than burying the body that was supposedly Tibby that came off an airplane. In the spring, Alice said, they'd know what to do. Alice had given them relentless permission not to come, but only Bridget had taken it. "I'll come in the spring," Bridget had said woodenly, and Carmen had known it would hurt Bee worse not to be there, but she hadn't been able to bridge the gap to tell her so.

Carmen had thought that when the burial was over there would be some relief, but there wasn't. Before, she had been able to aim the terrible feelings at the burial, so where was she supposed to aim them now? What was she supposed to do? She couldn't haul this misery around through her normal life. She couldn't fit it through the door of her loft. But what other life did she have?

She could stay here, curled up in the dark on her mother's bed.

But she couldn't. The skin of her back had begun to feel irritated under her mother's hand. Her whole body felt uncomfortable. The pressure in Carmen's chest forced her to sit up.

Christina withdrew her hand and she looked at Carmen sorrowfully. She knew she wasn't helping. Her face was full of compassion, but Carmen could see that her mother was spooked and uncertain too.

Not even you can reach me here, Carmen thought.

Perry and Violet were too quiet. They talked quietly. They ate quietly. When they played music it was quiet.

Bridget was loud. She stomped around loudly, wanting to drown out her loud thoughts, but it didn't work. By the second week she couldn't take it anymore. She left them a note and set off on her bike in the dark toward Sacramento.

She saw the neon lights of a pool bar on the outskirts of the city and pulled her bike into the parking lot. She locked her bike, heaved her pack onto her shoulder, and walked in. Now, this was loud.

She pulled her hair from its elastic and shook it out before she went up to the bar. She smiled at the fifty-some-year-old bartender and lifted her pack. "Do you think you could keep this back there for me?" she asked him sweetly. She smiled, and whatever reservation he had seemed to dissipate.

"Just this once," he said, and swung it under the bar. "What can I get you, sweetheart?"

"I'll take a Bud," she said. She didn't drink very often, and when she did, she wasn't prissy about it. She thought of Carmen and her white wine spritzers.

It was far from her last drink of the evening, but it was the last one she paid for. The guy who sent over the next two beers looked like he was barely out of high school. When he came over to ask her to dance he had an insistent look on his face and she didn't like it. "No thanks," she said with no coyness whatsoever.

He looked more irritated than hurt. "Come on, girl. I bought you two beers."

"And I thanked you for the beers. You didn't buy me."

She left him at the bar and went over to the area with the pool tables. It was crowded and the music was loud.

A waitress materialized with a tray and a bottle of beer on it. "This is from the gentleman over by the jukebox," she said, giving Bridget a little wink.

Bridget looked in the direction she pointed. The guy tipped his hat to her. He had tanned skin, straight dark hair down to his shoulders, and a worn cowboy hat. He wore a plaid shirt rolled up at the sleeves, revealing tattoos on both forearms. She walked over to him. "Hey, thanks."

"With pleasure." He studied her with obvious interest. "Can I talk you into a game of pool, beautiful?"

He was entirely relaxed and confident in the asking. He wasn't old, probably in his midthirties, but his skin was weathered in a way that made her think he probably worked at a local farm or ranch. Where the collar of his shirt was unbuttoned, she could see another tattoo winding up from his chest. She wondered what it was a picture of.

"Sure thing."

By the speed with which a table cleared when he made his intentions known, Bridget guessed he was a regular here and a serious player.

He saw Bridget pausing over the array of cues. "Is this a game or a lesson?"

Bridget feigned innocence. "Do you need me to show you how to play?"

He laughed, and it was a great big laugh. It was the first thing Bridget had enjoyed in many days.

She stuck out her hand. "My name is Bridget," she said.

He shook it, mildly surprised by her sudden formality. "Travis," he said.

"Travis," she repeated. "I like to know the name of my opponent before I beat him."

Travis bought Bridget two more beers while she beat him three games in a row. She was getting giddy. Giddy from drinking, giddy from winning, giddy from the crowd that had gathered around the table, giddy at the way Travis looked at her.

She was so giddy she lost the fourth game. She laughed as he got the whole bar involved in his victory lap.

He was obviously a local guy and well loved. He was as good a player as she was, if not better. But she'd taken advantage of his initial surprise and disorientation to win the first games. She was naturally gifted, and she'd played a shameful number of hours while getting Cs at Brown and in the first aimless years after she'd graduated.

"What do you say we team up?" he suggested. "We'll hold this table all night."

Their first opponents were two serious older Mexicans, and they gave them a long fight. When Bridget nailed the final shot, the entire population of the bar erupted. Travis picked her up off her feet and kissed her on the lips.

He might have expected her to pull away first, but she didn't. The kiss lengthened and deepened as the cheering of the spectators faded. Bridget felt the blood pounding in her head, rushing down into her abdomen. She felt the beer sloshing around behind her eyes and she could barely remember what had broken her heart two and a half weeks ago. She could almost forget that the burial had taken place and she hadn't been there.

They didn't hold the table all night. They were far more interested in each other than pool after that. They couldn't keep their hands off each other. She clutched another beer as Travis led her outside. If she kept drinking and he kept kissing her, she could keep the sadness away longer.

He took her around to the side of the bar, where it was dark and quiet. He took off his hat and dropped it on the grass. He took her in his arms and pushed her against the wall. He kissed her like she hadn't been kissed in a long time and she was breathless. The feeling was so strong she could lose herself in it.

She felt his hands on her back, then under her shirt. His hands came around the front. He pulled open her bra and then her shirt and she startled. It had been a long time since she'd had unfamiliar hands on her skin.

You are drunk, she informed herself drunkenly, feeling the spin starting in the middle of her head.

She unbuttoned his shirt so she could see his tattoo, but it seemed to spread all around and she was too close to his chest to be able to tell what it was. He was pushing himself against her and she could feel his hardness through her jeans and his. She meant to ask him about the tattoo, but she forgot the question before she could.

His hands were on the waistband of her jeans and then he was pulling at the button. *Am I really gonna do this? Right here, right now?* the least drunk part of her was asking, while the rest of her was barreling along.

He undid the button and zipper before she could pay attention. She felt his two hands on her bare ass.

Intoxicated as she was, there was something she needed to know. She pulled her mouth away from his. "Do you have something?" she asked. "A rubber or something?"

"No. Do we need it?"

"We need it," she said.

"Aw, shit," he said. He took his hands out of her pants. "You sure?"

"I'm sure."

"All right." He looked agonized in his impatience. "I'll go in there and find one. You stay here."

Bridget felt the first tendril of shame as she buttoned her pants, the second as she fastened her bra and closed her shirt. She sat down on the grass. She looked up at the sky to a moon that was barely a sliver. She felt tears running down her face.

What am I doing?

Travis came back. He recognized the change in her mood. "Are you okay?"

"No," she said. "I'm not." Beer told the truth.

She wrapped her arms around her knees. Her body was closed for business.

"You gonna be sick?" he asked.

"No, it's not that." She paused and considered. "Yes, I guess I am." She went around to the back of the bar and retched her guts out. She felt better in one way and worse in another. Nausea abated, reality came back.

She returned to sit on the grass and Travis sat next to her. "Feel better?"

"Not much," she said. She put her arms around her knees again. She rested her head on them. *God, I hate myself.*

He patted her hair very sweetly. "You're a beautiful girl and a fine pool player," he said.

"Thanks," she said into her knee.

"You want to go out sometime? Tomorrow?" he asked. "We can take it slow if you like."

She lifted her head and tried to muster a smile for him. If she was going to have a hideously destructive one-night stand, she had at least picked a nice guy for it.

"I've got a boyfriend," she said.

"Well." He nodded. "Of course you do. Lucky guy."

She shook her head. "I don't think he feels so lucky."

You have to be someone.

—Bob Marley

"I don't know if we should go forward with the wedding," Carmen said to Jones.

She sat at the table in the kitchen of their loft. The kitchen table at home with her mom was pine or cherry wood or something like that, with a million rings and scars on it. It was soft. This table, like everything else in their kitchen, was stainless steel. You could wipe off any marks, but it was hard under her mug, hard and cold under her elbow. Had Jones picked this one? Had she? Probably Annaliese, the designer, had picked it. *It turns out I hate this table,* Carmen thought.

Jones looked up from the espresso machine. She could tell he was about to press the button, but that he decided it would be unseemly to start up all the boiling, steaming racket when such a serious statement had been laid down.

"Carmen."

"How can I think about that now? How can I think about flowers and hors d'oeuvres? I can't."

"How can you not? Come on. We've talked about this. What *are* you going to think about? Tibby? Are you going to think about her all day long? About your friendship? How many days or weeks in a row are you going to do that? And do you really think it's helping, at this point?"

The tears were so warm in Carmen's eyes and so cold by the time they got to her chin and dribbled down her neck or dropped onto the table. "I don't know what else to do."

"Move on. Call your agents. Call your manager. Set up some auditions. Look at flowers, visit caterers, buy yourself the most gorgeous, most expensive fucking wedding dress in New York City."

Carmen studied a teardrop as it sat pertly on the metal surface of the table as if it were the only one. Well, there were more where that came from. She wiped it into a wet stripe with the tip of her finger. "I don't know if I can."

Jones knew about grief. You couldn't say he didn't. His brother had died at eighteen of a drug overdose when Jones was sixteen. "You can't let it define you," he'd said at the time he told her about it, maybe three months after they'd met, and then he'd never spoken of it again. He was either very good at grieving or very bad, and Carmen wasn't sure which.

"Do you think that sitting here in your sweatpants day after day is some kind of tribute to her?"

Carmen shook her head.

"Carmen, I could see it for the first week. Ten days. I get it. But you're not helping anybody here."

Carmen shook her head again.

"I'm not saying you try to forget about it. Of course you can't. But you take the sadness with you, you keep moving and you integrate it into your life, and the burden gets lighter over time."

Carmen nodded. He'd given this speech before.

"Okay?" he said, like a coach sending her back onto the field.

She shrugged. "I don't know if I can."

Jones stood there staring at her for an extra moment. She knew her hair was wild and her face looked sallow. The sweatpants were not attractive. He was probably thinking how ugly she really was. It was probably a relief not to have to get married to her. She thought of the beautiful girls in Jones's office who were constantly fluttering around him with their straight, silky hair.

He dropped his coffee cup into the sink with a clang and it startled her.

"All right, Carmen. If you don't want to get married, that's your decision." He walked to the door, then turned around. "I love you.

I want to marry you. I'd marry you today. I want to keep moving forward. You know how I am. But if you don't want to, that's for you to decide."

Carmen put her hands over her face.

"But I'm not moving backward," he said as he put on his coat. He opened the front door to leave. "That's one thing I'm not going to do."

Bridget slept in a field for the third straight night and woke up under a hot, damning sun. This bit of earth was positively the sunniest place in the state of California, and she was not enjoying it.

She was still nursing the hangover from the night at the bar, and she couldn't shake it. Too much time had passed to blame the alcohol anymore. Was it the guilt? The self-loathing? She biked into Sacramento to look for something to eat that might settle her stomach. After she ate a sourdough roll and drank a cup of jasmine tea she rode by a Planned Parenthood office and stopped her bike.

There was a part of her that cringed at what she had almost done that night and a part of her that wished she had done it. She wanted to cross a boundary, not stay on this side of her life anymore. She wanted to tear it all down and dare herself to feel any worse.

She walked into the office with a long-haired swagger and signed her name on the sheet. As instructed, she went to the bathroom and left a urine sample. She penned a little drawing of the sun on her warm plastic cup. An ancient Earth, Wind & Fire song was playing when she went back to the waiting room, and she found herself dancing to it. She didn't feel like sitting down.

She was free. She had that, at least. She had nowhere to be, no one to answer to. She slept under the stars. If she was going to be wrecked, at least she'd be free.

The nurse came into the waiting room and called her name. "Bridget Vreeland."

"Me," she said. Her name was one thing she was left with, and she had mixed feelings about it. Maybe she could change it. She'd call herself Sunny. Sunny Rollins, like the saxophone player. Or Sunny Tomko. She'd borrowed Tibby's old name once before when she'd needed to be someone different; Tibby would let her borrow it again.

She followed the nurse to an examining room. "Should I change into one of those gowns?" she asked. She wasn't afraid of anything.

"Let's just talk to begin with," the nurse said. She was pretty old. In her sixties at least. She had hopeful eyes, Bridget thought, but sort of sad. It was hard to say which they were more. "What can I do for you?"

"I need birth control."

"Are you using any now?"

"I had one of the rings you put on your cervix. I think it's expired. I can't remember exactly the date when I was supposed to change it, but I think it passed."

"Can you give me the date of your last period?"

Bridget thought back. She had no idea. It wasn't exactly at the front of her mind these days. "I have no idea," she said honestly.

"Are you sexually active?"

"Now? Today?"

"Well. Not today necessarily. Over the last two or three months."

She hadn't had sex with Eric since the night before Greece. "Not in the last couple of weeks, but before that, yes."

"Are you married? In a relationship?"

"I have a boyfriend." She didn't know why she kept saying that. She had left that alleged boyfriend without a decent explanation. He could probably not reasonably be called her boyfriend anymore.

"Do you think you want the cervical ring again?"

"Yeah. I guess."

"All right. Is there any chance you are pregnant?"

"No."

"Okay. Go ahead and put the robe on, opening at the front. I'll do a quick exam and get you on your way." More hopeful, her eyes, Bridget decided. They were oddly fragile for a person who'd been around so long.

"Great. Thanks." This was easy.

"Did you leave a urine sample?"

"Yes, ma'am."

The nurse came back in once Bridget had gotten into the robe and her expression was different.

"Do you think the ring is wrong for me?" Bridget asked chattily. "Maybe the pill would be better? But I might forget to take it. You see, that's why I got the ring instead."

"Bridget."

She turned at the sober sound of her name. "Yes?"

"Sit down."

Bridget hopped on the table. She gathered her papery robe in a bunch in front of her and fitted her heels into the stirrups.

"No, you don't need to do that yet. Just sit and talk to me for a minute."

Bridget sat up. She let her feet dangle.

"I can't give you a new cervix ring or any other kind of birth control because you are pregnant."

Bridget watched the nurse's face. She watched her eyes. She looked into them to find some other way of interpreting that word.

"You think I'm pregnant?"

"I know you're pregnant. I had them run the test twice. False positives are extremely rare after four or five weeks."

"I don't think I am. I don't think I could be. Are you sure you got the right cup of pee?" Bridget's feet were rattling; her lungs felt shallow. She crossed her arms over her chest.

"If you want to leave another sample, you can. But I feel almost certain that the result will be the same."

"But I have that ring."

"The ring emits a hormone that keeps you from conceiving for a certain length of time. You are right that it expired."

Her lungs were turning inside out again, not catching any air. The air gave her some hope of deniability and she couldn't seem to get any. Her breasts felt big and achy and had for many days. Her stomach had felt vaguely unsettled, but she accounted for it with the obvious facts that her heart was broken and her life was in ruins, not to mention her long-running hangover.

She thought of her stomach, her uterus, where this thing was supposedly happening. *Oh, my God.* She put her hands over her face. She felt horribly claustrophobic in here. "I have to go," she said. Her voice didn't sound right.

"Bridget."

Bridget realized at the door that she was still wearing the paper robe and that her clothes were in a pile in the corner. She froze. She didn't know what to do. It seemed overwhelming to walk to the corner and put them on.

She felt the nurse behind her. The nurse took her hand. Bridget felt herself shaking all over. Her hand was frozen and the nurse's hand was dry and warm. The hand pulled her back to the table and sat her down. The nurse sat down next to her and put her arm around Bridget's shoulders. The world was too strange for awkwardness anymore. Bridget caught some air, finally, and it helped her think a little bit.

"Can I just get rid of it?" she asked. She knew those weren't the kind of words you were supposed to use.

The nurse nodded slowly. "You can end the pregnancy."

"So let's do that," Bridget said quickly. "Can we do it right now?"

"Bridget, it's a somber choice. I've done this a long time and I've learned many things in the course of it. You won't forgive yourself if you do it without thinking it through first."

Bridget shook her head. She didn't want to make a somber choice. She didn't want to think about anything. She wanted this to be over.

"Go home. Tell your boyfriend. Let him help you talk it through. Come back if you decide you're ready and bring him along to hold your hand."

Bridget had no choice but to see Eric in her mind. The tears came up from somewhere deep. They weren't only for Eric but for everything she had lost or ruined or was about to lose or ruin. Because she didn't deserve anything. She didn't deserve him or anyone. She deserved to be alone.

The nurse stroked Bridget's head patiently and let her cry. After a while she moved to stroking her back. She held Bridget's hand and passed her Kleenexes. Bridget didn't deserve this kindness either, but she took it.

"I don't think I can tell him," she finally said.

"If you love him, then you have to try," the nurse said soothingly. "Whether or not you'll ever want to have a baby together, I can almost promise you the relationship won't survive if you don't tell him."

I don't think it survived, Bridget thought, but she respected this nurse too much not to walk out of here promising to make a somber choice. And if she needed to do it thoughtlessly, at least she'd go somewhere else.

The nurse walked her to the front entrance. Bridget realized she was still holding her hand. The nurse took a card out of her pocket. She wrote her cellphone number on the back. "You call me anytime, all right? I mean *anytime.*"

"Thanks," Bridget said. She looked down at the name on the card and up at the little name tag affixed to her breast pocket. For the first time she saw that the nurse's name was Tabitha.

The couch where Carmen did her crying was midcentury chrome covered in shiny orange material with a fancy name that was basically plastic. Unlike the one in the apartment where she'd lived with her mother, the old chenille chesterfield that kept a permanent record of every spill and every tear, nothing here stuck.

When Carmen finally got up and trudged to the bathroom to blow her nose and pee, she looked in the mirror and she was hideous. A hideous hideosity. For the first week after Greece, she had looked in the mirror and felt sorry for herself. Now she despised herself.

What was she going to do? Was she really going to end this thing with Jones because she was too sad and too crazy and too chicken to get married? Would she say goodbye to him that night? Move out, stay in a hotel for a couple of weeks, find a new place?

What did she have without him? Without this place? Nothing.

She'd be alone. Who did she have to cry to? No one. Not Lena. Not Bee. She didn't even know how to talk to them now.

She felt the tears starting again. Not Paul. Not her dad. The world was full of death, full of sadness, full of people too broken to lean on.

There was her mom. Her mom didn't know what to offer and Carmen didn't know what to ask for. Her mom had returned to busy mode, redecorating her house and trying to get Ryan into a new school. She was grateful for quick problems like flowers and hors d'oeuvres. She liked Jones. She was scared of Carmen's despair.

What about other friends? Her New York friends?

Her New York friends consisted of her stylist and her makeup artist and her manager and her publicist and the PA who got her lattes. They were people who expected something of her. They were audience members. They were not people you fell apart in front of.

And actor friends? They were impossible. They had a drink with you, maybe, but you stayed in bullshit cheek-kissing-acquaintance purgatory forever. Like her, they all had their real friends from "before." Nobody needed any new ones.

At seven o'clock in the evening, Carmen was wearing her Catherine Malandrino; she put on Billie Holiday and made Jones a martini for when he walked in the door. It was pretty corny, but effective.

Jones waltzed her around the room. "Are we on for September?" he asked happily.

"I was thinking more like April."

He stopped midwaltz. "This April?"

"This April."

His smile got big. He put up his hand to give her a high five. "Now we're *talkin'*, baby."

After the high five, he carried her into the bedroom and made love to her without even folding down the fancy bedcover or taking off her dress. His phone bleeped and buzzed and spasmed and for once he ignored it.

Afterward, they lay for a long time and talked about the venue and the guest list and where was the most beautiful place to go in April on your honeymoon. Carmen was a pretty darned good actress if she did say so herself.

———

For a long time after Bridget left the Planned Parenthood office she searched for her bike. She was dazed; her head was pounding and her eyes were stinging. Maybe she'd left it by the bakery.

She walked up and down the streets in the blazing afternoon sun, trying to retrace her steps. Again the world seemed to have stopped and started anew. First there was the world that had Tibby and the Septembers in it, a fundamental center to her life and a source of deepest comfort. In a single moment that world had ended and a new one had started without them. A sadder world had started with just Eric and a mattress on the floor, but she'd left that behind too.

And so had opened the world in which she was itinerant, filthy, and pregnant but had a bike. And apparently now even that world had come to an end.

She stumbled upon her broken lock lying on the sidewalk a dozen yards from Planned Parenthood. So that was what happened to her bike.

She didn't even stop for it. She kept walking. She pointed her body west and just kept going. She wondered if she could join one of the lower orders, like shrimp or termites, which were not burdened with consciousness.

By the following afternoon, her pack was too heavy and the sun felt too hot. Even the lower orders felt pain. Bridget stuck out her thumb. With her hair blowing around behind her, even messy as it was, she knew it wouldn't take long to get a ride. She let the first two cars that slowed go by. The third had a man and a woman in it. She got in the backseat.

"Where are you headed?" the driver asked. He was in his late forties, probably, with a neatly trimmed goatee and a Hawaiian shirt.

"Where are *you* headed?" she asked.

"Sonoma."

"That sounds fine."

The wife turned around. She had frizzy light brown hair and a look of motherly concern. "Where do you live?"

Even with the mind of a termite, Bridget knew not to set off the alarms of kind, concerned people who were giving her a lift. "San Francisco," she said.

"Do you want us to drop you there?" the woman asked.

"No thanks. I'm on vacation," Bridget said.

"So are we," the man said. "I'm Tom and this is my wife, Cheryl."

"Sunny," she said. "Nice to meet you. Thanks for the ride."

Bridget parted ways with Tom and Cheryl at a gas station off Route 80, a bit south of Sonoma. She walked in the direction of the setting sun. By the time it dunked into the ocean, she'd made it all the way to Petaluma. She sat on a bench outside a bank and wondered about Eric's cousin Anna and her wedding. It was the day after tomorrow, she thought. Or would have been the day after tomorrow. Anna belonged to the old world, along with Bridget's bike and her empty uterus and her sanity. She wondered if Anna was even getting married anymore.

Bridget bought a slice of pizza on her way out of town and walked westward in the dark. Cars zoomed by and she figured one of them might kill her.

Over the next blur of days she slept in state parks, ate at diners and from vending machines, and slowly made her way as far west as she could, and that was the Pacific Ocean at Point Reyes. Her arms were dark red from sunburn, and her hair was dirty and matted, but she couldn't feel anything anymore. She'd descended down through shrimp and termites to an even lower order, a thing without a central nervous system. Maybe a germ, an amoeba, blue-green algae.

She'd gotten to the ocean, but she couldn't stop walking, so she turned south. She spent her days sleeping and walking from Inverness to Dogtown to Bolinas to Stinson Beach. You could go a long way in this direction. You could go all the way down to Mexico. She pictured herself walking through Half Moon Bay, Big Sur, San Luis Obispo, Redondo Beach, Ensenada, all the way out to Cabo at the tip of Baja, and even though she couldn't feel anything she started to cry. It was an involuntary thing her body did, like the sweat that rolled down her back. She cried for a mile or so, and then she stopped and sat down.

At Stinson Beach she threw her pack on the sand. She realized she did feel something after all, but it wasn't sad. It was angry. She was pissed. The more she thought about it, the angrier she felt. She was furious at the stupid bed. She was furious at Eric for getting it and thinking she would like it.

She was furious at her uterus. She was in no position to be dealing with anything, not even herself. Didn't it know that? This captain was letting her ship go down, she didn't care who was on board.

She was furious at her bike for getting stolen. She was furious at the lock for failing. She was furious at her dad for getting rid of her old bike without even asking her. She was furious at him for getting rid of all their stuff, even her mom's shoes, when he sold their house and moved into an apartment.

She thought of her mom's shoes and how they'd been keeping them for so many years. They were a size and a half too small for Bridget, and she probably wouldn't have worn them anyway, but you couldn't just throw them away.

The churn of anger got rougher. How could her mom have just left them with all those shoes, not knowing what they were supposed to do with them? Or her clothes? Or her gardenias, every one of which slowly died in a dark room? All the stuff Marly left behind—what did she think was supposed to happen to it? Did she even care? Did she think the world ended when she decided to leave it?

And Bridget was mad at Tibby. She was *furious* at Tibby. She kicked the sand into a shower that got into her eyes and mouth and hair. *"How could you do that?"* she screamed at the ocean. *"I wouldn't do that to you!"*

She fell onto the sand and lay there without moving. Hours passed and she didn't bother getting her sleeping bag. She lay on her back looking at the sky.

Hadn't Tibby loved her at all?

If one synchronized swimmer drowns,

do all the rest

have to drown too?

—Steven Wright

Some people said the first month was the worst. Others said it was really the first three months. Grief was like a newborn, and the first three months were hard as hell, but by six months you'd recognized defeat, shifted your life around, and made room for it.

As Lena walked along the river in Providence, shivering in a wool coat long overdue for retirement, she felt like she was going in the wrong direction. She grieved about as well as she did everything else, backward and badly.

The first month hadn't been the worst. She'd been horrified, blinking and confused, like she'd been whacked in the back of the head by a shovel, but she hadn't really believed Tibby was gone. This December morning fell somewhere after the middle of the second month, and by now she believed it. Nature abhorred a vacuum, and in that empty space, the nothing in the middle of her, had come to settle a black, drab something.

Each day that passed took her further from the time when Tibby was alive and made her incrementally more dead. Each day that passed buried deeper Lena's old ideas about the world.

That morning she'd woken up feeling sorry for Carmen. It was a feeling she kept out, but her early-morning mind was half dreaming and vulnerable, and somehow the sympathy had gotten in. It was a flickering image of Carmen's damned iPhone that had gotten to Lena. Every time Carmen looked at her phone there was that old picture coming to life of the four of them as toddlers peeking over the back of a sofa, looking like a miniature girl band. Carmen looked at it five hundred times a day. How could she take it?

As Lena cried for Carmen and the picture on her phone, she knew why she tried so hard all the time not to feel sorry for Carmen and Bee. Because it was the same as feeling sorry for herself, and if she allowed that, the surge of it would carry her away.

At this rate she couldn't imagine what she would be like at six months. She would be a black shriveled ball. Blacker and more shriveled, with hopes buried too deep ever to come out. Her life wouldn't have shifted to make room for her grief, it would simply have shriveled and surrendered.

These days she walked a lot. Often along the river without really seeing the river. Somewhere she possessed the idea that if she was moving, the saddest images couldn't settle on her as heavily. It didn't really work. But being still was intolerable.

Her fingers ached with red cold as she put her key in the lock. They hurt all the time, but she lost track of them and failed to replace her lost mittens. The lesser pains like the ones in her fingers and toes vied for attention, but like fifth- and sixth-born children in a very large family, they didn't get much of it. It was the firstborn pain and the most recently born pain you tended to think of.

There were messages on her phone. She was down to two regular check-ins, by her mother and Effie, not Carmen anymore, and their messages had grown more pitying and patronizing, if that was possible. She didn't want to listen to the messages. She let them pile up.

In her tiny apartment she sat down at her desk, still in her coat. She crossed her arms and looked up at the ceiling. She didn't like to look at anything. On the walls were the photographs, the ones she hadn't taken down or hidden away. There were the drawings, all from a different time, reminding her of ways she used to feel but couldn't anymore. There was nothing she wanted to feel or taste or see or even imagine.

She jiggled the mouse of her big, lumbering desktop computer, watched it wake, and subjected herself to her own version of Carmen's phone, her daily punishment. Bright on the big screen was one of the few pictures she hadn't flipped over or put away: the four of them on the day they graduated from high school. There they were with those thick, oily rented gowns, holding or tossing those weird hats. Surrounding them were all their family members, their nearest and dearest. The picture represented her whole life at a moment when it had seemed biggest, most complete, most hopeful. Her arm was around Tibby, clutching her ardently and without reserve, her face so animated and free in its joy she couldn't even recognize it as her own.

There had been a break, a rupture in the seam of her identity, and it happened sometime after that. She wasn't the same person she used to be. She looked at the faces in the picture, from Tibby to Bee to Carmen and back to Tibby.

Those were the people who made her something, and without them she was different. She'd held on to them and to that old self tenaciously, though. She clung to it, celebrated it, worshipped it even, instead of constructing a new grown-up life for herself. For years she'd been eating the cold crumbs left over from a great feast, living on them as though they could last her forever.

But what was that great feast? It was the idea of their friendship, their shared strength, their unconditional love for one another, their support, their security, their honesty and the freedom it seemed to promise. It was an idea big enough to sustain her through years of poverty.

Now it was unquestionably gone. And deeper questions gnawed at her. Had it really been such a feast? Had it ever been real? How could this have happened if it had been? How could Tibby have kept so much from them? If the strength and support had been real, how could Tibby have given up? How could they have let her? How could they have let her get so far away from them?

There was a clear and dreaded answer to all these questions: If it had been real, they couldn't have. She couldn't have. It hadn't been real.

Lena hadn't been eating leftovers from a feast; she hadn't been eating at all. She'd been starving, and so devoted to her delusions she'd become incapable of feeding herself in the most basic way.

She eyed the letter Tibby had left for her. It stood perched on her desk, day after day. She studied Tibby's writing, just Lena's name on the front, and a note to open it after December 15 on the back, but it had no more secrets to tell her. She'd looked at it too often, too long, too fearfully for it to say any more. *I could open it now,* she told herself, and instantly recoiled at the thought, as she always did. Later was the time she would open it, never now. Tibby wanted her to open it after December 15. She didn't specify how long after.

The phone rang and jolted her from her thoughts. She stared at it without even considering the idea of sticking out her hand and picking it up. After a few seconds, she poked the button and the message began playing. She hadn't realized it was Christmas Eve until her robot-voiced message machine told her the date.

"Len, it's me. I'm on the train right now, because you are not allowed to spend Christmas alone. I'm passing through . . . I don't know, New Haven? I think that was the last stop. I said in the last message I'd be at your place by one, but it looks more like one thirty. Call me back and let me know you got this."

Lena felt as if she were choking on her tongue. Effie was on her way. She was coming here to keep her company for Christmas, and that was about the last thing Lena wanted.

She should have known she couldn't get away without acknowledging Christmas. Her parents had finally let the matter drop after badgering her endlessly about coming home to Bethesda, but she should have known she hadn't heard the last of it.

Why hadn't she listened to her messages? If she had she could have caught Effie while she was still safely in New York, not racing past New Haven. She could have somehow talked her into staying there or doing something else. Now Effie was coming here, and what was Lena supposed to do?

She knew Effie all too well. Effie was going to pester her with questions and confidences and take her out to dinner and make a big fuss about exchanging presents and sleep in her bed with her. Effie wouldn't leave her alone. She would crawl into Lena's precious quiet like a tapeworm.

Lena put her face in her hands. Should she call Effie right away? Before she entered the state of Rhode Island? Lena racked her brain for excuses to make Effie turn around and go back home. Leprosy? Bedbugs? No heat or hot water?

No, Effie was on the move. She couldn't be turned away. Lena suspected that her parents were a big part of the impetus for this visit and probably the ones financing it. If Lena wasn't careful, Effie would book them a hotel room with massages and manicures all around.

There was only one thing Lena could do. She could be so arduously, painfully boring that Effie would leave the next day. And that, at least, came naturally.

Jones decided, somewhat impulsively, that they should spend Christmas in Fresno, California. Christmas needed to be celebrated, and his parents needed to meet his fiancée before the wedding, so that was what they did.

Which was how Carmen found herself sitting at a dining room table in a modest ranch house in suburban Fresno on Christmas Eve, between the elderly Mr. and Mrs. Jones.

There was an artificial tree in the living room, a fruitcake on the kitchen counter, but as they sat down to dinner, Carmen was surprised by how little ceremony there was. There were no prayers or toasts, they just started eating. They didn't even remember to turn the TV off.

"I can't hear what he's saying," Mr. Jones said with some irritation after he'd eaten most of his ham.

Carmen wasn't sure Jones was saying much of anything, but she jumped out of her chair to turn the volume down on the television so they could all hear it in case he did.

"No. The other way," Mr. Jones directed her, and she realized the person Mr. Jones couldn't hear was the man on the TV.

"Oh. Okay. Sorry." Carmen remembered how, as a child, she'd longed to be able to watch TV during dinner and her mother had never let her do it one time, not even when she was sick.

"Delicious," Carmen said to Mrs. Jones, pointing at the ham.

"Thank you. I use a maple glaze."

"Right. It's very good."

"I can give you the recipe if you'd like."

"Okay. Yes. I don't cook much these days, but I'd like to learn."

She wondered if she should have said that. She glanced over at Jones, but he was staring at the TV.

"Do you enjoy cooking?" Carmen asked, and then she felt doubly stupid at the blank look Mrs. Jones gave her. She knew how alien and spoiled she probably sounded, as if cooking were a hobby you chose or didn't.

"Is that a lemon tree?" Carmen asked, pointing out the window. "Yes."

"That's the great thing about living in California, isn't it?" Carmen knew she was talking too fast. She suffered the length of the pause and felt herself grow a pair of antennae in the meantime.

"I suppose it is."

After a while Carmen shut up and let the TV take over. No wonder Jones had gone into the business.

As Carmen spread the noodle casserole around on her plate she let her mind turn to Bridget. She'd calculated the distance from Fresno to San Francisco on a map online. She imagined she might call, she'd thought about it a lot, but now that she was here she knew she wouldn't. If she could have thought of the first sentence to say, she might have, but she couldn't. She couldn't ask Bee how she was. She couldn't mention what she was up to. Every casual opening seemed intolerably phony, and the deeper conversation was impossible.

"We can spend tomorrow at the movie theater," Jones mentioned to her later, after they'd said goodnight to his parents.

On their way upstairs to the bedrooms Carmen noticed there was a picture in the stairwell that must have been of Jones with his older brother. It was the only picture of the deceased brother she had seen so far in the house. The two boys were sitting at a picnic table, with big slices of watermelon on their plates. Jones looked about seven. Carmen paused to look at it, but Jones didn't wait for her. He kept going up the stairs. She stared at his back and wondered if he or his parents ever talked about his brother anymore. She tried to picture such a conversation at the dinner table, with the TV going.

Carmen had often wondered how it turned out, the Jones style of mourning. Maybe now she knew.

Bridget woke on Stinson Beach sometime after the sun rose. She sat up and looked at the waves. She imagined each one coming at her, like the bar of a swinging trapeze, toward her and away, toward her and away, inviting her to come in and take hold. She could do that. She could walk right in and keep going, swinging from one wave to the next. Tibby had done it. Why not her?

She thought of Tabitha the nurse. Now, *this* was a somber choice. It was the mother of somber choices, by which you could take care of all the smaller somber choices at once.

Tabitha would be disappointed in her, and strangely, it was Nurse Tabitha's disapprobation that got to her more than her father's or Carmen's or Lena's or Eric's.

I wouldn't do that to you, she thought, as she had thought before.

The morning sun was burning a hole in the top of her head. So much for sun; why didn't it ever rain here? For the first time in her life she wished for a crashing, brawling East Coast–style thunderstorm.

She opened her pack and took out the envelope Tibby had left for her. She wasn't supposed to open it for another two weeks, but that was bullshit. Tibby didn't get to decide anything anymore. If she'd wanted the rights of friendship, she should have stuck around for them. Bridget considered tossing it in the water unread, but she couldn't make herself do it.

She tore it open. Inside was a letter and another sealed envelope marked with another later date. She unfolded the letter.

Dearest Honey Bee,

I'm trying to picture you reading this. Somewhere in the sunshine, at least a week or two before the date I wrote on the envelope.

I know you feel abandoned by me, and I understand. You've probably gotten to the point of feeling mad at me, and if you haven't, you will. Or you ought to. You trusted me to be around and I'm not. And God, I would give anything if I could be. Please believe that. The thought of missing out on the later life of my magnificent friend Bee is almost more than I can take. Everything feels like more than I can take right now.

Of all of us, I suspect this is hardest on you, and I wish I could cushion it. I wish I could make you feel as strong and as loved as you are. You'll find your way, because of that, and because you have the thing that so often wavered in me. You have faith. Not in God necessarily, but in the thing with feathers. You are brightness, Bee. You are hope. No matter how far down you get, you'll always have it. That's what makes you different from your mother and, I fear, different from me.

I picture your spirit as a yellow, fluttering, buzzing, flying thing, and no matter how down you feel, it is in there. It is who you are.

Bridget's anger evaporated and the sadness came back. The anger was easier. She owned and controlled it, whereas the sadness owned her.

It felt like a torrent so strong it could sweep her into the ocean, and not because she chose to go, but because she was powerless to resist it. Maybe that was what had happened to Tibby. Maybe she couldn't help it.

"Why do you keep making that face?" Effie asked, sitting cross-legged on Lena's bed. It was not yet four o'clock and Lena was running out of deflecting conversation topics.

"Why do you talk so loud?" Lena wondered if the close walls of her apartment felt as jarred and uncomfortable as she did being disrupted after so many weeks of solitary quiet.

"I'm not talking loud. I'm just talking."

Lena didn't argue. Effie thrived on arguments. Better to be flat boring than argue.

Effie's phone buzzed every few minutes, but she seemed to have made a commitment not to answer it. She glanced at it constantly, though. "How's that guy?"

Lena took a few extra seconds to answer. Words were like oxygen to Effie, and if Lena cut them off maybe she'd go home a little sooner. "What guy?"

"The guy who looks like the pot-smoking Scooby-Doo character."

"What are you talking about?"

"The guy with the scraggly beard. The guy who makes sandwiches."

Lena preferred to keep pretending she didn't know, but the suspense could come to seem interesting if she wasn't careful. "You mean Drew," she said flatly.

"Yes. Exactly. Drew. What happened to him?"

"Nothing happened. He still works at the sandwich place. He's still putting together work for a show."

Effie shook her head impatiently. "Do you still go out with him?"

Lena sighed boringly. She pulled the laundry basket over and started folding. "I see him now and then."

The truth was she'd seen him once since she'd gotten back, and that was to tell him she needed to take a break for a while, as though the relationship were strenuous in some way. It was the classic it's-not-you-it's-me conversation, and he had acceded without a fight.

"Do you hook up?"

No fireworks. No arguing. Lena shrugged.

Effie punched a couple of buttons on her phone and put it down again. "Honestly, I'm not sure which answer I'm hoping for. I hate for you to waste your time on such a loser, but it would be comforting to think you were actually having contact with another human being. Mom and Dad would be comforted by that, I know. Even Dad. I'm not kidding."

No fireworks. Lena clamped her teeth together. Effie was the human equivalent of gasoline sprayed all over the kitchen. It was hard to avoid not only fireworks but complete conflagration.

"You don't need to worry, Ef. I'm fine. I have human contact.

You all should calm down," she said calmly, boringly. "I teach two afternoons, one morning, and one evening a week. I spend time in the studio. I see other instructors and professors all the time." Effie looked bored, so she went on. "I go to a demo or a lecture pretty much every week. I helped Susan, um, Murphy do this PowerPoint slide show. . . ." Lena was running out of material and she wished she had more. Effie's eyes had drifted to her phone but she hadn't picked it up yet. "I have lots of human contact."

"Do you have any friends?"

It was so like Effie to cut her to the quick, to push aside her feeble maneuverings, to destroy her complacency, however lame. Lena swallowed and hoped her eyes didn't show anything. "Sure."

"I don't mean old friends, but friends here. That you see."

This was why Lena wished she had checked her messages and somehow derailed this visit. She wished her sister would go home. She wished she had never come.

"Sure," Lena said again, bending down to pick up the laundry basket. She carried it over to her bureau and set it down again. Slowly, laboriously, sock by sock, she went about putting her clothes away.

When she'd organized her face again, she turned to Effie. She cleared her throat. It took a lot for her to voluntarily bring up the subject of Effie's job at *OK!* magazine, because Effie's tales of low-ranking celebrity and the absurdly vain girls she worked with made Lena want to pull her own hair out. And furthermore, Effie would find it stimulating.

But here, under two and a half hours into Effie's visit, Lena had come to that. She sighed again and sat down on the floor. "So how's work?"

We are masters of the unsaid words,

but

slaves of those we let slip out.

—Winston Churchill

Lena submitted to dinner at a restaurant. She picked a place that was bustling, cramped, and loud, the kind of place that didn't take reservations, so as the evening wore on you found yourself sitting and eating among standing-up people who were hungry and wanted your table. She knew it would be hard on her nerves, but she also knew it could potentially spare her the devastation of Effie's laser beams and gasoline fires.

First Effie ordered a martini and smoked salmon and then a shell steak and two glasses of expensive red wine. She was at least as poor as Lena, but she dressed a lot better and she had a real knack for taking advantage of free food. Lena wondered if her parents knew what kind of meal they were underwriting.

Lena had one glass of red wine, and halfway through it she felt red-faced and slightly woozy. She was beginning to find the Christmas decorations infinitely depressing. When had she last had a drink? She thought back to Kostos and the couch in her grandparents' house. She put her hand on her red cheek.

The lights got dimmer and the music got slower. It was Ella Fitzgerald singing Christmas carols. Effie ordered a molten chocolate cake with vanilla ice cream for them to share.

"I'm happy to be with you, Len. You need your family at times like this."

Lena looked around the room. Effie was getting sappy and serious just when the restaurant was clearing out. Just when Lena had imagined and hoped for noisy hordes demanding their table, the place had turned perfectly intimate.

"Like with Valia, you know. You were a big help to me. I really took her for granted. I really didn't know how much she meant to me, how much she taught me." Effie closed her eyes for several dramatic seconds and heaved a sigh. If Effie was talking about Valia, Lena knew that the dangerous subjects and God-knew-what-else couldn't be too far behind.

Lena looked desperately at the door, wishing for the place to fill up. Where was everybody? What was wrong with this place? You couldn't count on Providence for anything ever.

Effie looked like she was going to cry. She reached out her hand to Lena's. "First Valia and then Tibby," she said. "It's really hard to believe."

Lena was frozen. She felt an upheaval taking place somewhere down deep, and she hoped that if she stayed very, very still it could be contained. She thought of the time she'd gotten food poisoning from kung pao shrimp, how she lay completely still in her bed, suffering the nausea, hoping if she didn't move it wouldn't all have to come up.

Valia had been ninety-two. Tibby had been twenty-nine. Valia had had children and grandchildren, a restaurant to run, and a long happy marriage. Tibby, with her talent, her wit, her love, had been denied everything. Valia had lived a full life, while Tibby had suffered a secret hole in hers so devastating she couldn't go on. *Don't move. Don't move.* It was going to come up.

"I'm really sorry about Tibby. I really am." It was the martini and all the wine talking. Lena hoped her wine wouldn't answer.

"I know how much you miss her, Len. I miss her too."

"What. Are you. Talking about." Lena's words came through her clenched jaw. It couldn't be contained. It was coming up.

"I am. I do. Tibby and I might have had a few conflicts, but that doesn't mean I didn't love her."

Oh, God. Here it came. Lena was effectively leaning over the toilet at this point. Her mouth was filled with saliva. Her stomach was heaving. You just had to get it out and pray you would feel better when it was over.

"You didn't *love* her," Lena erupted, all bile and nastiness. "How can you even say that? You know you didn't."

Effie looked injured. It was a look she was good at. Lena didn't let herself consider the idea that it was real.

"You were angry about the stupid thing with Brian." Another wave. Lena couldn't hold it back. "He loved Tibby and he didn't love you, and you never let go of it. You still blamed her for that. I know you did." It was nasty, finally, when it came up.

Effie's eyes were shiny. "How small do you think I am?"

"You stole our pants because of that! And you lost them!" As this bilious memory came up and out, Lena recognized the strange, childlike belief that was nesting right inside it. If they'd still had the Traveling Pants, this couldn't have happened. The pants wouldn't have let this happen to Tibby or to any of them. The pants would have protected them.

"You still haven't forgiven me for that! You said you did, but you never did and you obviously never will."

Lena pressed her mouth together. She wiped the tears off her cheeks with her fingers. She and Effie were shouting and both of them were crying, Lena realized, and it was probably a good thing the place was mostly empty. Ella Fitzgerald sang on about Frosty the Snowman and Lena trembled in her chair.

"That's not true," Lena said, more quietly.

"Anyway, I wasn't mad at Tibby," Effie spat out. "I wasn't mad at Brian. I was mad at you."

Lena felt her chin wobbling, her shoulders shaking.

"I was mad at you for choosing her over me. I was mad at you for choosing your friends over me *every time*. I am your *sister*! That never meant anything to you, did it?"

Lena watched helplessly as Effie stood. "Yes, it did," Lena said.

"No, it didn't!"

"Effie."

"I came here because I wanted to help you, Lena, but I can't. I don't matter enough to you to be able to help."

Lena was crying hard. She put her face in her hands. "That's not true," she tried to say.

Effie rooted around her bag and pressed five twenties onto the table. Her eyes were still streaming as she hitched her bag over her shoulder and walked out.

Lena watched her sister's back, and after Effie was gone she stared at the door of the restaurant with the diminishing hope that Effie might come back through it.

Bridget walked slowly back to Bolinas and into the Sea Star Inn. She was starving, and it was the first place she came to. She ordered eggs and sausages and buttered toast and more toast.

She didn't realize until she saw the tinsel strewn around the place and heard the well-wishers on the radio that it was Christmas.

"Do you know if there are any rooms available tonight?" she asked the waitress, who also appeared to be the innkeeper. The place was ramshackle enough that Bee hoped it was in her price range.

She got a tiny room and use of a bathroom in the hall for forty dollars a night. That evening she got into the creaky bed as the sun was setting. When she woke up in the middle of the night she could hear rain beating against the window.

By the second day of sleeping in a bed and eating cooked food, she'd run out of money. The waitress/innkeeper, Sheila, saw Bridget in the lobby with her pack on her shoulders.

"You going already? I'm sorry to see it."

"I'd like to stay," Bridget said. "But I ran out of money."

She saw the look on the woman's face. "I mean," Bridget said quickly, "I can pay my bill." She took out her wallet. "I've got enough here. I just don't have any more to spend."

Sheila nodded. She wore a bandana tied over her hair just the way Bridget's grandmother Greta sometimes did. "I've got some odd jobs around here," she said. "I could spot you a few days' room and board if you're prepared to work."

For some reason, the way it came out of Sheila's mouth, the word "work" sparkled like a new pair of cleats, a banana milk shake.

"I'd love to work," Bridget said.

"All right, then." Sheila nodded. "Go put your stuff in your room and we'll get started in the kitchen."

That night Bridget used the ancient pay phone in the lobby to call

Eric. She called him at work, knowing he wouldn't be there. She left him a message wishing him a merry Christmas and telling him she loved him. She thought she might say something else, but she couldn't. Her heart was pounding as she hung up the phone.

The next morning she used it again to call Nurse Tabitha.

"Did you talk to your boyfriend?" Tabitha asked.

"Not yet. No."

"Are you going to?"

"I don't know." Bridget poked her finger in the swinging hatch of the change slot. "How long do I have?"

"How long do you have?"

"To make the decision. To, you know, end it."

"Bridget, you are probably about nine weeks pregnant. That's early. According to California law, you can terminate the pregnancy at up to twenty-four weeks. But once you've thought it through and made up your mind, I do not recommend waiting. Based on my experience, if you go past fourteen weeks, it's a whole lot worse for you."

"Worse for your body?" Bridget asked.

"Worse for your heart."

Back in the quiet crypt of her room, Lena carefully packed Effie's things in a cardboard box. Although they were spread around the place, each of Effie's possessions stood out. The bottles of magenta and turquoise nail polish, the chartreuse tights, two Christmas stockings, the high-heeled gold boots, the lacy pink thong still in its package, the three different kinds of hair product in neon green plastic, a tub of makeup. It was as though Lena's drab apartment was incapable of digesting objects so colorful, fragrant, and festive.

Lena gazed wretchedly at the cheerful array in the box. Effie had come armed to celebrate Christmas with manicures, pedicures, facials, and makeovers. She was going to remake Lena's underwear drawer. She was going to give Lena a new hairstyle. She'd threatened to download new songs onto Lena's iPod. She had come because she wanted to make Lena feel better. These were the things Effie knew how to do.

"You just have to let people love you in the way they can," Tibby had said to Lena once.

Lena carefully taped the seams of the box and left it by the door to take to the post office. Effie had come bearing intimacy and joy and Lena could tolerate none of it. Effie was far above anything Lena deserved.

It's not that you don't matter; it's that you do, Lena told her sister silently.

Now Lena's drab silence was fully regained, her misery preserved. She perched on the edge of her bed, sitting on her hands. This was just what she had wished for, wasn't it? Effie was gone, without even spending a night. Lena's fingers and toes were unpainted. A holiday was uncelebrated. Her hair was as plain as before. Lena was all alone, dismal and withdrawn once again. She'd done what it had taken to scare Effie away, maybe for good.

Lena tipped over and lay with her cheek pressed into the itchy top blanket. She wondered again about her inclination to wish for things that made her so deeply unhappy.

Lena woke with a jolt in the middle of the night. She stared at the ceiling for a time, her eyes as wide and clear as if it were the middle of the day. She got up and walked the four steps to her desk and sat down in the chair.

Her apartment featured one large window, which faced the air shaft. For about an hour during the day and an hour at night, the sun and then the moon, respectively, found their way into her room. Now the moonlight brushed in through the dirty chicken-wire panes and illuminated the letter that stood there unopened day after day, night after night.

She glanced at the brown box by the door, waiting to be taken to the post office. She thought of Effie. She looked at her hands and watched them as they picked up the thick envelope and eased it open. She considered her actions with a distant sense of disbelief, but what else was there to do? What was there to wait for? Who else was there to be?

You thought you had the choice to stay still or move forward, but you didn't. As long as your heart kept pumping and your blood kept flowing and your lungs kept filling, you didn't. The pang she felt for Tibby carried something like envy. You couldn't stand still for anything short of death, and God knew she had tried.

Moving forward was hard enough, but to do it without Tibby felt intolerable. How could she keep going when Tibby couldn't? It wasn't the same world without Tibby. She didn't know how to live in it. She wasn't sure she wanted to. But did she have a choice?

And then came the harder thoughts. Tibby had thought she had a choice and she'd chosen no. She had rejected her life. And them. And Lena. Somewhere inside Lena was the infant who couldn't believe that Tibby would leave her on purpose.

Why? Why had she done it? Why hadn't she told them what was happening? Why had she let it get so far? Had she wanted to hurt them as much as possible?

No. Lena couldn't accept that. Even if it was true, she couldn't make that idea fit. And as a consequence the world split in two and there she perched, one foot on either side of the divide, incapable of moving one way or the other. She could not accept what had happened. But what was the alternative?

Her tendency was to hide from information, because every scrap of information she'd learned so far had been ruthless.

She looked at the box by the door. She pictured Effie alone in her fancy going-out clothes on the late train on Christmas. What would become of them? She couldn't stand still anymore.

Her hands were sweating as she opened the envelope and pulled out its contents. There was a letter, typed, covering the front and back of two pages. There were two more, smaller envelopes, sealed. One said *Lena* on it, and the other, bewilderingly, was labeled for Kostos.

Lenny,

> *Hard as it is to think of your life going along without me, I've forced myself to do it, but I'm too attached to you not to put myself in the picture even after I can't be there in body.*

What you leave behind is the people you loved. You leave yourself in them. I couldn't be happier than to be in you, Len. I'd like to picture myself and see your beautiful face. If you can put up with me, that's where I'd like to live. In you and Bee and Carmen. But for the most part, that's where I've always lived.

I can't stand not being there to goad, challenge, and annoy you, Len, so please forgive me for doing it anyway. There's something I need you to do. You'll see I included a pair of letters for you and Kostos. I don't want to be needlessly mysterious, but I also want to avoid the famous Lena obstructionism. So please, please be willing to deliver the one for Kostos to him: from your hand to his hand, in person, face-to-face. It's a lot to ask, I know. But I also know you'll do it, because that's the kind of person you are.

I put a date on them, and I want you to wait until then to open them. I know I'm a huge pain in the ass, and because I'm gone you feel like you have to do what I say, but I have thought this through a little.

You'll either hate me for it or you'll love me, but please know I did it because I love you. Whether it goes brilliantly or badly, I hope you'll forgive my intrusions.

There's another thing too. Would you stop by and see Alice once in a while? Not often, just every few months or so. I don't want you to talk about anything serious or sad. And of course I'd like you to hang out with Nicky and Katherine and my dad too, but it's Alice who might need it most.

Now instead of having one sealed letter to haunt her, Lena had two. Two sealed envelopes marked with a date in March. Instead of just herself and Tibby to hide from, she now also had Kostos.

But as much as she dreaded it, she had a project to do for Tibby. Two projects, including seeing Alice. Projects were things, like her flowing blood and her pumping heart, that would keep her going forward whether she wanted to or not.

No pen, no ink,

no table,

no room,

no time,

no quiet,

no inclination.

—James Joyce

There was something about a wedding. No matter how much you put into it, you could always put in more. There was always someone else you could call, some other question you could ask, something else you could buy. You could put every worry, every desire, every whim, every *moment* of your waking day into a wedding, and it was big enough to absorb them all.

And weddings were cheerful. Wedding planning was cheerful. The colors were bright and the people you talked to laughed and smiled easily. They cheerfully and laughingly took your money.

A wedding was an opportunity for control. You could present yourself and your life and your husband-to-be exactly as you chose, and there would be a million pictures to document it. For as long as you lived you could imagine that your wedding was what you really were and not just what you labored and paid to have it look like.

Control meant there were also things you could leave out of a wedding.

"Mom, do you know when Big Carmen's going to be in Puerto Rico?" Carmen asked casually, when she called her mother from the set.

"First of March to mid-April."

"Do you know the exact date in April? Are we talking the twelfth? The sixteenth?"

"I don't know—more like the sixteenth. You could call her. Why?"

"I'm just trying to nail down the date for the wedding."

"It won't be before the sixteenth, will it?"

"Well . . ."

"Carmen."

"What?"

"You are not attempting to have this wedding without Abuela, are you?" Her mother could be annoyingly perceptive on occasion.

"Well, if she's going to be in Puerto Rico, then I'm not going to expect her to—"

"Carmen, I don't care if your grandmother is in Timbuktu, there is no way she is missing your wedding. If she has to crawl to the church, she will be there."

Carmen decided this wasn't the best time to mention that it wasn't going to be in a church. "Well, *Mom.*" She sounded like she was five. "What if it's a really small wedding?"

Her mother sighed. "Even if your wedding is so small you don't have a *groom*, Abuela will expect to be there. Honestly, Carmen, banish the thought. She has been talking about your wedding since the day you were born."

Carmen slid her eyes down the long list of calls she had teed up. She huffed out her breath. "Fine."

"Carmen?"

Carmen pressed the end call button as a new PA poked his head into the makeup trailer. "Yeah?" She couldn't think of the guy's name.

"They need you on set."

"Now?" she asked grumpily, as though she were being prettied up and paid to do nothing more than plan her wedding on her iPhone.

By day Bridget weeded the unimpressive garden of the Sea Star Inn and repaired a stone wall. By night she washed glasses and plates in the cocktail lounge, where the smells were really killing her. Through all the hours she found herself thinking of Tibby. She'd kept those thoughts at bay before, but now she let them come. She remembered and wondered and conjectured.

Some days she started with the earliest memories of childhood and worked forward through high school, college. The Traveling Pants years. And then after they graduated, Tibby living in New York and waiting tables and writing her scripts. And then about nine months later, both herself and Carmen landing in New York too. She remembered the two-plus years she and Tibby and Carmen and unofficially Lena had been roommates on Avenue C. And then Tibby moved in with Brian, first to Long Island City, then to Green-point, then to Bedford-Stuyvesant, always in search of cheaper apartments, as Tibby tried to get her screenplays bought and her films produced and Brian tried to get his software company off the ground.

About a year later, shortly after their twenty-seventh birthdays, was when Tibby disappeared. With almost no warning she moved to Australia. Bridget remembered going to surprise her at her and Brian's ground-floor apartment in Bed-Stuy on Halloween. Bridget was in her full Indiana Jones costume, including the hat and the whip, carrying a box of caramel apples, ringing their buzzer and banging on the door, but no one was home. Finally Bridget climbed up to peer in the front window and saw that the apartment was empty.

Tibby emailed her and Carmen and Lena a short while later ex-plaining the move. It was a project for Brian's work. It paid really well. It would probably be only three or four months. *Radical, huh?* she'd written. *Australia!*

Tibby emailed pretty regularly for those first couple of months. Cellphone service was tricky, but she wasn't out of touch. She sent comically sappy ecards for each of them at Christmas. But then three months had gone by. And then four and six and eight. They kept waiting for her to come home, but she didn't. They pes-tered her endlessly about it. *When are you coming home?* That was the subject line of every email Bridget sent her. *When? When? When?*

Tibby's communication fell off about four months after she'd gone, just at the time they thought she'd be coming back. There were very few emails from her after that, and the tone of them changed. Suddenly she was noncommittal about when she'd return.

It took them a couple of months to pick up on this change, to register that it wasn't just one but all of them who'd experienced it. In June, they finally convened at a diner in New York to discuss it. They talked themselves down from crisis mode.

"She's probably working on something big," Carmen hypothesized. "You know how she gets when she's in the middle of a script."

"Maybe since she and Brian are already over there, they decided to spend the summer in the bush or diving along the Great Barrier Reef," Bridget had suggested. "That's what I would do. And there's no calling or emailing from there."

Tibby's birthday emails in September didn't really *say* anything; they were without information or intimacy. In retrospect, they were hauntingly vacant.

That was where the real troubles must have started, as best Bridget could tell. They weren't prepared for Tibby's departure. They didn't know how to handle it. They couldn't even acknowledge to themselves that it was real, that Tibby was far away. It wasn't the physical distance; they'd managed that before. It was the fact that for the first time in their lives one of them was really, purposely, extensively out of touch. They couldn't bring themselves to imagine it was true.

As she looked back, Bridget had the distinct sense of them all being stuck in time from that point forward. They never said it out loud, but it seemed implicitly disloyal to have fun together in Tibby's absence, to make any big changes, to allow anything significant to happen without Tibby being part of it. They waited for Tibby to come back, spiritually if not physically, so they could resume their lives. They'd never accepted her absence. They didn't know how to live if it wasn't together.

That was why Bridget, why all of them, had been so thrilled and relieved about the Greece trip, why they'd thought this bewildering, isolating era of their lives was finally coming to an end. *Thank God we'll be together again.* It had never been Bridget's idea to fall apart, but they certainly had. She understood that now.

Why had Tibby done it? Why had she left like that? That was the part Bridget couldn't understand.

Some days she worked backward, starting with the time just before the tickets for Greece came. She tried to connect those days to the days before and the days before that, to try to find some thread back to the time when she'd felt like she understood Tibby and lived a mostly rational life.

In her mind she looked for an explanation, a missing piece. Maybe Brian left Tibby and broke her heart. Maybe that was the cause of her falling out of touch. But wouldn't she have confided her sorrows to them?

The two people Bridget would have wanted to ask were Brian himself and Alice, Tibby's mother. What did they know? But her desire to find out was overwhelmed by her apprehension that neither of them knew what had really happened. Bridget had managed to call Alice a few nights before, but the conversation went nowhere. As far as she could tell, Alice believed Tibby had simply drowned. It was a senseless tragedy, an accident, and that was all. Maybe Tibby didn't want anyone else to know the truth, and Bridget didn't want to be the person to tell it.

One night Bridget borrowed Sheila's computer and searched for Tibby's name in Australia. It took a few rounds and refinements, but eventually her name came up, along with an address. Bridget's hands shook as she located the address on the map. She zeroed in closer and closer, and when she got right into the middle of town, she turned the map to the satellite setting. It was a small town. A village, really. Bridget could navigate over each of the buildings and study every street. She saw the figures in the satellite images and wondered how long ago the pictures had been taken, whether one of them could be Tibby.

That was when the idea came to her. She knew what she would do. It was something she wished, with excruciating remorse, that she'd done when Tibby was alive.

It would seem cowardly to make sure Effie wasn't going to be home the weekend Lena picked to go back to Bethesda, but Lena was pretty cowardly. She called both her mom and her dad separately to tell them she was coming and to fish around a little. Her mom might be tricky enough to push her and Effie together without their knowledge, but her dad wasn't. He always blurted out the thing he wasn't supposed to say and forgot to tell you the thing he was supposed to say. He wasn't trying to make trouble, she knew. He was just bad at keeping track, and the forbidden things stayed closer to the front of his mind.

"Sweetheart, I'm so happy you came," her mother said for the third time as Lena sat in their big, shiny kitchen and drank the tea her mother had made. The tea had more milk and honey than Lena would have put in, but it tasted good.

"I'm happy too," Lena said. She wanted to express herself honestly without indicating that she was open to a full examination.

Anticipating this trip, Lena had expected her mother to jump down her throat at the first possible opportunity, to ask a million jarring questions, to shine her maternal klieg light on all the tender, hidden spots. But she hadn't. She was companionably quiet. She put some groceries away.

"Did you set a time with Alice?" Ari asked after the last bag was balled up in the recycling bin.

Lena shook her head. This was the part of her weekend where the real dread kicked in. "No, I just told her I'd stop by in the afternoon."

Her mother nodded. "Do you want me to go with you?"

Lena looked up, surprised by the offer. She had forgotten, at her age, that her mother could do something like that for her, that there was anything truly helpful her mother could do to solve her problems. She could see the strain in her mother's face, but also the willingness, and she admired her for it.

Lena considered. "Thank you for offering. I really appreciate it. But I think I should go on my own."

"Okay," Ari said.

"You've been over?"

"A couple of times."

Lena nodded. "I bet you brought food."

"Loads of it."

Lena pictured it and it made her hungry. "Spanakopita, I bet. Nicky loves that."

"And other things."

Her mother sat down, something she rarely did. Her expression was thoughtful. "It's hard to know what to do."

Lena wondered if it was too late to turn out like her mother. "At least you try," she said. "At least you do something."

First they sat in the kitchen while Alice attempted to make them coffee. Lena sat at the table and watched Alice search for one thing and then another. The coffee filters. No coffee filters. She looked in a harried way in hopeless places, like in the refrigerator and under the sink. A piece of the grinder was broken. The instructions were around there somewhere. And the milk? They were just out of milk. It was a strange reversal for Lena.

"It's okay. I didn't really want any coffee anyway," Lena said.

Alice was squatting on the floor, unloading the contents of the lower pantry by then. "I think we have instant."

Lena wished she could say something to Alice to get her to relax and sit down at the table with her, but by that time Alice was on the phone to Loretta, the housekeeper they'd had for over a million years, asking where the instant coffee was, and Lena understood that Alice didn't want to sit down at the table with her. Lena understood because she knew very well what ants-in-your-pants evasion looked like. It was what she herself did all the time.

Alice didn't want to meet her eyes or hazard a bit of quiet creeping between them. She didn't want a space to open where they might have to talk about Tibby and what had happened and how it had happened and how much they missed her. In fact, Alice clearly dreaded it.

Lena looked at Alice finding the yellowed instructions for the grinder on the high shelf, and in Alice she saw herself. Lena always thought she masked it so cleverly, but seeing it across the room, it struck her as tragically transparent.

Lena didn't want to make Alice talk about anything she didn't want to talk about—Lena of all people wouldn't do that to her.

Lena didn't want to introduce anything hard or sad. She just wanted Alice to sit down. She just wanted Alice to know that she cared about her. Was this how it was for the people who cared about Lena? Like her mom? Like Carmen, Effie, and Bee? Like Tibby?

"How's Nicky liking the new school?" Lena asked casually. She knew he'd switched to Maret for his junior year, leaving the public high school where they'd all gone.

For the first time Alice looked up at her. "Not too bad. Pretty good," she said.

"It's supposed to be a great school," Lena said. "And hard. Harder than Bethesda, I'm sure."

"Yes. It is." There was a glimmer of pride in Alice's face as she stood and drifted toward the table where Lena sat. "He's working a lot harder than he's worked before and getting Bs. He got an A in physics. He was proud of that."

Lena shook her head ruefully. "I remember physics. I didn't get an A."

Alice rested her hip against the table tentatively. "It's a different ball game at this school. Nicky pulled two all-nighters before his American history exam."

"Wow," Lena said.

Alice laughed and shook her head. "Not like you girls, sunbathing on our roof all afternoon before your history exams . . ." Alice stopped herself. Her face got complicated and her eyes began to fill. She looked down at her hand and began to twist her ring around.

Lena heard the gnashing gears of the dread machine starting up again and she wished she could silence them. But this time, for once, it wasn't her gears making all the noise. The volume of Alice's dread drowned Lena's out. It made Lena more empathetic, a little bolder.

We'll just have to feel our way through this, she thought.

Perry didn't have the money to lend her. Bridget knew because she called and asked him.

"I wish I could," he told her. "We've got credit card debt and we can barely scrape the rent together this month. Ask me again in July when I'm done with school and have a job, and I'll give you whatever I have."

She called her father twice and got impatient. He never answered his phone, and she had no good way for him to call her back whenever he got around to it, so she didn't bother leaving messages.

She sucked it up, took a bus to San Francisco, and marched into Eric's office. She'd worn clean clothes for the occasion. She'd failed at brushing her hair, which was heading precariously toward dreadlocks, but at least she had tied it back neatly. When she'd hugged Sheila and made her goodbyes after nearly three weeks at the Sea Star Inn, Sheila had held her at arm's length and given her an approving once-over. "My, you clean up nice."

Eric was surprised to see her, so surprised that his face registered joy and relief before anything else. He immediately wrapped her in his arms. "I'm so glad to see you," he said. "I'm so glad you're all right."

When they sat down together, there were tears in their eyes, but no recriminations. "I've been a wreck about you."

"I'm sorry," she said. She was moved by his love for her, even after what she'd done. She was aching over the things she wasn't telling him. "I'm sorry I just left like that. I'm sorry I haven't called. I'm sorry for why I'm here."

He took her hand and studied her fingers one at a time. He had a knowing look, but not a damning one. He was sorry for her. He knew her history. He knew what this had done to her. "Why are you here?"

"I'm not staying. I came because I need to borrow money."

He nodded. She expected him to ask why and what for, but he held back. She almost wished he would ask and demand and blame, because then maybe she could feel angry at him instead of this terrible missing.

"How much?"

She hadn't even thought this far. "I guess . . ." She calculated. How much did it cost to get to Australia? She could buy a one-way ticket if it came to that and figure out the rest later. "A thousand? Eight hundred might be all right."

"Okay." His face was not only handsome, but a part of her. He had sweat circles under his arms and a splotch of ink on his fingers. "Will you walk with me to the bank?"

"Of course."

He put his arm around her shoulders as they walked, and they fell into a comfortable step together. It felt sad and good to be with him.

She waited in the bank's lobby while he went to a window and spoke with a teller. He came back to her and handed her an envelope.

She looked down so he wouldn't see the emotion in her face. "Thanks," she said. "I don't deserve it."

"Are you going right away?"

She stared at his slightly wrinkled pants, his scuffed office shoes. She was tempted to stay. They could walk to Chinatown and get dim sum together. They could slip into the bathroom and make love.

With a pang, Bridget thought of Tabitha. She put a hand to her abdomen. She could tell him. She could tell him the whole thing. Could she do that? She tried to think of one or two starting words, and she felt her vision closing in as though she might faint. She felt the agonizing restlessness in her joints and a tingling like an attack of red ants on the bottoms of her feet.

She couldn't. "Yes, I am leaving right away," she said. She leaned in and kissed him on the lips. There was obvious passion in it, even after all this. If she stayed near him too much longer, she wouldn't be able to go, and she knew she couldn't stay.

She walked away down Pine Street, toward Powell. Her chest ached. She meant not to look back, but she couldn't help it. She turned and he was standing there, watching her go. He didn't wave or smile. He looked sad. When she turned a second time he was gone.

She didn't open the envelope until she'd gotten to the bus station and needed to pay for her ticket. He hadn't given her the thousand dollars she'd asked for—he'd given her ten thousand.

———

Lena's parents didn't torture her with questions or advice, as she had dreaded. They took her out for dinner to the Lebanese Taverna, ordered seven plates of food and a bottle of wine, and talked about the troubling state of Greece's economy.

"It's not going to be easy, selling a house in this market," her father said.

Lena allowed her mind to take a slow walk up the hill to her grandparents' house. She had to see how much it hurt before she went inside.

Lena cleared her throat. "The tourist places will be okay. If any place will survive this, it's Santorini."

Ari nodded. "That's what I said too."

"I've got to go over," her father said resignedly. He looked exhausted at having uttered the sentence. "We can't just let the place sit there moldering for another year."

Lena thought of Kostos sitting on the ground, surrounded by tools and bits of hardware, taking apart the hinges of the back door. There was pleasure in the image to balance out the pain. She nodded.

"He's canceled the trip twice already," Ari said.

"I had a case go to trial."

Lena nodded sympathetically. But she knew it wasn't the case going to trial that gave her father the haggard look. She imagined how it would be for him, confronting his parents' world, their clothes, their smells, and confronting the guilt for having left them so completely and so long ago, always vowing that there would be a time when the office got calm and he would go for a good long visit, maybe even a sabbatical, but never doing it.

Her dad wouldn't talk about any of that. He'd talk about the case that went to trial or nothing at all. Was it too late not to be like him?

Lena thought of the two sealed letters stuck between the pages of her sketchbook. With an accelerating heartbeat she thought of her project.

"If you want, I could go," she said.

Her father turned to her as though she'd disappeared and resurfaced in her chair with a new face on. "What do you mean?"

"I could go and take care of selling the house."

"By yourself?"

He said it as though she were still twelve.

"Of course."

A look of eagerness and relief was mixing into his cramped features. "Do you think you can?"

"I do. I know the house. I know the island reasonably well. I don't think you need to be a native or a lawyer to figure out how to sell a house."

"You do need to speak Greek," her mother pointed out.

Her father raised his hand. "Not necessarily. Everybody is speaking English there these days."

"You wouldn't want to get cheated or manipulated. It's helpful to be able to read all the paperwork," her mother cautioned.

Her father had now seized on this and he wasn't going to let it go. Lena didn't even get the chance to mention that she did, in fact, speak pretty good Greek these days. He was suddenly so flushed with the prospect of not having to go himself, he'd probably have sent Bubbles, the neighbors' cat, over to do it.

"Lena can fax the paperwork or send it electronically. I can look over everything. Anyway, I'm not expecting to get top dollar for the place."

He probably would have authorized Bubbles to sell the house for any offer over five euros and a willingness to take it furnished.

Her mother was considerably less enthusiastic. "Lena, are you sure it's a place you want to go back to right away?" she asked with honest concern.

Her father opened his mouth to respond too, and Ari shut him up with a look.

"I know," Lena said quickly. "I was considering that also."

Ari put her hand on Lena's. "Sweetheart, it's a generous offer. It really is. But why don't you take a little time to think it over and make sure it feels right." She cast another stern glance at her husband, who looked like he was going to explode.

Lena nodded.

"Because selling the house could take a while, you know," her mom added.

"Not so long," her dad spat out.

"It's a big job."

"Not necessarily so big."

"And expensive to get there, of course."

"I'll pay for the plane ticket," said her father.

Lena was tempted to laugh. "I've actually been thinking about it for a while. This isn't the first time it's occurred to me." She sat back in her chair, oddly relaxed. "It's a place with a lot of painful memories, no question about that. But I feel like I need to do something different than what I've been doing. It's not good for me to be in Providence right now." She was surprised at her own openness and hoped she could leave it where she wanted to.

Her parents looked surprised too. Instead of jumping in with queries they waited for her to say more, so she did. "I can't keep avoiding it. I need to do something, and the idea of this feels all right."

Ari nodded. She looked as though she had fifty questions and a hundred comments, but she didn't say any of them, and Lena was grateful that she held back.

Lena thought of herself as Alice, turning the kitchen inside out so as not to have to engage, and her mother just wishing she would relax and sit down.

Her father clapped his hands together. "I think it sounds like a *great* idea," he said.

I had seen birth and death,
But had thought they were different.

—T. S. Eliot

There was a list 119 items long of the things Carmen was doing. There was a list one item long of the things she wasn't doing. And it was the second list she thought of more.

She'd put the envelope Tibby had left for her unopened in her underwear drawer. At first it was so she would see it there, and then she tried to cover it so she wouldn't see it there, but it turned out her underwear was too flimsy to cover anything.

Sometimes she held the envelope, felt its weight, shook it, tried to guess its contents. Sometimes she studied Tibby's writing and wondered if she'd been in a hurry when she'd addressed it. Sometimes she carried it with her from place to place. The one thing she didn't do with it was open it.

Until the night she came home from drinks with her publicist, having had a gin and tonic and two glasses of wine on an empty stomach.

She'd eaten so little for three days in a row, she felt fierce and impermeable. She hadn't said or thought anything substantial in over a week, so she felt shallow. And Jones wasn't home, so she felt sort of like an adult. She felt like nothing could hurt her. Or she felt like nothing could hurt her for a few more drunken minutes, at least.

She got the envelope out of her underwear drawer and pulled it open. *Hit me with your best shot,* she thought, so shallow she could only think in Pat Benatar lyrics. She dumped the contents out on the bed.

To her amazement an iPhone dropped out. She looked it over quickly. It was the newest kind, with the biggest memory, the fastest processing, the better camera with video. It was exactly the one she'd been yearning to get but hadn't, because she wasn't eligible for an upgrade yet and it cost six hundred bucks. Here she'd been girding to have her heart broken more and instead she got an iPhone.

There was a brief note with it.

Carma,

    Brian got this for me and I have no use for it, but I thought you might.

Love,
Tibby

That was it? That was too easy. There was another note folded up in the envelope. She opened it.

Carmen,

    I'm keeping this short, my dearest Carma Carmeena, because I can't make the feelings I have for you fit on this page, I can't even try, so I'm just going to ask you one thing. Will you come to the address written below on or soon after April 2? Of course you don't have to if you don't want to. I know you're really busy. But it's less than an hour and a half from NYC. Come if you can, because there's someone I want you to meet.

Love,
Tibby

Carmen looked in the envelope for something else, but there was nothing. There was nothing to wallow in, nothing to cry over. She was so hyped up and drunk and hungry and prepared to cry she put her head down on the bed and cried anyway.

Bridget had used one of the kiosks at SFO airport to buy the cheapest plane ticket to Sydney, Australia.

She got a flight out early the next morning. She looked down at the last bit of coast as it disappeared into seven thousand miles of water. Checking out her window every few hours of daylight made her wonder whether the earth was really made of anything besides water. She didn't know what she'd find where she was going. She didn't even know what she was looking for. It was a long way to go for nothing. But it felt good to be moving hundreds of miles an hour, thousands of feet up in the air.

She remembered again that juncture of uncertainty starting around age twenty-five, after they'd had to give up the apartment on Avenue C, where she'd been happy. That was one place she could remember that she hadn't wanted to leave.

Tibby had moved in with Brian. Carmen had gotten her fancy agent and started getting real parts. Lena had gotten promoted to a teaching gig that kept her in Providence five days a week. Eric had graduated from NYU law school and gotten a job that kept him busy twelve hours a day. And what had Bridget been doing? Moving from one temporary living situation to another, walking dogs for money, working for a city landscape company in good weather, learning how to dance on Rollerblades from a dazzlingly crazy man in Central Park—nothing that was remunerative or ambitious, anything that kept her outside.

Leaving that apartment had clearly been a moment to grow up, but had she looked at her options and thought them all through? Had she searched for a job or a living situation that would suit her needs? Nope. She'd managed to amble from couch to floor, from apartment to apartment, from one impulse to the next for a year and a half, before she hopped on a plane and moved across the country. When in doubt, keep moving.

She looked down at the ocean. She'd thought going across a continent was something. But going across the planet—now you were talking.

She got a train from the airport to the central station in Sydney and took CityRail two hours south to the town of Bowral, New South Wales. It was a pretty town with cafés, shops, a couple of art galleries. It was less alien than she'd expected it to be, having come across the planet for it. Maybe because she'd studied it so long on the screen of the computer in Sheila's office at the Sea Star Inn.

The address matched a bungalow not unlike Perry and Violet's, but the inverse, other-side-of-the-world version. Where Perry's was purply gray, this one was butter yellow. Where Perry's was held close by a matching house on either side, this one was surrounded by its own little meadow. Perry's tiny backyard was bordered by a line of old dark-leaved eucalyptus trees. Spreading behind this one were young woods, topped by a cloud of green so green it seemed to pulse. The pink late-day light slanted differently here, the shadows spread differently under her feet.

Had Tibby lived here? Vacationed here? For a short time? A long time? Was this the place she'd lived most recently or had she left it long before?

It was opposite world, turned upside down. The toilets flushed the other way, the guy on the train had told her, and you just had to see Bowral's famous spring tulips—in September. Fall was spring, winter was summer, gray was yellow, night was morning. Maybe death was life. Maybe Tibby was here.

Bridget floated along the concrete walk. She was tired and disoriented. There was nothing that could surprise her, nothing she wouldn't let happen.

She noticed a car parked in the driveway behind the house. She walked up a few steps to the shaded porch. The screen was closed, but the door was open. She knocked on the wooden trim. She heard a voice talking from the back of the house. She opened the screen door a couple of feet.

"Hello?" she called. She felt yet another old version of the world ending, a new one opening up.

She saw him walking toward her down the hallway. The sun was setting behind the house, making a silhouette of him against the back windows, so she could make out his shape but not his features at first. The gait was both familiar and strange. It took until his face was within a couple of yards for her to know it was him.

"Bee," he said.

He came out onto the porch, barefoot and also disoriented. She put her arms around him, and he felt thinner and more brittle than she'd expected him to.

"Tibby said you would find us," Brian said as they came apart. "But I didn't think you'd come all the way down here."

Before Bridget could formulate a question, another shape emerged from the back of the house, a very small one. Bridget was mesmerized by it as it came into focus.

The tiny shape reached to pull open the screen door and let it slap behind her. The shape turned into a tiny girl, who came up beside Brian and wrapped her arm around Brian's knee.

Bridget stared at the girl in astonishment—the large hazel eyes, the pointy face, the serious mouth. This was a person she knew. Death was life and the present was the past. She'd gone back to her earliest childhood to find her friend again.

Brian took the little girl's hand and led her forward. "Bee, this is Bailey. This is Tibby's and my daughter."

Lena was back in Providence, back in her tiny, dark studio apartment, back to long, quiet, mostly empty days, but one important thing was different: she had a project.

When you had a project it was much easier to pretend to be someone else. You could pretend to be Nancy Drew, for instance, or Maria from *The Sound of Music,* or the sensible wisecracking housekeeper on *The Brady Bunch.*

In her Nancy Drew persona, Lena looked up the phone number of Kostos's so-called vacation house in Santorini and called it. She couldn't hold on to the persona long enough to leave a message on voice mail, but she called three times over the course of the week, and the third time the phone was answered by a live person, a woman who greeted her in Greek. Lena asked in timid Greek if Kostos was home.

"No, he's not here. He doesn't come back until the middle of February." The voice was rough and deep, that of an older woman, probably large in stature.

"I'm Lena Kaligaris, an old friend."

"You have an American accent."

"Yes. I'm American. My family is Greek."

"I am Aleta. I take care of the house. You should call him in London."

"Okay." Would Nancy Drew ask for the number?

"Lena, right? If I talk to him should I tell him you called?"

"No, no, that's okay," she answered quickly and fearfully, one hundred percent Lena and zero percent Nancy Drew.

When she hung up, her heart was pounding. Her heart wasn't buying the persona yet.

Now what? She couldn't wait that long to leave for Greece. She couldn't go all the way across the Atlantic and not deliver Tibby's letter. She woke up her computer and checked the cheap travel sites. There were about as many flights to Santorini stopping in London as any other way. It was less expensive than trying to fly nonstop to Athens, and it broke the trip up a little.

From the back of her underwear drawer she retrieved the letter of condolence Kostos had sent about Valia. The return address was London. She confirmed it on the Internet, but the phone number wasn't listed.

It would be better to call first, before she went ahead and bought the ticket through London. When she pictured herself picking up the phone and calling him, though, she was frankly relieved that neither she nor any of her new personas had his number.

She had his address. She'd get his number in some way or other, even if she had to call Aleta again. Being a plucky risk-taker in her Maria–from–*The Sound of Music* persona, she bought her ticket on the strength of that.

Bridget watched in pure wonder as Brian fed Bailey the last of her dinner. She watched as he cleaned her up.

Bailey sat on the edge of the kitchen sink, her feet in the basin and her hands stuck under the flowing faucet. She shouted when the water felt hot and laughed when it felt too cold. When the water was right, Brian plugged the drain.

Bailey stood on the counter and Brian pulled her dress over her head and took off her diaper. She was tiny enough to fit in the sink. Brian turned off the water and pushed the faucet aside so she wouldn't hit her head.

Occasionally Bailey turned her curious, somewhat suspicious eyes on Bridget. Bridget stared back without a gesture or a word.

Brian told Bridget she should go ahead and put her pack in the guest room. He showed her the closet where the extra sheets and towels were. When he invited Bridget to join them for Bailey's pajamas and bedtime story, she followed them up the stairs mutely. She lay on the floor of Bailey's room, her mind a whirl of incoherence, listening to *Goodnight Moon* twice.

Bridget didn't try to talk to Bailey or touch her. When Brian kissed Bailey goodnight, Bridget stood shyly in the doorway. She could hardly say anything. It wasn't Bailey's baby diffidence that was the problem; it was her own.

Bridget went to the kitchen and mindlessly tidied up from Bailey's dinner. She couldn't find her voice. She couldn't shake the feeling that she'd passed through a time portal and found Tibby in the midst of their joint childhood. She couldn't help feeling that this tiny former Tibby was her peer.

She was on the underside of the world and she couldn't remember where she was in the time line of her own life. She felt like she could close her eyes and open them and be in any part of it.

She drifted out to the front porch and sat on the steps. She watched the dark. They had lightning bugs here too. No matter where you went in time or space you could find them.

Brian came out and joined her. She thought of when he had entered the story, an oddball character in Tibby's "suckumentary" the summer they turned sixteen. *You don't come into the story just yet,* she felt like telling him. *We are still small.*

They sat in silence as Bridget tried to remember how the story went, how to put all the parts back in the right order.

"How old is she?" she finally asked.

"Twenty months." His face showed strain and exhaustion. She could see the web of blue-purple veins under his eyes and at his temples.

"You're her father. I can't believe you're a father."

"I can't remember not being one."

"Tibby is her mother." Bridget looked quickly at Brian and he looked away. "Was her mother."

Brian's face stayed turned away. She could see the wariness in his posture.

"She looks so much like Tibby it scares me."

Brian nodded, but still didn't look at her. He didn't want to talk about that, she understood. She could see by the way his head tipped how much he didn't.

For the first time since Greece, Bridget couldn't force away the presence of Carmen and Lena in her mind. They didn't know about this. They needed to know.

"Would you mind if— Could I tell Carmen and Lena about her?"

"About Bailey?" He looked uncomfortable. "Tibby didn't say anything?"

"No, she—"

"Then I'd rather wait till we get back to the States next month. Tibby wanted to make the introductions in person."

"She did?" Bridget swallowed painfully. How could you make any sense of what Tibby wanted?

"That's why we're moving back," he said.

"Oh." There was an opening here and she was too unsettled to know what to do with it.

"Next month. The truck comes on the twenty-first of March."

"Where will you go?"

"We bought a place in Pennsylvania. A farm. Tibby picked it."

She waited for him to say more, but he was quiet.

"How did you find us here?" he asked after a while.

"I found the address on the Internet." She was somewhat ashamed to admit it. But she hadn't known what she'd be finding.

She'd imagined the address would only be the first step of a long, roundabout search for Tibby's lost years. She hadn't expected to hit it right off.

"I was figuring you would wait and find us at the new place," Brian said.

"Why?"

"Because Tibby said she was sending you an invitation to come there."

The word "invitation" rang in her ears. "She probably did. I didn't open the letter yet." As Bridget said it, she realized how typically impulsive it sounded and how badly she had misfired yet again. "I'm sorry for just showing up like this," she said.

Brian shook his head. "It's okay that you're here. I was just surprised."

He pulled apart a fraying bit of his shoelace, and she watched the side of his face. She wondered what dark thing had happened to him and Tibby. Had their relationship become a source of misery? Had the baby been an unwelcome trial?

Brian was the only source of information she had, and with his stiff body and his face turned away, she didn't know if he even realized the worst of it, or how to ask him. "I just want to know what happened," she began gracelessly. "Can you tell me about her life here? Because I just wish I knew—"

Brian got to his feet. He looked at her and then looked away again. "Bridget, I don't think I can handle this right now."

"But can you just . . ." Bridget stood too. "Did the two of you fight? Was she sorry about moving all the way out here?" Even as she said these things she knew they were the wrong questions.

Helplessly she watched Brian step into the house and let the screen door bang behind him. She felt injured and oversized and she couldn't follow him. What could she do?

Maybe he blamed her. Maybe he thought she was blaming him. Maybe he didn't want to compare notes on their failures.

Maybe he didn't know what had really happened. Maybe, like Alice, he thought it was simply a terrible accident. Or maybe he knew the truth and was as blindsided, confused, and miserable as

Bridget was. Maybe Tibby's death had shattered his idea of the world as it had hers.

She waited until the house was quiet before she walked silently to the guest room and collected her things. She was halfway down the front walk when he caught up with her.

"Bridget, don't leave," he said.

She could see that he'd been crying and she felt sorry. She'd come here expecting him to be a role player in her tragedy, to give her that missing piece that would make her life bearable. But he had his own tragedy to get through, and a kid besides. Was he supposed to relive his torment for her benefit?

"I should go," she said.

"No, you shouldn't. Tibby would never forgive me if I sent you away." Some small part of his face had opened toward her.

"I know you want to be left alone." She felt genuinely terrible for him. Over the last three months she'd taken the opportunity to fall apart, but he hadn't been able to do that, had he? He looked like he wasn't far from it, like a skeleton with slippery joints. She couldn't push him for answers. It was wrong of her to think she could find what she needed here.

"Listen." He was at least talking to her now, and not to the side of the porch. "I have a project for work hanging over my head. It was due a couple of months ago, but I—well— Anyway, it's a big software job I have to do and I need to hold myself together and finish it before we move. It's not that I don't want to talk about Tibby, but I wasn't prepared for this. I can't do it now."

There was something about Brian. The sincerity of his eyebrows and the way his eyes hardly blinked. She couldn't help but feel sympathy for him and shame at her selfishness. And strangely she felt a little bit afraid of him, for the unhappiness he had allowed to grow under his roof.

She looked up at the sky. If she was going to reconstruct the steps that had led Tibby to the bottom of the world, she was going to do it without his help.

———

Bridget forgot until she got into bed in Brian's guest room that night the thing that was going on in her uterus. She didn't remember it in a panicky way. She remembered it as an abstraction. And even as an abstraction, it didn't suit her at all.

She pictured the sure way Brian bathed Bailey and read to her and knew when to put on a new diaper and what she was supposed to eat and wear to bed. She couldn't imagine knowing or doing any of that. If felt as foreign to her as standing up in front of a college classroom and lecturing on chemistry. She had nothing to say about it.

She wondered if her own mother had felt that way. She could remember how her mother's face looked when confronted with lacing Bridget's skates or getting gum out of her hair. It was just too taxing, too foreign, too much. She wondered if that was the way Tibby had felt.

Look up . . . and see them.

The teaching stars,

beyond worship

and commonplace tongues.

—Dorothy Dunnett

It was strange for Lena to attempt to dress herself and do her makeup in an attractive way without calling Effie or Carmen for help, but attempt it Lena did. She piled all her clothes up on her bed and tried on every defensible outfit she could come up with.

In between the navy blue shirtdress and the black and white patterned skirt with the white blouse, she stood still in her underwear. She turned to the mirror and studied her image carefully and honestly, in a way she hadn't done in a long time. She'd spent a lot of years dressing down, being every quiet and serious thing other than pretty.

"God, your looks are wasted on you," Effie used to say.

But was that true anymore? Was she even pretty anymore? Was there any point in spending energy pushing away something she didn't even have?

She stepped closer to the mirror, so close her two eyes became one stretched cyclops eye, and then she stepped back again. She couldn't tell, honestly. Her hair was still thick and shiny, but was long and shapeless from not having been cut in a couple of years. Her eyes were still that odd pale celery color. If anything, they were getting lighter as she got older. It was hard to say they were pretty, exactly.

She was thinner than she used to be. She was thin by her own standards, by normal people standards, but certainly not by Kate

Moss standards. Not even by the new Carmen Lowell standards. She squinted and felt insecure. She wanted Kostos to think she was pretty. That was about all the use she had for pretty.

This year she'd be thirty. Maybe when she was forty or fifty she'd look back and think, *Why didn't I enjoy it when I had it? Why did I spend my pretty years in dark clothes looking down at the sidewalk? Why didn't I wear red or fuchsia and submit to the makeup Effie was always trying to put on me?*

Lena trudged back to her closet to look for something red. She had one thing, and she didn't know if she could bring herself to put her hands on it. It was a red silk dress—or maybe rayon—simple but fitted and kind of short. Tibby and Carmen had bought it for her to wear to her first gallery opening, a group show at Larker, but Lena had chickened out at the last minute and worn brown.

Effie would have had ten things to lend Lena on the spot, and she would have given them generously. They would be big on Lena, but Effie would belt them or pin them in her magical way, and they would transform her. Lena would look ten times prettier and also uncomfortable.

The thought of making peace with Effie felt about like embarking on an Ironman triathlon: absurdly grueling, but Lena knew the steps it would take to accomplish it, even badly. The thought of trying to be close to Carmen again felt more like trying to design a time machine using only the things in her kitchen. She had no idea how to go about it and no faith that such a thing could be done.

Some nights when she lay in bed, she imagined her way through Carmen's day. Other nights, she went through Bee's. She could picture them doing the regular things. She could picture Bee pedaling up hills on her bike, buying falafel from a truck parked at the edge of Dolores Park or eating a burrito from Pancho Villa the size of a newborn baby. She pictured Carmen in her trailer parked on the Bowery or Seventh Avenue, in the makeup chair with a cup of coffee in one hand, her script in the other, her iPhone on her lap. She pictured Carmen sweeping into crowded restaurants alongside Jones and his pretentious glasses.

But when she tried to see into their minds, to think their thoughts, she couldn't. When she tried to imagine how they were making sense of things, what they might know that she didn't, how they fit the brutal facts into their lives, what memories they were carrying around, she couldn't. That exercise had been effortless for most of her life, and now it wasn't. They seemed almost like strangers to her; she could only see them from the outside.

Bridget was the one she worried about, even from the outside. Bridget was the one with the deepest fault lines. She was the one least able to diagnose or treat her own condition.

As the days passed, there was some robotically maternal part of Lena that couldn't quite let Bee go. Every few days Lena left a message for Bridget or wrote an email, certain as she did that it was going straight into the digital abyss. But she didn't know what else to do.

She'd even called Bee's dad once and left a message. She hadn't said anything important and wasn't so surprised he hadn't called back, but still. Lena thought it was tough having parents who tried too zealously to fix your troubles, but how would it be to have a parent who didn't even notice them?

When the phone rang on Lena's desk amid all her packing, she was so surprised that she answered it. She was down to one regular caller, her mother, and Ari had taken to leaving messages on her cellphone, because the mailbox—unlike the one on her home phone— wasn't full.

"Lena?"

"Yes."

"Why is it you can't meet for the next two weeks?" The voice was loud and speaking Greek.

"Eudoxia. Hi."

"Are you going somewhere?"

"Yes."

"Why didn't you tell me? Where?" Usually they confirmed and occasionally canceled their Wednesday-afternoon coffee by email. They hadn't spoken on the phone in years.

Lena took a breath. She tried to summon Ann B. Davis playing the sensible *Brady Bunch* maid. In Greek. "To Santorini."

"You are going back? Why?"

She remembered with some longing the comfort of Eudoxia as a disembodied Greek-speaking voice on the phone and then Eudoxia as a large, kind, pastry-eating stranger. But Eudoxia was long past being a stranger now. It was frustrating how when people loved you they took an interest in you and sometimes worried about you and personally cared what you did with yourself. Lena wished that love were something you could flip on and off. You could turn it on when you felt good about yourself and worthy of it and generous enough to return it. You could flip it off when you needed to hide or self-destruct and had nothing at all to give.

"I'm going to try to sell my grandparents' house finally."

"Oh." It was a complicated "oh." Eudoxia wasn't going to leave it at that.

"I think my dad was pretty happy that I volunteered."

"I am sure he was. When do you go?"

"Tomorrow."

"Dear me. And return?"

"I bought an open ticket for the way back. I don't know how long it's going to take."

"You don't mind going back there? After what happened?"

Lena didn't stop to think how to say these things in Greek, she just said them in Greek. "Of course I do. I mind everything after what happened. I mind being here or being there. I mind thinking about it and not thinking about it. I mind walking and I can't stand still. I need to do something."

"Oh, my dear one," Eudoxia cooed sympathetically.

Lena felt her eyes filling with tears. She thought of Tibby's mother. "It's hard for everyone," she said.

"Do you want me to come with you?"

Lena was stunned, but the way Eudoxia said it made Lena know she meant it. Slowly in Lena's mind a picture evolved of the two of them trundling through the airports and climbing the steep paths of Oia. "Doxie, you are very kind to offer."

"I have savings, you know. I could keep you company. I could help sell the house. I know something about real estate. Anatole says I could sell a Bible to the Pope."

Lena pictured the two of them side by side, hand-delivering Tibby's letter to Kostos in London. She almost smiled at the thought. Imagine if Eudoxia met Kostos. Then Lena would never, never hear the end of it.

"The plane leaves early tomorrow morning," Lena said.

"I can pack quickly. I am a light traveler. You don't even know that about me."

The tears in Lena's eyes spilled over. "I am touched that you offered. I really am. But I can't take you from Anatole for so long. What would he do? He might starve. He might die of loneliness. And besides, I will be fine. I don't mind going by myself at all."

Eudoxia sighed. She was quiet for a few moments. "All right, then. But if you change your mind you can call me anytime tonight. I will be home."

"Thank you, Doxie. I will."

"It will be good practice for your Greek."

Lena hung up the phone and lay down on her bed and cried a puzzling brew of tears. It was probably good you couldn't flip the love switch, because sometimes it was what you needed, even if you didn't want it.

"I had an idea," Brian said to Bridget on her second strange morning in Bowral.

She looked up from the kitchen computer, where she was trying to find a flight back to the States and ruefully facing up to the fact that she had come on a one-way ticket, had made no provision for the future, and had not one single plan for what happened next.

"Well, more like a favor," he said.

"Okay," Bridget said. She was in penance mode. She was ready to do a favor.

"You know that software project I told you about."

"Right."

"Well, I was wondering if you could give me some help."

She turned to him. "I don't really know anything about software," she began, "but—"

"No." He sort of smiled. "I was wondering if you could look after Bailey for a few days. So I could work."

"Oh." Now she felt embarrassed. She was unused to the feeling.

"Right. Well." There was no way she was going to come right out and say no to him. "I don't actually know anything about taking care of kids either. I'm worried I would mess it up."

"Bee, it's not like there's any science to it. Figure she's like you but wears a diaper and needs to sleep and eat a bit more often."

Bridget nodded hesitantly, wondering if this statement was strictly informative or if there was an insult in it.

"But if you don't want to, I understand."

"No, I will. I'll do it. I'll try." She heard herself agreeing before she'd quite talked herself into it.

"Thanks. It would make a big difference to me," he said. He looked like he meant it.

"I'm happy to," she said. It was rare that she spoke dishonestly. She wondered if she looked as diminished as Brian did.

Carmen was standing in the Vera Wang boutique attempting to buy the most expensive wedding dress in New York City when she heard the special ring tone of her agent, Lynn.

"Hi, Lynn."

"Sweetie! I've got an unbelievable piece of news. Grantley Arden is casting for his Katrina opus and he wants to meet with you. They've already set up the production office in New Orleans. He wants you to go down there and talk to him and a couple of the producers. They've already got Matt Damon committed."

"You're kidding me."

"No."

"When?"

"They want to meet next month on the twenty-eighth. That gives you some time. But I think you should go a few days early and get a feel for the place. Have you been?"

"No."

"Well, you need to go. Listen to the accents, walk around, eat some food, absorb everything you can. It's a film about the city. You really need to take it in. That's what Grant kept telling me. I'll email you the script as soon as I get it."

"I'm working until March twenty-fourth."

"So leave as soon as you finish. And plan to stay an extra week in case they want to get you on film or have you meet the studio people. I don't want you coming home without an offer."

When Carmen hung up, her heart was pounding. The saleslady wheeled in a rack of dresses, but Carmen couldn't look at them. How could she think about wedding dresses at a time like this?

Carmen thanked the saleslady and apologized and walked out to the street. She walked up and down Madison Avenue calling every member of her team, and then she called Jones.

"I'm blown away," he said. "Do you know anything about the part?"

"No. Not yet."

"Carmen, this is big. This could be the biggest thing you've ever done by far." She had to hold the phone away from her ear because he was shouting.

"I know." After Jones she called her mom.

"Is it like, an audition?" her mom asked.

"They want to meet me," Carmen said impatiently. "You aren't really expected to audition at my level," she heard herself adding somewhat haughtily. She realized she sounded like Jones when she said it.

"Oh. Right." Her mother was on her heels, which was a place Carmen was constantly trying to put her but never wanted her to be once she was there.

Carmen relented. "But it's basically like an audition."

"Are they meeting with other people for the part?" her mom asked, which Carmen interpreted to mean "You haven't really got anything worth bragging about yet, have you?"

When she hung up with her mother she considered calling her father but decided not to. Unlike her mother, her dad would assume she had the part won and the contracts signed. He would probably go around telling people she'd landed the starring role. So it went, when you were an idea.

Carmen felt hollow and unsatisfied as she walked downtown. She felt like she'd just left a three-star restaurant with no food in her stomach. Her fingers ached to make a few more calls. But she couldn't call Bee. She couldn't call Lena, and God knew she couldn't call Tibby. How fast her sweet wine turned to vinegar.

It was that old feeling: if she hadn't told the Septembers yet, it hadn't really happened. She thought of her alleged wedding, her robotic efforts to push it forward. Her life as it unspooled without her friends was no life at all.

Lena wore brown and put the red dress in her carry-on bag. She worked up her courage through seven hours in the air, such that after the plane landed at Heathrow she marched directly to the women's restroom. She wriggled out of her sweater, T-shirt, and pants. The stall was tiny, of course, and she kept whacking her elbow into the metal wall.

"Hello?" came a voice from the next stall over.

"Nothing. Sorry," Lena said, half undressed and fully discombobulated.

The red dress was hitched up on one side and twisted when she came out of the stall. In the mirror she saw that her hair was sticking up in back. There were dark circles under her eyes. The black tights did not look good at all. She thought despondently of the nickname she'd had in high school, Aphrodite. *What the hell happened to you?* she wondered.

She went back into the stall and banged around until she'd gotten the tights off and the ballet flats back on. She looked down at her bare legs. They were pale, but at least she'd shaved them the day before. How cold was London in February? She looked down again. Her skin was already mottled and goose pimply. *I am terrible at this,* she thought.

She brushed her hair. She put on mascara and lipstick. She tried to put on eye shadow, but it made her look like she'd been in a fistfight. She washed it off and tried again. By the third time, she gave up on the eye shadow. She put on gold hoop earrings.

After several dozen people had come and gone, babies had cried and been changed, and a toilet had overflowed, Lena gazed unhappily at the final product. She reached into her bag and took out the envelope with the precious address.

I should call first, she thought. But she didn't have the number, and according to a live, living London operator it was indeed unlisted. She felt idiotically grateful talking to a real voice on the other end of the London telephone.

It was weird to just show up at his address. But it was weird to do this in the first place. It was weird for Tibby to have written Kostos a letter. It was weird for Lena to travel thousands of miles to deliver it in person when she didn't even know what was in it. But this was her project, and she was doing it, God help her, in a red dress.

She pictured Tibby's face as it looked in the graduation picture that haunted her every day from her computer screen. *I wish I could have loved you better than this,* Lena thought, *but this is what I've got.*

Don't wear fear
or nobody will know you're there
You're there.

—Cat Stevens

London was cold in February. That wasn't surprising. Lena sat in the back of the train with her threadbare wool coat wrapped around her. She practically ran, regretting the decision to ditch the tights, from the train station to the Underground.

She had mapped this route carefully several days before and checked it over many times since. It involved the airport train to the Underground, and a few bursts of walking in between.

Kostos lived in a place called Eaton Square, off the King's Road. When he'd lived in London long before, after the summer they'd met, he'd lived in a place called Brixton, over a pub and diagonally across from a place called the Speedy Noodle. She remembered so distinctly the feeling in her chest when she saw a letter come through the mail slot with the address written on it in Kostos's neat-for-a-boy handwriting. She remembered so distinctly the feeling of writing that address out carefully on one envelope after another.

Brixton Hill, Lambeth. That was the start of a poem for her. It captured a feeling. Eaton Square, less so. It was newer to her, and time and memory helped bestow poetry. It was a little colder-sounding, she thought, less evocative. It had its power, though. How many times had she stared at the address, trying to picture it, trying to picture the Kostos who lived there and the moods and ranges of the place?

She spent a few moments orienting herself after she emerged from the Tube stop called Sloane Square. She walked the wrong way a couple of times before she found a street name that seemed right.

She found the street and a row of houses with relevant numbers that appeared to be going in the right direction.

Fourteen, sixteen, eighteen. She stopped and checked the map she had printed out. His house was apparently five numbers farther down a row of stunningly posh and handsome town houses. Did that mean he lived in one of these?

She slowed her pace. Eaton Square was seeming colder by the minute. Her legs were not simply cold, but numb. She checked her map and then the address as he'd written it on the envelope again.

She tentatively walked past another house and another, wondering if these were the kinds of buildings that were divided into flats. They were awfully big to belong to one owner, weren't they? If they were flats, she hoped Kostos's name would be indicated on the buzzer or mailbox or something.

She carried on very slowly, as though a powerful wind were pressing against her, until she reached number twenty-eight. She looked up at it. It was a sort of glowing white limestone with a portico, and ornamental trees on either side of a grand and glossy black door.

She scanned the area around the door for a panel of buzzers, but there was just one, an elegant button set in a polished brass plate. There weren't numerous mailboxes, there was one, also brass. Was this his front door; were these his perfect little trees, his upstairs windows? Could she really walk those three steps up to his door and push that button?

Her feeling of intimidation had melted away in his presence in Oia, but now it was back in force. He was a rich and successful man. He lived in a mansion in the middle of London. He had lunch with the treasury minister. What was Tibby thinking, sending him this letter? What was Lena thinking, delivering it?

In fact, what in the world was she doing here? There was no sense in which she belonged. She felt like she'd been Photoshopped into the scene. The whole enterprise struck her as childish, akin to passing notes in seventh grade.

She looked up at the house again. It was six forty-five London time. There were lights on. He was probably home.

She glanced again at the mailbox. Could she just leave it there? How strictly did Tibby intend the "in person"?

She walked up the first stair. She put her hand in her bag and took out the letter. She took another step. She looked at the mailbox. She took another step and carefully eased it open. Without breathing she put the letter inside and turned around. She walked down the three steps and stopped.

No, she couldn't do this. What if she'd made a mistake? What if he didn't live here anymore? And more importantly, she'd come all the way here to deliver a goddamned letter in person and she was going to deliver a letter in person.

Tibby was trying to get her not to be a chicken, obviously, and Lena wasn't going to go and subvert Tibby after all this. What did she have to lose anymore?

Lena turned around and walked back up the steps. She plucked the envelope out of the mailbox and pushed the doorbell before she could think another thought.

Her heart was throbbing. She pictured Kostos only three months before, lying on the couch across from her, his arms around her ankles.

She could do this. It didn't matter that his house was gigantic and he had multibillion-dollar deals to make. He cared about her. He'd loved her once—so much that he'd bought her a ring and thought he wanted to marry her. Granted, he'd thrown the ring into the Caldera and sworn against her name, but she had been important once.

She held on to the image of his sleepy face on her grandparents' couch as she waited for the door to open.

The door opened, but it wasn't his face that appeared. It was the face of a dark-haired woman in a black cocktail dress and heels. It was a beautiful face wearing dark pink lipstick, made up for a night out. Maybe this wasn't where Kostos lived anymore.

Lena had to reach down to find her voice. "Is this the residence of Kostos Dounas?" she asked. She was shivering inside her coat.

"Yes, it is. Can I help you?"

The woman's face appeared suspicious to Lena, and not welcoming. Lena looked down at the envelope in her hand. "I have something for him," she said faintly.

The woman put out her hand. "I can take it."

Lena looked at the white manicured hand with the glinting sapphire ring on the third finger. She looked again at the letter, addressed in Tibby's handwriting. This was far worse than the mailbox. She knew this was not what Tibby had intended.

"Is he here, by any chance?" Lena asked timidly.

The woman sized her up, and Lena felt unbelievably cold and self-conscious. "Are you a friend of his?" she asked.

"Yes. An old friend," Lena answered courageously.

The woman seemed to be considering. She took in Lena's old coat and her bare legs. She took a step back and turned toward the stairs. "Darling, you have a caller," she shouted merrily, as though Lena were no more than a puzzling, weirdly dressed joke to her.

Lena stood frozen. Why hadn't she thought of this? Of course he was "darling." Of course. He wasn't a student, living with four roommates in a flat across from the Speedy Noodle, writing longing letters to Lena. He was a powerful man living in a big glittering house in a fancy neighborhood, the darling of a woman with a sapphire ring and a mean stare.

Lena crossed her arms, clutching herself protectively, and finally permitted herself an unsettling and obvious question: Was this woman his wife?

Kostos hadn't said he was married when they were in Santorini together, but what was the need? He was being nice to her, pitying her out of devotion to her dead grandparents, and besides, she hadn't asked him one single question about his life. It wasn't like he'd been hiding anything. The idea that she was any longer a potential match probably hadn't occurred to him.

Lena's eyes sought the stairs behind the woman, because she saw some movement there. She watched in a strangely serene state of self-punishment as Kostos walked down the grand staircase. He was also dressed for an evening out, but his shirt was not yet buttoned to the top and his tie was not yet tied. His hair was still wet, presumably from a shower.

She caught the whole picture, the stunning yet mean woman standing inside the door, the glorious Kostos descending the stairs, the glowing interior of this gorgeous house of theirs, the mass of pink lilies on the hall table. Click. She got it all in a single frame, and the picture of it all together was devastating.

Lena felt like a child. Worse than a child and less valuable. She felt like a mouse. No, smaller than a mouse and less alive. Her life seemed so small and crumpled you could shoot it through a straw like a spitball.

Kostos stopped near the bottom of the stairs as it slowly dawned on him who was there. He was surprised, undoubtedly. She didn't know what else he was, because she couldn't look any longer. She looked away.

She held out Tibby's letter with a shaking hand, and the woman took it. "I am so sorry for disturbing you," she said earnestly. She turned and walked down the three stairs and away from that house as fast as her numb legs would take her.

As soon as Brian had shut the door to his study at the rear of the house, Bridget embarked on her journey back through time.

It began with Bridget and Bailey staring at each other over cereal.

"Bee," Bailey said to her. "Beebee. Beeeee. Bee."

"Right," Bridget said with a note of pride. "That's me." She hadn't realized she had a name that fit perfectly into the mouth of a toddler.

Bailey tipped her bowl over and sent milk and Rice Krispies all over table. She laughed.

Bridget thought of Brian's advice. But here was another way Bailey was different from her—Bridget wouldn't have done that.

Bridget cleaned up the mess and felt the day stretching out for a thousand years in front of her. She tried to think back. What had she liked to do?

"Let's go outside," she said. She lifted Bailey from her high chair and put her on the ground. She took her hand and led her out to the backyard.

The grass seemed to glow. The little forest buzzed. The world felt early and young out here, a place where none of the serious things could have happened yet.

"Oh, my gosh. You have a creek!" Bridget exclaimed.

"Creek," Bailey repeated.

Bridget led her under the canopy of leaves to the edge of the water. It was a perfect creek, just like the one that ran through the little woods at the end of Tibby's old street. Time passed so slowly at that place Bee couldn't begin to calculate the number of hours they'd spent there.

"Look, you can step over it. You can walk on the stones." She swung Bailey from one rock to another, as Bailey slipped and slid.

Bridget liked how Bailey was careful, but her balance wasn't very good. Bridget hoped she would not pull Bailey's small arm right out of its socket. Bailey's eyes were large and uncertain as she looked down at the water going past her feet. Bridget wondered if she was scared.

"Again," Bailey said as soon as they got to the other side.

"Okay," Bridget said. They went across again, slipping and sliding. Bridget couldn't tell from Bailey's face whether she liked it or hated it.

"Again," Bailey said again, and so they did.

They went back and forth and back and forth with complete solemnity until a foot went wrong and landed in the shallow flow. Bailey looked up at Bridget to see how they felt about it. Bridget smiled. "Ha! Cold!" she said.

Bailey's serious face transformed into an expression of pure glee. "Ha!" she said. "Ha ha!"

Bridget felt her face mirroring Bailey's. "Ha ha!"

Once they made friends with the water, they started looking for things to catch. At first it was just a stringy bug that Bridget picked up from the surface. She held it out on her palm as it wriggled. Bailey touched it in fascination. Bridget couldn't think of a specific name for it. "Bug," she said.

"Bug," Bailey repeated, digging into the "g" sound, looking at

Bridget as though she were a genius. It was nice to be around some-one so easily impressed.

Bridget put the bug back gently. As much as she felt like a child, she realized that as a child she would have just as easily crushed it in her hand or smashed it against a rock. She never thought of the bug fitting into a larger perspective back then.

They perched on neighboring rocks, Bridget holding Bailey's hand, and dangled their free hands in the water to sieve for crayfish. Bridget caught one and triumphantly held it up, all its little legs going.

"Big bug," Bailey intoned carefully. There was so much motion she was timid about touching it.

"It doesn't bite." Bridget put Bailey's finger on it so she could enjoy its sliminess.

"Bite," Bailey said. She got a slightly vicious look on her face and snapped her jaws together.

"No, it doesn't bite us. And we don't bite it."

Bailey thought this was funny. Or seemed to think it should be funny. She opened her mouth in a wide and somewhat fake laugh. Bridget saw she only had about eight teeth, all crowded to the front, and big spaces where the molars would go.

"Here. You can throw it back," Bridget said. She carefully put it in Bailey's palm. "Gentle," Bridget said as Bailey's fingers closed around it with a crunching sound.

"Okay, say goodbye."

Bailey flung the disfigured, mostly dead crayfish. "Bye! Bye-bye!" she shouted gaily.

Why did you want this for me, Tib? Why did you make me do it?

Lena walked for blocks and blocks. So much for her carefully la-beled map of London. She didn't have any direction in mind and she barely looked up.

Maybe it was so Lena could finally see what was obviously true to everyone else: Kostos had moved on. He was far out of her league.

Tibby wouldn't think of it that way, exactly, because she had always overvalued Lena. But she would want Lena to understand that it was time for her to move on too.

Lena passed unthinkingly through one neighborhood and then another.

At last she was too cold and tired to go on. She didn't want to sit at a restaurant or drink at a bar by herself. She ducked into a supermarket that was open late.

Sightlessly she walked up and down the aisles, and eventually stood by the front window. It was dark on the street and brightly lit in the store, so she couldn't see the outside; she saw only her forlorn reflection. She wanted to distract herself with the life on the sidewalk, but instead she saw her red dress and felt embarrassed.

There had been a fantasy. She hadn't wanted to acknowledge it, but there absolutely had been. She would wear her red dress, and Kostos would see her anew. He would see her here in London and realize he loved her again, maybe had loved her all along. He would grasp not just the letter but her. He would take her in his arms and overwhelm all of her fears and misgivings. In some way she longed to turn herself over to him, to let him take over the running of her, because she didn't know how to do it anymore.

She'd been trying to look glamorous and magnetic, but in the context of Kostos's home and his wife (or girlfriend or maybe fiancée), her efforts seemed pathetic. Red dress or brown, she looked like what she was: a timid cipher. She was usually good at keeping her hopes down, but even that small gift had failed her this time.

It was the time they'd spent together in Santorini that had done it to her. She'd felt so close to him; closer than she'd even known. She'd told herself she wanted nothing more from him, but it wasn't true.

As angry as she was at herself, she realized she had some anger left over for Kostos too.

"Can I help you?" a young woman behind a register asked her.

Lena turned her head to stare at her and remembered where she was.

"No. Thank you. Sorry," she said with her head down. She went back outside to the cold and resumed her walking.

She thought maybe if she walked long enough she might eventually pass into Brixton, but now she had the sad feeling that there was no way to get there from here.

She remembered back almost ten years ago to her moonlit walk up the hill in Oia to meet him in their special olive grove.

"Someday," he'd said to her in Greek. She hadn't been able to speak Greek at all then, and it had taken her great effort to figure out what the word meant.

The word had seemed like a precious gift at the time, a keepsake or an inheritance. She'd tucked it away and treasured it accordingly, waiting for the right time to cash it in.

Waiting and waiting. That was her thing. The word gave her an excuse to wait and do little else. The word wasn't so much a gift as a terminal virus with a long period of latency.

In her heart she thought he had meant it, but of course he hadn't. She remembered other parts of that long-ago conversation word for word. He'd asked her if she loved somebody else and she'd said, "I don't know if I can." And in return he'd said, "I know I can't."

She had been pretending she'd more or less forgotten the whole episode, but she hadn't. She had still been a teenager at the time, he not much older, and that gave everybody an automatic out, didn't it?

No, it didn't. Not in her lockbox of a heart. *I know I can't.* She'd held on to that declaration as if it were a signed affidavit.

And yet it was total crap. She thought of the beautiful, scornful woman in the black dress. *Oh, yes, you can,* Lena thought.

People said things they didn't mean all the time. Everybody else in the world seemed able to factor it in. But not Lena. Why did she believe the things people said? Why did she cling to them so literally? Why did she think she knew people when she clearly didn't? Why did she imagine that the world didn't change, when it did?

Maybe because she didn't change. She believed what people said and she stayed the same.

I was ador'd once too.

—William Shakespeare

Naturally it started raining. Around ten o'clock that night, freezing and wet in a place called Houndsditch, Lena finally stopped. She stood under a bus shelter and took stock. Her flight did not leave for Greece until ten past ten in the morning.

She had consciously planned a lot of things, but not where she would stay the night. Why not? Perhaps that was where the unconscious planning had come in. Somewhere buried under a few layers in her mind had been the idea that the moment she saw Kostos, everything else would fall into place. It was to be the happily-ever-after part in the story that took place after the velvety red curtains closed and was never strictly specified.

Now that she was taking stock in Houndsditch, she decided to confront that too. What had she really thought? He would see her and take her in his arms? Was that really it? He would carry her to his bed and they would make love all night?

She blushed at the thought, more from shame than desire. Maybe she hadn't quite thought that. Not even her subconscious fantasies were quite that brave.

A group of men in suits cast her long looks as they went by. One of them said something she couldn't quite hear and the group of them laughed. In her red dress and bare legs, and with what was left of her makeup running down her face, she probably looked like a streetwalker.

She didn't want to find a hotel at this hour, nor did she have the cash on hand to pay for it. Out of principal, she carried a debit card instead of a credit card, and her checking account didn't have much of a balance. She hadn't thought she'd need it. Her dad had prepaid for most aspects of this trip, including airfare and the special service for her cellphone so it would work over here. She'd brought a couple hundred dollars in traveler's checks, but she didn't want to blow it all on her first night.

What could she do? She took the train schedule from her bag and unfolded it. Two trains left Houndsditch that night, and she had to hurry if she was going to catch the last one.

The map of the Underground showed the way to Aldgate, a Tube stop a short distance away. She had to push herself out of the dry shelter of her bus stop and into the post-disappointment stage of this adventure.

Bridget got hungry for lunch before Bailey did, which made her question Brian's advice once again. She wasn't sure what they should eat. "What do you like to eat for lunch?" she asked Bailey.

Bailey stared back at her impassively.

"Do you like yogurt?"

"Yes."

"Do you like apples?"

"Yes."

"Do you like crackers?"

"Yes."

"Do you like spinach?"

"Yes."

"Do you like poisonous mushrooms?"

"Yes."

"Okay. Never mind." Bridget put out crackers and sliced up an apple. She found some hard cheese in the refrigerator and sliced that up too.

Bailey had stuffed several things in her mouth before Bridget realized she was eating as much dirt as anything else. She took Bailey back out of her high chair and carried her to the sink under her arm like a football. She put her hand under the faucet to test the temperature. "We should probably wash these," she said, gathering Bailey's fingers in the water.

When she sat Bailey back down, Bailey's cheeks were still full. "Are you chewing any of that?" she asked. She remembered the lack of molars.

She ended up excavating Bailey's packed mouth, throwing out the contents, cutting everything on the plates up finer, and starting again.

They both ate the little bits of things hungrily. *We are about the same, but I have quite a few more teeth*, Bridget thought.

They shared a cup of strawberry yogurt. Bridget got them each a spoon. Bridget ate hers and Bailey flung most of hers on the table and on the floor. Bridget considered the options. *I can see doing that.*

After lunch Bailey was desperate to go back to the creek. This time she was the one to grab Bridget's hand and lead the way. When they got to the squelchy mud at the edge they dug their toes into it. Bridget squished her toes down deeper and Bailey copied her. Bridget had a brainstorm. They both sat down in the mud. Why not? They were already dirty and the air was warm.

It was perfect, because she and Tibby used to love to make mud pies. Bridget dug in and pulled up a heaping handful. She brought her hands together and shaped it. "It's a pie. Yum," she said, bringing it to her mouth.

Bailey took to this idea right away. She got her own clump of mud and brought it directly to her mouth. When she looked up at Bridget there was already a mud mustache under her nose.

Bridget laughed. "No, you don't actually eat it. You just *pretend*."

Bailey liked that equally well. They pretended to eat several pounds of mud and then Bridget made a mud turtle and a mud starfish. After Bailey got the idea that these were not to be pretend eaten, but played with, she made her own versions, which weren't very good.

Bridget's fingernails were as stuffed with mud as they had ever been, and her hair as snarled. Feeling the creep of the wet earth through her pants and the sun on her head, Bridget closed her eyes and believed she was small again, sitting with her friend Tibby by the creek. And opening her eyes did nothing to undermine her image. This little person next to her had the same intensity, the same quickness to be won over, the same pixie face and flyaway hair that never seemed to grow past a certain point.

Bridget had marched through her portal to a simple time, and she was back with Tibby doing the things she and Tibby liked to do. Her mind seemed to vibrate more and more slowly into something like silence, and that was all she could ask for right now.

Lena arrived at her gate exactly eleven hours before her plane was scheduled to depart. In the annals of travel she didn't think anybody had ever gotten to a gate earlier than her father, but now she had. She brushed her teeth and washed off the makeup at a row of fourteen sinks (she counted) in the women's bathroom.

Back at the gate, she sat on the ground by the big window where you could watch the planes taxi away, but there wasn't much going on at this hour. She wanted to stay awake. It seemed important to stay awake, because otherwise, what might happen to her? She put her arms around her bag, just in case.

She may or may not have been dozing, she wasn't sure, when her bag started buzzing. It took her a moment to realize it was her phone. She'd forgotten that anyone could call her here. She grabbed it and answered without looking at the number. It was either her mom or her dad. Who else called her anymore?

"Lena?"

"Yes?"

Her mind was spinning. It wasn't her dad and it definitely wasn't her mom.

"Where are you?"

She was groggy and confused. "Who is this?" she asked.

"It's Kostos."

Her mind spun faster and in a different direction. How did he get her number? "How did you get my number?"

"I called your mother."

Oh, shit. Well, she knew who would be calling next.

"Why are you in London?" he asked.

To see him. To deliver a letter. To fall into his arms and then have the lights go dark and the red curtain fall. There was no part of the truth she could tell him. "I'm just on a layover."

"Going where?"

She couldn't tell him the truth about that either. Between London and Santorini it would seem like she was stalking him. She closed her eyes and searched for a lie. "To Italy. To look at art." She sounded like she was reading from a script. She hated lying.

"How long are you here?" he asked.

"I fly out tomorrow morning."

"Lena, you came all the way to my house. Why did you run away like that?"

Because you live in a mansion with a beautiful and scary wife. Because you crushed my hopes and hurt my feelings. Because you promised me Someday, *and you didn't even mean it.* "I just wanted to deliver the letter. I felt like I was disturbing you and your . . ."

"My?"

"Your . . ." Lena didn't know what she was. She didn't want to be forced to ask.

"Do you mean Harriet?"

"I mean the woman who opened the door. We didn't introduce ourselves."

"Yes, that's Harriet." He sounded uncomfortable.

"Are you married? Do you live together?" Lena wasn't so much amazed by her masochism as by her boldness. Anyway, she knew the answer. There was something about the flowers in the front hall that made her know at least part of it.

"No, we are not married. Yes, we live together. Lena, where are you staying? I know it's late, but do you mind if I come by? I'd really like to talk to you in person."

She knew exactly what he wanted to talk to her about and she didn't want to listen. Somewhere his own words were probably ringing in his head, the words he'd said to her more than ten years before, after he'd shocked and devastated her by getting married to Mariana less than a month after he'd promised to love Lena forever. *I love you. I'll never stop. I never will.*

He probably felt bad about hurting her now, just as he'd felt bad about it then. He must have seen by her face how she felt. She'd tried to hide it, but she'd never been good at that. Especially not around him. At least she hadn't collapsed this time.

This time. How many times could you let one man break your heart? What was the matter with her? And if she was being honest with herself she also had to ask, how many times had she broken his?

He was going to try to ease this painful reality on her, make a few excuses, attempt to salvage her pride and preserve their old friendship. He wanted to continue to feel good about himself. Not cause Valia to roll over in her grave.

But seeing him wouldn't help anything. Not for Lena anyway. It would only make everything worse.

"Just tell me where you are and I will come."

God knew she wasn't going to tell him where she was staying. That she was too poor and delusional to have booked a hotel. "You've got a life, Kostos, and I respect that. I should have called before I came. I'm sorry I didn't."

"Please, Lena? Please tell me where you are. I need to see you." His voice sounded strange, distorted. She wondered if he'd been drinking with "Harriet" on their big night out.

She realized that the reason her throat ached so badly was because she was going to cry. She was grateful that he couldn't see. That nobody could see, except the janitor rolling her mop and bucket out of the women's room.

"I can't. I don't want to. I made a mistake by coming here."

"Lena, you didn't. If you would just give me a chance."

"I can't," she said again. She needed badly to blow her nose. She hoped he couldn't hear the wetness of tears and mucus.

He was silent for a moment. "Can I call you again? Tomorrow?"

She closed her eyes and willed her voice not to sound as wet and sad as it felt. "Please don't."

"But you don't understand anything."

She wished she could hold herself back, but she couldn't. She was crying hard, and he was going to know it. "Understand what? There's nothing you can say that changes anything."

They were both quiet for a moment. She held the phone away until she could pull herself together.

When he spoke again he sounded subdued. She had observed this transition in him before. His voice had flattened. "All right. If you don't want me to, I won't."

She was scared to say anything. She stayed quiet.

"So what about this letter?" he said, clearly perplexed by it and its origin.

She tried to even out her breathing. "It's from Tibby. I don't know what it says. She left one just like it for me too. She left me instructions to deliver yours to you in person."

"I see," he said. "I guess that explains it." It was that flat voice.

Lena wasn't sure what it explained, and she didn't have the wherewithal to ask.

"Are we supposed to be together when we open them, or something like that?" he asked. She wasn't sure if his voice sounded mocking.

"No, that wasn't part of it."

"It says on the back I'm not supposed to open it until the middle of March."

"I know," she said. "That's what mine says too."

The angels come to visit us,
 and we only know them
when they are gone.

—George Eliot

Carmen had never dreaded an audition before. Usually she went with a kick of her expensive heels and a kind of ferocity in her heart. *I'll show them a thing or two,* she would think, with all the delusional verve of an only child. If she didn't get the role, they didn't get her. That was that. But she felt sober and wary when she thought of this one.

"The wedding is on April seventeenth. How can I possibly get everything ready if I'm in New Orleans at the end of March for a week and a half?" she complained to Jones from the bathroom a few evenings later as she slogged through the removal of her makeup.

"You'll have your phone. You can do it from there." She noticed he didn't offer to do it himself.

"What about tasting the menu? What about trying on the dress? I can't do that from there."

Jones was trying to read something in bed and not savoring her pouty diatribes. "Listen," he said finally. "You need to concentrate on this meeting. I'm serious. You need to get your head into it. If you want to postpone the wedding for a month or two, we can do that."

Carmen looked down at the cotton ball blackened with stuff from her eyes. Jones wouldn't have wanted to postpone the wedding for her grandmother, but he instantly tossed it aside for an audition. Grant Arden was a lot more important in his world than Big Carmen.

Did she want to postpone it? Or did she just want to get it over with? If she rushed into the wedding headlong, she wouldn't have to think very much. Things like what to do about Tibby's family, whether to involve bridesmaids or just blindly skip that whole morass, those questions could be largely avoided. Thoughts like *God, Carmen, what in the world are you doing?* could be politely stepped over on her way up the aisle. It was a built-in excuse for herself and everyone else—*We just slapped it together.* Maybe it was even an excuse in case she needed one later. *We probably should have taken more time with it.* She could almost hear herself five years in the future saying it.

"How'd you two do?" Brian asked at the end of the first day when he emerged from his office and found Bridget and Bailey exhausted at the kitchen table.

Bridget shrugged. "Pretty good. I don't know." She looked at Bailey. "How'd we do?"

Bailey copied Bridget's shrug.

Brian looked Bailey over carefully and kissed her pink ear. "Usually we change out of pajamas at some point in the day. And sunscreen is always a plus. But otherwise she looks good, I think."

Bailey was eager to be back in her father's arms and put to bed right after dinner. Bridget slept a longer and more innocent sleep than she had in a long time.

In the morning, Bee and Bailey carried their breakfast outside, and both screamed in delight when a yellow bird flew down and landed on the edge of Bailey's cereal bowl and ate a Cheerio. They talked about it for the rest of the day.

They played for a couple of hours at the creek. They found a garter snake and taunted it with sticks. They tried to get it to eat a Cheerio, but it wouldn't. Bridget felt the old childlike brutishness rising in her again.

In the heat of the afternoon they lay on their stomachs on the front porch and scribbled with crayons. This was exactly as far as

Bridget's artistic talent had ever taken her, and she was satisfied with it.

Listening to the sticky click of the crayons going on and off the paper, breathing in that old waxy smell, Bridget realized she was enjoying herself.

She realized this job suited her in unexpected ways. It was like temping, in that each day contained different activities, so you didn't feel too tied down. It was better than temping in that you got to be outside and wear your oldest, dirtiest clothes. It was better than temping in that you got to follow your own ideas, and whatever you might say about toddlers, a two-year-old boss was a lot easier to please and impress than a representative from human resources.

Idly Bridget wondered what you needed to do to qualify for such a job and how much it paid by the hour.

Lena sold the house the third day she was in Greece. She called four different brokers the first day, cleaned like a madwoman the second day, and hosted an open house the third day, and by five o'clock she had accepted an offer for the place, furniture and all. The fourth day she signed papers, went to the bank, and faxed documents to her father. The fifth day she met with the moving company and worked alongside them boxing up papers, books, and personal effects to be shipped back to her parents in the States. She was astonished by the efficiency of it all.

On the sixth day she woke up without a project. She woke up in a cleaned-out house that didn't really belong to her anymore, in a bed she couldn't seem to get out of. She lay there and watched the sunlight creep over her blanket. She didn't have a message to deliver in Tibby's name anymore. She didn't have a house to sell anymore. She didn't have a man to contemplate a life with anymore.

She had . . . what did she have? She had large feet. She had self-pity. She had an ingrown toenail on her left big toe. She had four days until she could get on a flight back to the States.

She stayed in bed until after noon. She made herself an omelet. She sat cross-legged on the floor of Valia's closet for a while. Then she got up and looked through the last of the clothes in her grandmother's closet, the ones destined for the garbage. She tried on Valia's pink cotton bathrobe and then her Pucci-style housedress. She put both of them in her suitcase.

Her bapi had died long ago. Most of his stuff had been cleaned out and given away years before. But when she wandered into his closet she found a pair of silver cuff links in the shape of lions in the back of a drawer. She also saw, still pinned to the wall, two small drawings she had made that first summer, one of a church in the village and another of the fishing boats in Ammoudi. She remembered showing them to Bapi when she'd first made them, and his wordless appreciation. She'd left them in her room when she'd gone back to the States. It felt self-important or presumptuous of her to have given them to him, but she was moved that he had liked them enough to keep them and hang them in his closet. She was moved at the idea that he would have looked at them and thought of her when she wasn't there.

She sat on the windowsill of her bedroom and looked out at the sparkling blue water of the Caldera. The lost city of Atlantis was supposed to be under there. She imagined Tibby under there. She imagined the Traveling Pants under there. She imagined the ring that Kostos had bought for her when he still thought he loved her under there.

Her vision of the world under the water represented a beautiful stillness, a version of heaven. It was the lost city of Lena, her alternate universe, the life she yearned for but didn't get to have.

Later in the week, after a few morning hours in the creek, Bridget and Bailey found a bunch of wooden boards in the shed and tried to construct a tree house in a bush. After an hour it collapsed, which seemed to both of them much more entertaining than its staying intact. They built it again and again, shoddier each time, and laughed when it fell down.

That same evening, Brian worked late, and after dinner Bridget and Bailey went out to the back steps to watch the last of the sun fading away and the sky turning dark. They saw two bats, and then in the gloaming, the first zap of a firefly. Bridget shouted like a two-year-old and pointed. "Lightning bug! Did you see it? The light flash in the air?"

Bailey watched the air with suspicion and interest. Bridget could see her trying the words out in her mouth before she said them aloud. Even at this tiny age she was like her mother in not wanting to get out in front of something before she had a feel for it.

"Let's get a jar and we'll catch one," Bridget said excitedly. She ran into the kitchen with Bailey following. She found a glass jar on a high shelf. Bailey watched in wonder as she jammed a few holes in the lid with the point of a sharp knife. Bridget vaguely wondered how many decent knives she'd ruined over the years in this enterprise.

Bailey followed her back out to the yard. Standing on the grass in the falling dark, Bailey looked tentative. Bridget wondered if she'd been outside at night much.

"Let's pick a few blades of grass and put them in the jar to make it a nice home for when we catch one," she said ambitiously. "Here, like this." She plucked a blade of grass, unscrewed the lid, and put it in the jar.

This Bailey could do. She leaned down and plucked the blades one at a time and carefully put each one in the jar. It was hard to get her to stop.

"I see one," Bridget said. "Look." She pointed there and there and there. Bailey stood frozen in her white pajamas and bare feet in the middle of the grass. Her eyes were large and attentive.

"Watch this," Bridget said, putting the jar down. She chased a bug and grabbed it out of the air with cupped hands. She brought it back to Bailey, kneeled down, and opened her hands slowly. Bailey was eager to see but didn't want to get too close. "See it?" Bridget said when the bug's posterior lit up.

"See it," Bailey said, awed.

Bridget let it go and Bailey followed it with her eyes. Then Bailey started jumping around. "Catch! Catch!" she yelled.

Bridget ran around the lawn. Bailey ran around too, but in aimless excitement. "Got it!" Bridget cried when she caught another one.

Bailey rushed over. This time she peered down very close and made a little scream when it flashed.

"We could let it go or put it in the jar." She pointed to the jar lying on the grass.

Bailey made an excited mangle of sounds ending with "jar."

Bridget wasn't sure Bailey knew what it meant. Kneeling down so Bailey could see, she trapped the bug in one closed hand and opened the jar with the other hand while holding it between her knees. She opened her closed hand onto the top of the jar and held it flat until the bug flew in. She could hear Bailey breathing. "Now, quick, you put the lid back on so the bug doesn't fly out."

Once the lid was screwed shut Bridget handed the jar to Bailey. Bailey held it with two hands and gasped and dropped it as soon as the bug lit up. Bridget laughed and picked it up off the grass. She put it back in Bailey's eager hands.

"Pretty cool, huh?"

Bailey stared into the jar and then looked up at Bridget. "Again?"

"You want me to catch another one?"

Bailey nodded.

"Okay. You can try to catch one too."

Bailey was loath to let the jar go for the sake of catching, but finally relented. They both ran around the grass. Bailey flailed at the sky with cupped hands in rough imitation of Bridget.

As soon as Bridget caught and captured another one in the jar, Bailey looked at her greedily. "Again?"

"Another one?"

"Other one!"

They kept at it until there were nine lightning bugs in the jar. Bridget found it so thrilling that it was hard to stop, and Bailey was relentless.

"It'll get too crowded," Bridget finally said, laughing.

"Other one!" Bailey shouted.

"Too many in there. They might get in a fight."

Bailey paused and looked interested in that.

"They might bite each other."

Bailey looked concerned.

"No, I'm just kidding. They don't bite."

"No bite," Bailey proclaimed, snapping her jaws together.

"No bite."

Brian came out onto the back steps. "What are you doing out there?" he called.

Bailey went rushing for the steps, nearly hyperventilating in her eagerness to show her dad the bugs and the jar.

Bridget smiled and stood around, a little awkward about her own zeal, but proud at having caused the excitement and pleasure.

Bailey's words collapsed into such an eager muddle you couldn't understand one thing she was saying, but the blinking jar spoke for itself.

"Wow," Brian kept saying, carrying her into the house as she held the jar, still sputtering with her story. "Wow. Wow."

Bridget cleaned up the kitchen with a feeling of satisfaction, listening to Brian calming Bailey down and putting her to bed.

Yawning on her own way to bed an hour or two later, Bridget stopped at Bailey's bedroom and opened the door very quietly. She walked a few steps into the room and smiled to herself at the sight of Bailey in her crib, still clutching the lightning-bug jar, and the bugs still flashing faintly between her arms.

Bridget hoped for another long innocent night of sleep, but it didn't come. The longer she lay in the little twin bed in the extra room of this house that had been Tibby's house, the more agitated she felt. There were so many obvious sources for this feeling, she didn't feel any desire to dig. But her mind didn't go to the obvious things like Tibby or Eric or Nurse Tabitha or Carmen or Lena, it went further back, to her mother. The memories opened not in any logical order but in flashes, some sweetly nostalgic and others devastating.

And then, without warning, her mind skipped all the way back to the present. It flashed on the glass jar in Bailey's arms and then flashed ahead to the very near future, the morning right in front of them. The thought of it made her so restless she sat up in bed and put her feet on the floor. She imagined Bailey waking up and finding the bugs dead or dying among the bits of grass in the jar.

Bridget had killed enough lightning bugs in her life to know how it went. Whatever light they might muster in the context of the morning sun looked tawdry and pitiful, so you couldn't believe there had been any grandeur to it at all.

She couldn't tolerate the idea of Bailey's discovering them in that state. What would Bailey's delicate heart say about that? What would she think of Bridget's magic then?

How could Bridget have ever thought the lightning bugs were a good idea? What business had she to try to capture life and light? Why was she incapable of thinking anything through? She belonged in the lower orders with the termites and cockroaches. She belonged in a jar, small and powerless, where she couldn't do harm.

Bridget crept out of her room and into Bailey's. She carefully pried the jar from between Bailey's arms and crept back to the hallway. She went through the back door out onto the dampening grass. She unscrewed the lid and showed the poor bugs the sky, imagining they would fly to freedom. But they didn't. They were apparently so stunned by their twisting fate, the only way to get them out was to dump them on the grass. She watched them trying to reorient.

When Jones woke to a car alarm in the middle of the night, he looked at Carmen staring wide-eyed at the ceiling.

"What's the matter?" he asked.

"Tibby wants me to go to someplace in Pennsylvania on April second. If I go to New Orleans, I won't be able to get back in time."

"*If* you go to New Orleans?" He didn't even question the notion of how Tibby could ask her to go someplace.

"Yeah, if I go."

"You have to go."

"I don't *have* to go."

Jones lifted his head and propped it on his hand, looking at her in disbelief. "It would be career suicide not to. I mean, think of it. How would your reps feel? Do you think you'll be getting any more calls like this again?"

Carmen clamped her molars together. She could have these childish run-ins with Jones all she liked, but she could hear herself on the phone with her mother in the morning. Her mother would be saying, "You don't *have* to go," and Carmen would be saying, "It would be career suicide, Mom. What would my reps think?"

"Work's not the only thing in life," Carmen said petulantly.

"Of course it's not. But this is a once-in-a-career opportunity, and what would you be missing it for? What do you think you are going to find in Pennsylvania? You're not going to find Tibby, if that's what you're hoping for."

Carmen turned on her pillow to face away from him. She stuffed her arms under her pillow. She didn't want to admit to herself that she was even more afraid of Pennsylvania than she was of New Orleans. She didn't want him to see her cry anymore.

"You can go to Pennsylvania after you get back," he added in a softer voice. "After the wedding. Tibby wouldn't expect you to miss a casting meeting with one of the top directors in the world. She wouldn't want to get in the way of your wedding." He touched Carmen's shoulder blade. "These are important things. She would understand."

Tibby would understand what was important. Carmen agreed with that part. Tibby always understood. But as she struggled to see Tibby's face in her mind, Carmen also knew what was important, and it wasn't either of the things he said.

I'll let you be in my dreams

        if I can be in yours.

—Bob Dylan

Bridget woke the next morning to the sound of crying. She realized that there were tears on her face and there was panic in her chest but that the sobs didn't belong to her. She couldn't remember where she was. She gaped at the ceiling, trying to remember. Her mind spun through a series of beds in Mission apartments, at Perry and Violet's place, at the Sea Star Inn. She had to sit up and look around before her mind finally and fully joined her body in Australia. The sobs were Bailey's, coming from downstairs. She could hear Brian's soothing voice, trying to comfort her.

Bridget dressed quickly. When she arrived in the kitchen, Bailey was still clutching the glass jar where the lightning bugs had been and sobbing. Brian cast Bridget a drowning look.

Bailey sat in her high chair, holding up the jar so Bridget could see it, but she was incapable of forming any words. After Bridget had released the bugs the night before, she'd put some grass back into the jar and returned it to Bailey's crib.

Bridget pulled a chair close. "The bugs went away?" she said.

Bailey nodded. The look on her face rent Bridget's heart and she began questioning everything she had done. She tried to identify the moment when she'd done the worst wrong. It often happened without out clear warning. Was it the moment of abandon when she'd begun grabbing living things from the sky? Was the worst wrong opening the jar and letting them go? Had she sided with bugs against a child? Was the worst wrong returning the empty jar to Bailey's arms?

"We don't know how they escaped, but they did," Brian said. "They flew away." Bridget couldn't tell if there was a note of accusation in his voice.

Bailey nodded.

"I told her they're happy in the sky," Brian continued, "but she's still feeling sad."

Bailey was listening carefully. The sobs had stopped, but her face was still stricken, wet with tears and her runny nose.

"I'm sorry they went away," Bridget said. She understood Bailey wasn't looking for an explanation. Bailey didn't need Bridget to tell her they hadn't gotten out by themselves, and that if she'd left them in there they would have died. She put her hands out and lifted Bailey from her chair.

She wordlessly took the jar from Bailey's hands and put it on the counter. She folded Bailey into her side, held her firmly with one arm and stroked her head with the other as she walked back and forth across the kitchen. After two or three laps, Bailey gave the weight of her head to Bridget's shoulder.

Brian sent her a grateful look and tiptoed back to his office. Bridget didn't stop walking. She moved from stroking Bailey's head to stroking her back. She made the laps bigger.

Bailey wiped off her nose on Bridget's shirt, and Bridget felt strangely grateful for it. Bridget felt the violent hitch in Bailey's breathing begin to smooth out. After some time Bailey put her thumb in her mouth and got heavier.

When the loop grew to include the entire ground floor of the house and the front porch, Bridget began to understand the deeper thing Bailey was crying for. She wondered about the words Brian might have used. They probably involved going away and maybe even being in the sky, and Bridget was sure they were bewildering to Bailey and signaled nothing more than pure loss.

Bridget went out to the porch and lowered onto a wicker chair in the soft shade. She continued to rub Bailey's back as she felt Bailey's body settle deeply into hers.

She'd thought Bailey had fallen asleep until Bailey sat up on her lap. She took her thumb out of her mouth and formulated a question.

"Catch a-a-a-again?"

Bridget sighed. She was greatly tempted to tell Bailey they would catch more tonight. They could easily catch a dozen in their jar. They could catch them every night if they wanted to.

But Bridget thought again about the moment of worst wrong, such an unassuming juncture that she often swanned right past it. There was no way she was putting them through that again.

"They are always in the sky. In the summertime you can see them," Bridget said quietly. "Everywhere you go."

Bailey lay back down on her again, and Bridget resumed stroking her back.

Bridget had imagined it was better if the thing you loved just disappeared. But maybe Bailey would have been better off if she could have seen and known what happened. Either way, she and Bailey were the same. They were both broken in the same place.

I know how you feel, Bridget thought. And it wasn't just Tibby. She had lost her mother too.

The day Lena returned from Greece to nothing and no one, there was a letter waiting for her. She knew instantly who it was from by the way her name looked in the particular way he wrote it. It had been forwarded from her parents' address.

Dear Lena, it began in his beloved handwriting. *You said not to call, so I decided to write.*

The momentary ecstasy at seeing her name in his writing again was quickly replaced by a pang of dread.

With a girded heart she scanned the letter for the explanations and mollification regarding Harriet. On the phone he'd said they weren't married, but that was kind of a cop-out. He and Harriet lived together in an extravagant house and Harriet wore a big fat sapphire on her marriage finger. You didn't do that if you weren't planning to get married. At least, a girl like Harriet didn't; Lena felt pretty sure of that.

Lena looked through the neat lines for the apologetic language, the stilted sorrow for the ending of her hopes, such as they were, and the exhortation for friendship in the future. He'd say that they were like family, that he really cared for her and blah, blah, blah. This was exactly the conversation she didn't want to have and the one he was surely eager for. But when she paused her brain and actually read the words, she saw that they were nothing like that.

> As I walked along the river on my way home from work yesterday, I had a memory of Tibby, and I wanted to tell it to you.
>
> Do you remember that August, almost ten years ago, when you and your friends came to Santorini to look for your lost pants? Bridget saw me first on a street in the village and recognized me, I think. But it was Tibby who chased me down. I don't know if they even told you about it.
>
> Tibby said, "Lena is here, did you know that?" and I told her that I didn't. I was startled to hear it and startled to see her. She introduced herself, but I already knew who she was. "Do you want to see her?" Tibby asked.
>
> She had so much intensity and sweetness in her demeanor. I was a coward at first. "Does she want to see me?" I asked.
>
> And Tibby fixed me with quite a look. She was weighing my character at that moment, and I would have believed her judgment over anyone else's. "Do you want to see her?" she said again.
>
> I remember standing in the middle of the street, and there was Tibby right up in my face and Bee standing in puzzlement with her hands on her hips a few yards away. I could see the conflict with Bee. She didn't know if she would be betraying you by coming closer or by staying away.
>
> Seeing those girls, I knew you better. I understood you in a new way. After all that had happened earlier that summer, I guess I wondered about you: do you

even want to be loved? And when I saw them, I knew you did.

So there was Tibby, a stranger who didn't feel like a stranger, putting it to me. I wanted to hide from her, but I couldn't. I looked at her and said, "Of course I do. More than anything else."

And so Tibby considered me and then nodded. She said, "You should come to the house this afternoon." And I did.

In the morning and evenings here in London I like to walk to and from work alone, in part because I'm never actually alone. I always seem to walk with some-one, either living or gone.

Often I walk with my father, though I have almost no true memory of him. He's my adviser, fixed and principled, the man who tells me to do the right thing and knows I know what it is, regardless of any seeming complication. Occasionally it's my mother. My mem-ory of her is no better, so I fabricate. I project her, as an analyst might say. She looks or sounds different at dif-ferent times, changing according to my needs, I sup-pose. She is my empathizer.

On lesser days, when I'm surface bound, it's one of my colleagues or my secretary. Often it's a friend, Yusuf or Daniel from the old flat. Today, yesterday, the day before, maybe tomorrow, I walk with Tibby.

Lena didn't stare at the letter for hours at a time in her customary way. She didn't think, obsess, wonder, or tremble. Well, she did all of those things, but she was suddenly invested with some larger power. She sat down and wrote him back.

Having grown up perched over the Caldera, do you ever think of the lost city that supposedly slid into the sea?

I seem to think of it and dream of it all the time these days. I know it's infantile, but I imagine that Tibby was swimming out there, searching for our lost pants, and found the trick way in, and she's there, and it's beautiful and everything is slow and still and quiet, as I always wish the world to be.

That's my projection, as your analyst would say, I guess, and it keeps me company. Our pants do happen to be there too, and Tibby found them, so according to our old myth, she has us with her.

Tibby occasionally looks up, I think, and sees the sun the way it might come down to reach her, glowing gold and refracted. Now she knows the secrets they have down there that we don't understand.

I think there are other things of mine down there in the ancient city, and they all happen to have a common quality: that I lost them and wish for them. Under there is a life I could have had, but don't, and it's going on without me in it.

In reality I guess you would say it's me who goes on without Tibby, but I can't quite seem to do that. It feels more like she's gone somewhere without me.

Not only did Lena write the letter quickly, she didn't overconsider the introduction, conclusion, or sign-off. She copied his closing: *Your old friend, Lena.* And not only that, she stuck it in an envelope as soon as she'd finished it, sealed it, put two stamps on it, and delivered it to the mailbox around the corner before she could fail to do so.

It was a blessing and also a curse of handwritten letters that, unlike email, you couldn't obsessively reread what you'd written after you'd sent it. You couldn't attempt to unsend it. Once you'd sent it, it was gone. It was an object that no longer belonged to you, but belonged to your recipient to do with what he would. You tended to remember the feeling of what you'd said more than the words. You gave the object away, and left yourself with the memory. That was what it was to give.

———

After the lightning-bug incident, Bailey could not be detached from Bridget. She sat on Bridget's lap through dinner. She wanted Bridget to read her bedtime story. She wanted Bridget's kisses right after Brian's.

Bridget went to bed early as usual. She lay in bed and listened to the rain start up. She felt sad but serene. Her limbs were heavy and quiet. Far from agitated, she imagined it would take a crane through the roof to get her out of bed.

She thought about Eric and the way he had looked when she'd walked away from him down Pine Street. She thought of Carmen and Lena on the last terrible day in Greece when they couldn't let their eyes meet and said things to one another that were supposed to pass for a long goodbye.

She tried to picture them in their lives. Carmen in her glitzy loft with her cappuccino machine that cost more than all of Bridget's possessions put together. Was the cappuccino machine offering Carmen any comfort? Maybe it was. Maybe Carmen understood something Bridget had simply missed.

She pictured Lena in her dark, quiet little room. So dark you couldn't grow a plant, the only window thick with chicken wire. She pictured Lena drawing her feet until the drawing was so real there were four feet and you couldn't tell the difference. And here Bridget could barely muster a scribble. Maybe Lena understood something too.

For the first time Bridget felt a vague longing to talk to them, a hope that they were doing better than she was. It was a strange tingling she had that made her think of phantom limb syndrome, but the tingling was rooted much deeper. She felt like parts of her soul were missing, had left her body long ago. It had happened not in Greece three months ago, but long before that. It was in Greece that she'd realized those parts had left her and were not coming back.

Her mind turned to Eric again, when she heard a flutter of feet down the hallway. She sat up, feeling an unexpected surge of adrenaline. Had Bailey climbed out of her crib? Was she okay?

So maybe it wouldn't take a crane, Bridget recognized ruefully with her feet planted on the floor, as her door pushed open and a small figure crossed her room with the grace of an insect. Bailey appeared at the side of her bed, too short to climb up on her own. She raised her arms to be lifted, and Bridget obliged her.

Bailey crawled under the covers and molded her body against Bridget's. In some wonder Bridget heard the crinkle of Bailey's diaper, smelled her zincy ointment, and felt the moistness of her toes, which only came down to the top of Bridget's thigh. Bailey put her thumb in her mouth and closed her eyes.

Afraid of breaking this spell, Bridget barely breathed. She put her arm around Bailey, wanting to hold her, but afraid to burden her with any weight.

The rain pounded on the roof and trickled down the window. Bailey snorted and twitched and drooled and finally passed into such a deep stage of sleep, Bridget supposed she could dangle her by the ankles without waking her.

It wasn't a spell, Bridget realized, gathering Bailey closer. She needed a mother. *Like all of us,* Bridget thought. And like most of us, Bailey wanted to sleep in proximity to another warm body.

Bridget lay awake, but she wasn't restless. There weren't as many places to go as there were thoughts to think.

Sometime in the early-morning hours, Bridget felt Tibby's presence again. Not in the form of this look-alike old playmate, but separate from her. In Bridget's half-dream, Tibby seemed to lie in a symmetrical curve on the other side of Bailey, so that their knees practically touched under Bailey's feet. This time she took the form of a mother.

Honey,

you cannot wrestle a dove.

—The Shins

Nearly every aspect of the wedding planning had been a cheerful and much-needed distraction for Carmen until now. Now she sat at the kitchen table in her loft, bouncing her leg, staring at the pile of invitations, unable to pick up her pen.

Until now she'd been pleased with the invitations. They were expensively engraved, just the right shade of ecru, and one hundred percent tasteful. With the help of these invitations, she'd managed to waste at least four evenings, addressing them during the time when she otherwise might have had to spare a thought for how her life was going to feel the day after her meticulously planned honeymoon came to an end.

But when it came to the last two invitations, her pen dried up and her energy left her. She'd invited Lena's parents. She'd even invited Effie. Now she had to invite Lena. She'd invited Bee's dad and her brother and Violet, even though she felt pretty sure they wouldn't come. Now she had to invite Bee.

She knocked her pen against the metal table. The plan had been to call them first, resume contact before the invitations arrived, but she hadn't done that. The plan then became to write a little note in each of their invitations acknowledging, at least, how strange and difficult this was, but she hadn't managed that either.

What was she so scared of? She couldn't even frame it. She didn't want to have to talk about what happened. She didn't want to have to acknowledge the impenetrably dark thing that they three—maybe only they three—knew and could not say. *It isn't just that she drowned.*

Carmen didn't want to have to digest it any further. She couldn't.

The third plan was just to write out their addresses and stick the damned things in the mail, but even that proved too hard. She pictured their reactions when they got them. *You are seriously going ahead with this?* What would they think of her? They would think she'd had a lobotomy. That would be their kindest reaction.

What if she didn't invite them? That would be insane.

She tried to imagine the feeling of walking down the aisle, seeing their faces in the crowd as she and Jones took their vows, just two more random spectators. If only she could think of them that way. But she couldn't. She couldn't imagine them and not imagine their honesty along with them. They knew her better than anyone.

She tried to imagine the feeling of walking down the aisle without seeing their faces at all, and she simply couldn't do it.

Without them, her life was a farce. With them her life was a farce. Carmen sighed and put her head down on the cold table. Her life was a farce.

Kostos's return letter came in an extraordinarily brisk three days. It had many parts, all of them funny or sad, none of them having anything to do with his girlfriend/fiancée named Harriet.

> *I dreamed of your lost city last night. Isn't that strange. You gave me a dream. Thanks for it. It was lovely and serene and I saw some people I've really been missing, not all of them dead.*
>
> *Any scuba diving allowed? Any transubstantiation in one direction or the other? Can you at least just go down and say hi?*

Once again, Lena finished reading it, took out a piece of paper, and wrote him back. As she wrote to him, he didn't seem to her so much a corporeal presence, a confusingly desirable and disappointing man, but as a kindred consciousness floating out there alongside hers.

> *I put on Valia's housedress today. The one with the pink and purple squares. You probably remember it; she wore it all the time.*
>
> *I don't know why I did it. Maybe because there's a cold, gloomy rain outside. It's not a good fit, exactly, but it's made me strangely happy. I feel like it's still got some Oia sunshine in it, as well as Valia's indomitable energy. You know I've always been superstitious about clothing. Now I don't want to take it off. I'm going to wear it to teach figure painting today.*

Under the part in her letter about the housedress, Lena took out her colored pencils and made a drawing of Valia wearing it along with her absurd pink plastic house shoes. She placed Valia in the loosely sketched doorway of her house with one hand on her hip.

Lena became completely absorbed in the drawing, remembering and articulating every subtlety of Valia's fierce morning stance and her sleepy, wrinkly expression. There had been a running rivalry between Valia and her best friend, Rena Dounas, Kostos's grandmother, over which of them woke up earlier and made the first appearance in the morning.

"*I have been up for hours!*" Lena wrote as the caption.

Kostos's response came quickly.

> *I am torn between laughter and awe when I look at—or even think of—the extraordinary picture you made. It is sitting on my desk. You capture the seventy-year relationship between our two grandmothers in one image.*
>
> *Why, you must be an artist.*
>
> *You'll see I've enclosed my own slight creation, not to be compared to yours. It's a deck hinge, in case you weren't able to identify it immediately.*

I was in Oia this past weekend, and made a fish dinner for my grandparents. My grandfather took ambivalent note of my cooking skills and studied my hands with disapprobation. He has a deep respect for men with rough hands, and I could see he thought I was going soft.

So I went back to the forge for old time's sake, and perhaps to restore myself a little in his eyes or mine. The forge is hardly used anymore. Bapi has been retired for ten years. It took me senseless hours to get it going, and senseless more to make the small, shabby thing here enclosed. But I took my blackened hands to the office with pride this morning.

You may not have much urgent use for a deck hinge. And it's not a very good one, to boot. But short of enclosing an excellent fish dinner, which I didn't think would travel well, it's the best thing I could make for now.

In ten days' time, Lena realized she was getting and sending a letter almost every day.

Thank you for the deck hinge. From the moment I get my first fishing vessel, it will be in constant use.

Honestly, Lena didn't know what she had been doing with her life before the letters started. They filled her mind and the hours of her day almost completely.

Kostos, she decided, had more hours in his day than she had, probably at least five or six more. His letters were longer, more interesting, and cleverer than hers, and somehow he also managed to hold an important job and have a life.

Lena was teaching a total of four classes a week and spending time with no one but Eudoxia for an hour once a week. She'd had no desire to go into the studio and paint since October.

But more and more she was adding little drawings and designs to her letters. She made a sketch of her grandfather's famous white-tasseled shoes. She drew a picture of a fishing boat, the kind that docked in Ammoudi, with an inset drawing of a magnified deck hinge. She made a watercolor of an olive tree and let it dry by the window before she folded it up to send.

There were so many things she wasn't saying. There were so many memories pertaining to him and them in each of these images, many of them sad. Those were the only feelings, the only subject, that didn't go into her letters.

Kostos left them out too. Probably without the same careful intention; he might not have been wallowing in those memories at all. But whatever the reason, he didn't talk about love, good or bad, and that was a relief. Nor did he ever mention his fiancée/girlfriend. And that was a bigger relief.

Maybe this was the kind of relationship Lena and Kostos were meant for: abstract, contextual, but not intimate. She thought of Markos, the man her father had played tennis with every Saturday morning for the past twenty years. It was like a million other friendships in that it went along without their ever needing to talk about themselves or, God forbid, their relationship. Her father hadn't found out Markos had gotten divorced until two years after it happened.

I think you and I are the last two letter writers on earth, she'd written to Kostos a few days before. Neither of them was suited to phone conversations or jotty emails employing only lowercase letters. But clearly they had found their métier.

It was a strange joy to get to know him again, to reveal herself honestly again, without all the heat.

She looked up from the current letter, on which she'd spent two hours making a delicate border of olive leaves. It would be hard to say there was no love in these letters.

"You have been an unbelievable help to me. To both of us. I don't even know how to tell you."

Almost three weeks had passed, and Brian was sitting at the kitchen table with a bottle of beer after having put Bailey to sleep. It was rare that he and Bridget had a moment to talk. He worked late and she went to bed early. He was working with a team in California and a team in Kolkata, he said, so he kept odd hours. Maybe they were avoiding each other.

"You don't need to tell me," Bridget said, mashing up ripe bananas in a bowl. She'd discovered that Bailey would eat anything that involved bananas, so she'd made up a recipe for whole-wheat banana muffins. *Eric would like these,* she found herself thinking.

"I don't know how to thank you."

"You don't need to thank me." She mixed the dry ingredients together and got the eggs out of the refrigerator.

"A package came for you today. Did you see it?"

"I got it," Bridget said. She'd ordered a pile of books for Bailey. Bailey loved books about dogs and monsters, so she'd ordered all the ones she'd remembered loving, mostly from reading them at Tibby's house: *Good Dog, Carl; Martha Speaks; Harry the Dirty Dog; The Monster Bed; Marvin and the Monster.* She'd also ordered the entire Schoolhouse Rock collection on DVD.

She poured the batter into the muffin tin, imagining Tibby buying the muffin tin. "How's the project going?"

"It's going. I have maybe another week and a half of work. I have to send it out before the move."

He was silent and she knew he wanted her to stay. "Do you want me to stay?" she asked.

"Can you?"

"Yes." She didn't say she couldn't imagine leaving.

She noticed he'd brought home a huge pile of flattened cardboard boxes when he'd made a run to the supermarket that afternoon. "I can help you move if you want." She was really, really good at moving.

"Are you sure? You don't have somewhere else you need to be?"

Bridget shook her head. She had never been big on posturing or pretending she had anything she didn't.

She knew Brian probably wondered what had happened to her life, what had happened with Eric, why she didn't call anybody. But he didn't ask. The air was packed with the things they didn't ask each other.

"I wish I could repay you."

"You don't need to repay me." If she could have found a way to say it, she would have been honest and told him she wasn't doing it for him or Bailey or even Tibby as much as she seemed to be doing it for herself.

But by the time she'd finished cleaning up from the muffins, she'd thought of a payment she would exact. She would venture a question.

"Hey, Brian?" she asked.

"Yes."

She wouldn't risk opening the sky on him as she had at first. *What happened to you two? Why were you hiding from everyone who loved you? Why didn't you tell us about your daughter?* She'd ask him something specific and relatively easy.

"Were you and Tibby married?"

He looked up at her in some surprise. It was an easy one, but a breach of their tacit agreement nonetheless. His eyes were wary. Was she a fellow fugitive, as he'd come to hope, or really a spy after all? "No," he said.

He must have sensed her disappointment as she picked up her water glass and started for the door.

"We were planning to get married as soon as we got back to the States," he said. "Tibby wanted to wait to do it with her folks and the three of you."

Bridget floated back toward the table.

"But that didn't happen, of course." He seemed to be trying to fend off a lot of things with his "of course." A gulf was opening, and neither seemed to know how to close it.

"That's delayed me taking Bailey back," he added, more businesslike. "She was born here. Because we weren't married yet, there were some legal issues about guardianship to nail down before I could take her out of the country."

Bridget nodded.

"She hasn't met her grandparents yet, you know?" There was an almost undetectable crack in his voice.

Bridget had wondered about that. She nodded again.

"Or Nicky or Katherine. Or Carmen and Lena."

Bridget thought it was brave of him to say all the names of the missing in a row. "Right," she said.

"But now it's all settled. So that's the next thing, I guess." It was a wearying prospect. She could see it in his face.

"Right," she said again.

They were silent after that. She took the muffins out of the oven and left one on a plate for him. She'd wait until a couple of days to ask any more questions by way of payment.

After more than three weeks of obsessive letter-writing and at least twenty letters on each side, Lena got one from Kostos that ended in an absolutely breathtaking and unexpected way.

> *The second-best part of my day is writing a letter to you. The first-best part is receiving one from you. And all day long I think, "But wouldn't it be lovely just to wake up together in the same bed?"*

For the first time Lena didn't know what to write. Her head sizzled with a shock that killed every idea. She couldn't do so much as take out a piece of paper and lay it on her desk. She walked around with a roaring lawn mower in her chest.

The feelings were too noisy, moving too fast to be understood. So much for Markos the tennis partner. There was excitement and fear and a hundred other strands that she couldn't untangle.

She attempted to search the Internet for information about Harriet, knowing only her address and first name, and found nothing. She felt stupid.

Two days later another letter came from him and it was short. Lena tore it open before she lost courage. Her heart raced with hope. What was the hope?

It was one page, five words.

> *My mistake. Won't happen again.*

That wasn't the hope.

The lawn mower stopped. All the noise and energy drained out of her. She felt tired, all of a sudden, and nothing else. She slept through the late afternoon and night and didn't wake up until the next morning.

Still wearing Valia's robe, she took out a piece of paper and wrote a question.

Do you love Harriet?

She stared at it for a long time, and then she threw it in the garbage.

All morons hate it
when you call them a moron.

—J. D. Salinger

Bridget and Bailey played in the creek and weeded the flower bed alongside the house. They went to the neighbors' house to visit their cat, Springs. Bailey adored Springs but Springs did not adore Bailey, who was always trying to pick her up by the back legs.

After lunch Bridget and Bailey lay on the couch together and Bridget read *Good Dog, Carl* four times in a row, in four different accents.

Bailey fell asleep on Bridget's chest, and Bridget closed her eyes in contentment, feeling Bailey's body rising and falling on her breath.

Bridget heard a song floating in from Brian's study. It was a Beatles song she used to love, "I'll Follow the Sun," and with Bailey safely asleep, she let herself cry. They were tranquil tears, even philosophical ones, but deeply sad as they slid down from the corners of her eyes into her hair and ears.

How could you have left her, Tibby?

It was the question that poked and nicked and needled her a hundred times a day, but only now had she put it into words.

How could you choose to spend even one day away from her?

Bridget had thought maybe when faced with the daily tribulations of an actual child she would understand it better, what Tibby and Marly had done. But she didn't. She understood it less. Every day she spent with Bailey the mystery grew darker.

How could you have done it?

And because she was not completely without shame or self-awareness, Bridget thought of the thing in her uterus, not a thing but a person, a soul, and she felt chastened. Just look what she was willing to do. Had been willing to do.

The tears rolled on and Bailey rose and fell on her chest. Bridget cried for the leavers and the left. For the people, like herself, grimly forsaking what few precious gifts they would ever get. She cried for Bailey, for Tibby, for the resolute clump of cells making headway in her uterus, and for Marly, her poor, sad mother, who'd missed everything.

Lena half expected that the day known as Wednesday, March 15, would not occur. It would somehow get swallowed by the calendar. The earth would give a little heave in its orbit, and Tuesday would turn into Thursday. People across the globe would miss dentist appointments and soccer matches, but they would reschedule them and life would go on.

The time to open Tibby's portentious letter would be gone without ever having arrived, and life in the post-disappointment era would go on unchallenged.

Lena's life had come down to a very few things, and on the evening of March 14, even those were beyond her. She couldn't take in the words on the pages of her book. She couldn't hear the words of the songs she played. She couldn't taste her dinner. She couldn't fall asleep. She didn't want to cede what slight hold she had on the world in case the appointed day might just tiptoe past without her notice. But wouldn't that be easier, in a way?

At midnight she crept out of bed and woke her computer. Her computer wouldn't lie to her. If it skipped the day, it would at least let her know.

At 12:00 a.m. it recorded Wednesday, March 15. Was it being honest with her or just conventional?

She thought of Julius Caesar on this day. *So it has come,* she thought. *It has come, but it has not gone.*

Should she open it now? She thought of Kostos. What time was it where he was? Later. He hadn't already read it, had he? No, not that much later. He was probably asleep in his bed. She didn't want to picture his bed in the likely event he wasn't alone in it.

She picked up the letter. She could open it—it was the proper day. But somehow her desperate-in-the-middle-of-the-night-in-her-bare-feet status would seem to follow the letter of Tibby's law rather than the spirit. The spirit was what she was going for here.

She brought the letter into her bed and clutched it until morning.

At six o'clock in the morning she tried to be casual. She ate a bagel casually. She went out to the newspaper stand two blocks away and bought *The New York Times*. *Wednesday, March 15*, it said along the top. It was probably midday in London.

As soon as she got back to her apartment, she walked directly to the letter still lying in her bed and opened it. In the envelope were two things. First was a one-page letter, folded, and second was yet another small sealed envelope with her name on the front. On the back the envelope said *Please open on March 30*.

How long would this go on? She put the sealed envelope beside her on the bed, and unfolded the page to which she was now entitled. It was printed sort of like an invitation.

> *Someday is now. (Or it is never.)*
> *Please come to the following address on the Second of*
> * April*
> *at 4 o'clock p.m. Eastern Standard Time.*
> *If you choose to come, bring yourself, all of yourself,*
> * and no one else.*
> *Consider it a journey that could last the rest of your*
> * life.*
>
> *If you choose not to come, that's a different ending,*
> * but it's a beginning too.*

Bridget waited until three nights before the move, while she was helping Brian pack up the books in the living room, to ask another question.

"Did Tibby want to have a baby?" As payment went, this was a more expensive question, and she knew it.

He didn't answer at first. His book-boxing movements became robotic. "Yes. Of course."

"Did you?"

"Of course."

She stopped and looked at him with some impatience. Tibby was gone. It didn't seem so "of course" to her.

He walked out of the room, up the stairs, and into his bedroom, and she thought they were back to her first day in this house.

She waited for a door to bang shut, but a few seconds later she heard him walking down the stairs again. He was carrying something and he thrust it at her from several feet away. His face had changed to a completely different shape.

She took it from him and looked at it. She drew in a breath and felt her whole body shifting in response to it.

It was a photograph in a glass frame. It was black-and-white and must have been taken within a few days of Bailey's birth, because her tiny face was puffy and crumpled.

In the picture Tibby's hand cupped the baby's head and her cheek lay against her baby's cheek. Tibby's eyes were closed, her freckles were like dark snowflakes on her white skin, and her lovely pixie face showed something too ancient to name. It was her familiar Tibby, but also it was Tibby gone to a serious place where Bridget couldn't follow.

From the picture Bridget understood. She felt an uprising of tears, neither tranquil nor philosophical. The picture answered her question expensively.

She handed it back to Brian and saw he was crying too. He sat down in a chair, his jaw in his hands and his shoulders shaking. She went to the other chair and curled up like a fetus.

They stayed like that for a long time in their separate chairs. They didn't exchange a word, but unlike the first time she'd pushed too hard, she realized that the air felt strangely companionable.

She decided not to ask him any more questions for a while.

———

Lena thought of canceling her weekly coffee with Eudoxia, but for what? So she could sit on her bed and stare at the wall and ruminate. Was that really something she needed more of?

"My dear, what is it?" That was the first thing Eudoxia said. "Something is very wrong."

Lena looked at her coffee and looked at Eudoxia and looked back at her coffee. It seemed insane, on the face of it, to tell Eudoxia what was going on.

But why?

Because it wasn't the kind of thing she did.

But why?

Because she was raw and uncertain, and she liked to keep all the messy parts of herself to herself.

Lena realized she was kneading her hands in the manner of Valia if Valia had taken amphetamines. As much as Lena liked to hide the mess and display the finished product, by this point she was all mess and no product. She couldn't hide from everyone for the rest of her life. . . . Well, she could. That was the direction things were going. But she knew from long-ago experience that when you were uncertain and if you were courageous enough to let her in, a real friend could do a world of good.

"Tibby left a letter for me and one for Kostos. She gave a date and a time and meeting place, some place in Pennsylvania I've never heard of, and invited us both to show up."

Eudoxia looked purely puzzled. "To show up for what?"

It was so outlandish, Lena found it hard to answer. "I guess it's the chance to be together. To get together and stay together."

A dawning look was coming into Eudoxia's eyes. "And if you don't?"

"Then just give up and move on."

"Tibby wants you to make a choice, not just wait around for him to come."

"I'm not waiting around for him to come."

"Lena."

"That supposes that I want to be with him. Maybe I don't."

"I see your face when you say his name."

"What does that mean?"

Eudoxia cocked her head to one side. "Let me put it this way: do you want to be without him?"

Lena remembered the feeling of saying goodbye to Kostos at the ferry the last time. "But that doesn't mean I want to be with him." Why was everyone always trying to turn the world into binary choices, black or white, A or B, this or that?

Eudoxia looked unimpressed.

"We've caused each other more misery than anything else," Lena said hotly. "It's true. It's all suffering with the two of us. If you were to ask Kostos: Has Lena caused you more pleasure or pain? If he was honest, he'd answer the same way I would about him."

Eudoxia sat there shaking her head. "That's just silly."

Lena felt like Eudoxia had slapped her. "That's *silly*? Thanks a lot."

Eudoxia looked unrepentant. "You've been unhappy because you haven't been together. If you were together, you'd be happy."

Lena's mind raced over their long, tragic history, all wrenching goodbyes and longing letters. Kostos being with people besides her.

It couldn't possibly be that simple, could it? There was no possible way. Their torments were real and important, fateful and psychologically complex.

Weren't they?

Then the strangest thing happened. It was as though Lena's consciousness shifted from her body into Eudoxia's. Suddenly Lena's mind existed at the top of Eudoxia's big, generous body and looked out of her canny eyes.

From that perch Lena saw the whole thing differently, and it did seem silly. And dumb. It was another dumb thing Lena had been holding on to. Another part of her dreadful mythology that made her think even simple things were overwhelmingly complicated and worthy of dread.

Feeling dumb, Lena crept back wretchedly to her own body. If she'd been aiming to keep her personal mess off the table, this might have been a good time to pay the bill and go home, but she realized she couldn't anymore. She was all in.

Lena stared at Eudoxia's knowing face, and though she did feel silly, she did not feel appeased. There were other problems too. "In all the fourteen or something years we've known each other, we haven't done much more than kiss a few times. How can we make some big blind commitment when we don't even know how we are together?"

Eudoxia cast that off with a flick of her wrist. "Anatole and I had barely kissed. Most couples in the history of the world had barely kissed. It's when the world changed and people started doing everything else, that's when everybody got divorced."

"You think." Lena half intended to sound sassy and sarcastic, but it didn't come out like that.

"Of course. It's better this way. You have more to look forward to."

Lena was floundering in messy doubt and Eudoxia was sitting there like the queen of certainty.

"Oh, and another thing. I think he's getting married." Lena laid down the heavy card.

Eudoxia shrugged philosophically. "Then he probably won't come."

Lena shot up in her seat in protest. "He probably won't come! And that seems okay to you? You think I should go and yet you think he won't show up?"

"I don't think he won't show up."

"But you think it's possible."

"Of course it's possible."

"How can I go if he doesn't go? How terrible would it be to just wait there pathetically alone for him never to show up?"

Eudoxia's expression grew more serious. "That's what you're doing anyway, my dear."

Probably because she had no pride left, Lena called Eudoxia three hours after they'd said goodbye at the coffee shop.

"Do you think he'll come?"

"I don't know, dear one."

"You act so confident, like you know what's going to happen."

"I don't. I know what I want to happen."

"But what do you think *will* happen?" Lena recognized that she sounded like she was five.

"I think you need to make this decision on your own. I think you need to know what you want and try to get it. That's the only thing you can do. The other part is not in your control."

"Okay, okay, I know that."

"You get older and you learn there is one sentence, just four words long, and if you can say it to yourself it offers more comfort than almost any other. It goes like this. . . . Ready?"

"Ready."

"'At least I tried.'"

Lena sighed. "Okay. I get it. I do." She was too pathetic for words. "But will he come? I just want to know what you think the odds are. Tell me what you really think."

"I think Tibby was a wise girl. I think she loved you."

When we argue for our limitations,
we get to keep them.

—Evelyn Waugh

The afternoon she was getting on a plane to go to New Orleans, Carmen stopped in the Apple store downtown to switch her service from her old phone to the new one that Tibby had left for her.

She had to wait in line, and then wait endlessly for the so-called genius salesperson to transfer all her contacts, so that by the time she got out of there she was running really late.

She saw as she raced back to the loft that the black town car was already waiting to take her to the airport. She finished packing in a hurry. She went down to the car and then raced up to the loft again when she realized she'd forgotten her makeup bag. By the time the car pulled onto the FDR Drive she was half an hour later than she should have been.

It ought to be fine, Carmen told herself. Travel departments always loaded on extra time. She immediately thought to pass the time checking her email and making calls, but the new phone was not booting up properly. She turned it off. Maybe AT&T needed a little time to switch the service. Her fingers itched.

She grabbed a copy of *People* magazine from the seat pocket. She remembered how much she used to love these gossipy magazines. At Williams, between Dostoyevsky and Marx, she'd be gobbling up *Us Weekly* and *OK!* She'd believed they were faithfully recording the magical world of celebrity. But the more she knew the business, the less she enjoyed the magazines. Every page she turned, she saw the manipulations, the gears showing. She saw how much of the coverage was bartered and bought. She used to look at the red carpet pictures and be dazzled, but now she saw Botox and fake teeth, starvation and double-sided tape.

Maybe they lost their thrill the day she had seen herself in one of the pictures. It was a red carpet photo of her at the Golden Globes, and it probably looked as glamorous as the next one to the outside eye. But when she saw it all she could think of was the sweat that had been dripping down her back, the gross taste in her mouth from not eating for three days, the tape holding up her dress, her confusion at photographers barking her name, the smile pasted on her face. There had been nothing magical about it.

"What time is your flight?" the driver asked her.

Carmen looked up. "Uh. Five forty-five, I think?" She looked at her dead phone. The flight time was on the phone. The airline and terminal information was on the phone. She wondered what time it was. Damn, that was on the phone too. The phone company might as well have switched off her brain while they were at it.

"That might be tough," he said.

"What?" Now that he mentioned it, it did seem as though the car hadn't moved in a while. She looked out the window. She scooted up to look through the front windshield. "What's going on?"

"There must be an accident. Nobody's moving."

She could see the Triboro Bridge in the distance, but there were about a million other cars between them and it. She heard sirens behind them, trying to get through. The lanes of the FDR were so packed, no cars could get over to make way for them. A blast of honking began.

At last she spotted an old-fashioned clock on the dashboard. It was almost five. "Can you get off this?" she asked.

The driver looked over his shoulder at her. He couldn't get anywhere. It was too stupid a question to answer.

She tried to turn her phone on again, but it turned itself off. Was it the battery? Where could she charge it?

Another twenty minutes passed, and no one moved except two

police cars and an ambulance that finally broke the sclerosis. "Shit," Carmen said, as she did every couple of minutes. She stared at the phone in rising panic. What could she do? She couldn't call the airline, she couldn't call her manager, she couldn't call the travel contact. What had anybody ever done before they had iPhones?

She read every page of *People,* including the weird ads in the back. At five forty-five she paused and raised her head to acknowledge officially missing her flight.

"What do you want to do?" the driver asked.

"I guess go to the airport," she said. She felt like half a person without a phone to wield. "I'll have to catch a later flight."

The only saving grace was the fact that the official meeting wasn't until Tuesday. She'd simply have to absorb the local culture at a slightly faster rate.

She read *The New York Times* and even the *Financial Times,* God help her. She didn't get out of the car and into the airport until seven twenty. She went to the Delta counter and put herself at their mercy.

"Please just get me on the next flight to New Orleans," she said.

The Delta woman seemed to push every button on her keyboard at least a hundred times. "The next flight I can get you on is Tuesday afternoon."

"*What?*"

"I'm afraid so." She pushed a few more buttons.

"It's only Saturday. How can that be?"

She shrugged. "Can't say."

"Are you sure?"

She looked down at her screen again. Her name was Daisy and she had a very cheap dye job. Carmen could not afford to start hating her yet. "Sorry. Most of these are overbooked."

"Can you check another airline for me?"

"Well, I can't really. . . ."

"Please?" Carmen felt like she might vault over the desk and hijack the computer herself. She ached for some digital interaction.

"All right, let me look," Daisy said. She looked, shook her head, looked, shook her head. Carmen hated the sound of her fingernails clacking on the keys. Why did somebody who typed on a keyboard for a living grow such farcically long nails?

"What?" Carmen finally exploded bossily.

Daisy picked up her phone. She mumbled a few things and nod-ded a few more times. Finally she looked at Carmen. "There's some big music festival in New Orleans this weekend into next week. That seems to be what's going on. Nobody's got any seats until Tuesday."

"Nobody?"

"Nobody."

"What should I do?" Carmen wished she had somebody better than Daisy to throw her lot to.

Daisy seemed to wish she had somebody better than Carmen to assist. "Wait till Tuesday?"

"I can't wait until Tuesday!" Carmen exploded. "I have a meet-ing on Tuesday! It is the biggest meeting of my entire career."

Even Daisy was a human being. "You could drive."

"I don't have a car."

"You could rent one."

"I can't drive for a million hours by myself!" She wasn't even so sure she had a valid license. She drove about twice a year, when she went home to see her mom and David and Ryan.

Daisy gave her a look of maternal sympathy. Carmen realized you could turn almost anyone into a mother if you acted like enough of a baby. "Could you get a train?" Daisy asked.

"Is there a train to New Orleans?" Carmen had effectively for-gotten the existence of trains. She used to like trains. She once took the sleeping train to see her father in South Carolina, and she'd found it pretty thrilling.

"Sure. There must be. It would take a while."

"Can you look for me?"

"Can I?"

"Sure. On your computer."

"You'd probably do better to call Amtrak."

Would it help or hurt if Carmen started crying? "I don't have a phone. It's not working."

Daisy looked around to see if there was danger of someone catch-ing her engaging in a non-plane-related travel search. Carmen sud-denly loved Daisy.

Daisy opened up the Internet browser on her computer and tapped a few things in. She raised her eyebrows. "Well, believe it or not, there's a train leaving Penn Station at nine fifty-nine tonight that gets you into New Orleans at . . . five fifteen in the morning."

"Tomorrow morning?"

"Monday morning."

"You've got to be kidding me."

"No." Daisy made an understanding face. "You'd make your meeting."

Carmen considered. She'd do her local absorption at warp speed. What choice did she have?

"It's almost eight now. You probably ought to get going," Daisy counseled.

"Okay. You're right. Well, thanks."

"Good luck to you," Daisy said sincerely.

Carmen looked over her shoulder several times as she left the terminal. She found it strangely difficult to say goodbye to Daisy, and she wondered if maybe this meant she was lonely.

Lena walked along the river. Over the last few days, she'd taken many walks along the river. It was freezing, but she didn't feel it. It might have been hailing. The river might have leapt out of its banks and taken her under and she might not have noticed it.

What would she do? What would he do? No, no, no. What would she do? (What would he do?)

Stop! That wasn't what she got to decide. She only got to decide what she did. This was a version of the prisoner's dilemma: a lover's dilemma. She had to do what she was going to do regardless of what he was going to do. She had to do the right thing.

She thought back to something Effie had told her once long ago when it came to taking a risk on Kostos. *You have to have some faith,* Effie had said.

But Effie hadn't meant faith in Kostos, Lena realized. Not faith that Kostos would be there to meet her and throw his arms around her and want her more than anyone else. Effie meant faith in herself.

Faith that even if he didn't come, she would be all right. She had to have faith not just in trying, but in failing. Was she strong enough to fail? Was she strong enough not to?

"I'll give you a hundred bucks if you can make this phone work in the next ten minutes," Carmen thundered at the pimply young man in the phone store two blocks from Penn Station.

"We close in five minutes, ma'am," the pimply young man answered.

Carmen glared at him. Where was the ambition? Where was the greed? This country was going down the tubes if this kid was any indication. "I'll give you a hundred bucks if you can make it work in the next *five* minutes," she said slowly.

He looked scared of her. He was no Daisy. His Adam's apple bobbed. "I could try."

"Please try." Was she going to have to tell him about being on TV? She didn't want to, but that sometimes worked on guys like him.

He turned her phone on. He pushed a couple of buttons and then the home key. "I don't see anything wrong with it," he said.

"Are you serious?"

He pointed it at her. She snatched it from him.

"You don't have to pay me the hundred bucks," he said magnanimously.

"Thanks," she snapped, walking out the door.

She managed to buy her train ticket on her credit card without incident. There were no roomettes available, she discovered, but there was a car called the dinette where she could eat.

She passed by the newsstand and looked at the fashion magazines. She didn't need them. Her phone was working, she'd be fine. She could read the script, she could make calls. She could write emails and plan her wedding. She could play that game where you landed the airplanes. With a functioning phone in her hand she felt her confidence slowly returning.

She got on the train with time to spare. She put her head back and closed her eyes. It was hard to believe she'd had all these reversals without telling Jones about any of them. He was always the one she complained to first. He understood her bumbling and faltering. He seemed to expect it.

Carmen felt happy to have two seats to herself on the dark train. She was happy that there was no one in the seats directly across from her or behind her. If she could keep her phone charged then maybe this wouldn't be so bad.

She dozed a little until Newark, when the train stopped and more people got on. She put her big purse on the seat next to her. She watched a trickle of people come down the aisle, most of them, thankfully, passing her by. Finally a small group straggled up next to her. It was a man with a small boy and a baby. He was eyeing the seats directly across the aisle from her. *Please don't sit there,* she thought. She overheard the man talking in Spanish to his son.

Her heart sank as they settled in. She listened to the boy chirp excitedly to his father. Oh, God. How long before the baby woke up and started screaming? She wondered if she could get her seat reassigned. This was really the last thing she needed.

Eight days remained before the fateful meeting was meant to take place, five days before Lena was meant to open Tibby's last letter, and there was something Lena was doing, hour after hour, day after day, and it didn't feel right. She'd done it in her studio apartment and she'd done it alone and with far too much ease. It was the grueling habit she meant to overturn, and yet she had no choice but to do more of it: it was waiting.

But what else could she do? She felt unusually fitful, jumpy, and impulsive, yet she was stuck in a holding pattern and didn't know what to do other than fret and fret and fret and wait.

Many times she thought of reading back over the twenty precious letters Kostos had written, but something stopped her. *I don't want to turn those into memories, like everything else with him.* She didn't want them enshrined as further exhibits in the Lena and Kostos memorial museum. Maybe they would end up there, but she wanted them to stay real for at least a while longer.

She stared at Tibby's sealed envelope and had the strangest idea. What if she opened it right now? What if she didn't wait?

Could I just do that?

She felt a weird gonging in her head. She ripped the envelope open so fast she almost shredded the letter inside.

My dearest Lena,

I know I've made a blunt and probably unwelcome maneuver to wrest control of your life from you. And I know that you'll know that, misguided as it may be, it's out of love.

You don't have time, Len. That is the most bitter and the most beautiful piece of advice I can offer. If you don't have what you want now, you don't have what you want.

I know you've always hated an either-or decision. You always want to choose Option C, as you call it, the third way, which too often, my sweet Lenny, means no way at all. And here I am demanding A or B.

I'll be honest and tell you I want you to choose A. I feel like I understand Kostos. I don't think he's forgotten you. I think he's waiting too. He's holding back, because he knows if he comes to you he'll scare you off. And if he comes to you, there will always be doubt. You have to come half the way. I didn't think anybody could comprehend you and love you as well as we Septembers do, Lenny, but Kostos impresses me.

If you choose B, I promise to leave you alone, not to haunt you with further letters or demands. I promise I'll leave Kostos alone too. (And really, what choice do I have?) There will be no doubt or disappointment from me wherever I am. You can free yourself of that notion. Because you will have chosen your path and not put it off any longer, and that's all I really want.

Maybe you think you'll be entitled to more happiness later by forgoing all of it now, but it doesn't work that way. Happiness takes as much practice as unhappiness does. It's by living that you live more. By wait-

ing you wait more. Every waiting day makes your life a little less. Every lonely day makes you a little smaller. Every day you put off your life makes you less capable of living it. Sorry to pontificate, my friend, but my body is giving out and that's where my head is today.

(I admit to a secret wish that you'll open this letter before the date on the back.)

Live for me, my friend Lenny, because I can't anymore, and God, how I wish I could.

Two things happened over the next hour that made Carmen want to wrench open her window and jump off the train to her doom.

First was the crying. Just when Carmen had reclined her chair as far as it would go, gotten herself a pillow and a blanket from Coach Attendant Kevin, as his name tag said, and closed her eyes to rest, it started. First it was little barks a few seconds apart. They got closer and closer together until they turned into full-on crying.

You've got to be kidding, she thought. She cast a narrow-eyed look at the man, presumably the baby's father. Now that she thought of it, where was the mother of this group? Had she come on with them? Maybe she was in the bathroom and when she got back she could make the baby be quiet.

The second thing was the phone. Once Carmen was awake on account of the crying and there seemed no hope of going to sleep, on account of the crying, she grabbed her phone. But when she tried to wake it up it stayed black. *It's all right, don't panic,* she counseled herself. It was a slightly temperamental phone, was all. She held down the home button for a while. Still black. Okay, it was the charge. She unwound the charger and thankfully found an outlet. She plugged it in and waited. Sometimes this could take a minute or two. She knew the stubborn biorhythms of these phones better than the ones of her own body.

At last it lived. The little waiting circle spun and then the screen lit up. And when she saw the icon on the screen, the fear began, like the beat of a slow drum against the horror-movie sound track of the screaming baby.

There glowed the dreaded icon that instructed you to plug your phone into your iTunes mother ship or you were screwed. Well, she had no iTunes to plug into. The mother ship was sitting in the living room of her loft, giant-screened and cutting-edge and of no help to anyone. This daughter-phone was not so independent as she liked to pretend.

Carmen turned it off and turned it on again with no feeling of hope whatsoever. Same icon.

"Shit," Carmen muttered. She would have felt guilty about cursing near children, but they were the ones who should have felt guilty. "Shit," she said again. Her mind raced for possible solutions. Whom could she whine to? Whom could she bribe? Whom could she charm?

No one. She was down to zeroes and ones, and they really didn't care about her. She loved her phone, but her phone did not love her back.

She thought of Tibby with a feeling of pique. Some gift this was. And then she felt horrified. How could she be irritated at Tibby, who was dead?

She realized she was sweating. Her heart was pounding. She couldn't call anyone! She couldn't text anyone! She couldn't read the script! She needed desperately to call Jones and tell him she couldn't call him.

She looked up at the ceiling. She looked out at the darkness, at the billows of dark steamy pollution, at the grim lights of industrial New Jersey or Delaware or wherever she was. She couldn't spend thirty-two more hours on this train with no one to talk to and nothing to do. She couldn't.

You can't kill yourself over a phone, a sane voice in her head pointed out. *Oh, yes, you can,* a less sane voice answered.

She laid her head back on her pillow and tried to breathe deeply. She tried to steady her heart. Every little trick she had for self-comfort hit a wall. Call her mother? No. Check the weather? No. Update her Facebook status? No. Google her rivals? No. Find her horoscope? No.

Like a drug addict, she felt the itches and the tremors that made her want to claw her own skin. Like a drug addict, she found herself grasping at any fix no matter how self-destructive: she could get off in Baltimore and buy a new phone—who cared if she missed her meeting! She could offer a thousand dollars to anyone on the train who would sell her theirs! Better, she could steal one! Who cared that it wouldn't have her mail or her contacts? Who cared that the only numbers she knew by heart were Lena's, Bee's, and Tibby's?

Like a drug addict, Carmen felt waves of nausea and despair throughout the night. She might have seen hallucinations of spiders, she wasn't sure.

At some point in her misery, she realized that the baby had gone quiet and the mother still hadn't come back.

Not knowing

when the dawn will come

I open every door.

—Emily Dickinson

Throughout the early morning Carmen got several cups of coffee from the dinette. She flipped through the awful train magazine.

She spent a little time talking to Coach Attendant Kevin, who was from a town called Goose Creek, just west of Charleston, but had not heard of the street where her father lived.

Carmen went back to the dinette and got some walnuts in a bag. She begged the lady behind the counter, Inez, for reading material, but Inez had nothing. She had a pack of cards. Finally, Inez rooted through her own bag and handed Carmen the very issue of *People* magazine that Carmen had spent a full ninety minutes reading on the way to the airport.

Carmen trudged back to her seat. She had never in her adult life gone this long without checking her email, Facebook, or Twitter or making a call.

What had people done before they had phones? It was a serious question. She needed to know. What had she herself done, before she had a phone? She remembered the long car rides to Bethany Beach or the really long car rides to Fort Myers, Florida, to see her great-aunt and great-uncle. What had she done? She hadn't read— not even magazines. It made her carsick.

Carmen knew what she'd done. It seemed hard to fathom right now, but she did know. The younger, phone-free Carmen had looked out the window and thought about things.

Carmen wondered about that. She was too tired to be huffy and indignant any longer, so she wondered about it honestly. Did she even have thoughts anymore?

She looked out the window. She tried to think of where in the world she was. She thought she'd heard the conductor announce a stop in North Carolina not too long ago. She observed how the trees were getting fuzzier and greener as they went. In New York, the trees were still mostly gaunt and bare, but here, they were budding and blossoming like mad. As the train rumbled south they plunged into spring, passing through whole weeks in a matter of hours.

It made her feel a little homesick, because of the blossoms, the cherries and dogwoods and magnolias and those pink ones, whatever they were called. These were the flowers that burst out all over her old neighborhood growing up, that would drop into her hair like spring snow. They probably had them in New York too, maybe in the park, but she never saw any.

If the train was in North Carolina now, then South Carolina would be next. That gave her a pang of nostalgia too. If she'd been in a plane and flown over these places, she wouldn't have thought a single thing of it, but now she was going to be passing through the state where her dad had lived since she was six. It was the place she'd visited, fantasized about, been disappointed in, and grown up some in. It was the place where she'd met her stepbrother, Paul. And his sister, Krista, too, but Paul loomed larger here. He gave the whole state the stalwart suffering feeling that he had, even though she knew he didn't mean to. It was the place where Lydia and her dad had gotten married and where Lydia had been sick and died. It seemed sad to go through the state and not reach out to any of them.

When she heard the baby shout she looked up. She felt an ache in her throat, and wondered if she felt sadder about Lydia than she'd realized, or if the phone carried a contagion of sadness sent over from Tibby.

The baby wasn't crying, for once, but smiling and trying to say something. They were wordlike utterances that weren't actually words. The baby was a girl, Carmen observed. She had olive skin and very large dark eyes. Her hair made shiny delicate dark curls. *But you wait,* Carmen thought. *My hair looked like that too when I was your age.*

Carmen observed that the mother of the family had not, in fact, been in the bathroom for the last ten hours as she had thought, but was apparently not on the train at all. Carmen looked at the rumpled father and took pity on him. It was awfully bold of him to take two small children on this ride by himself. *Had you no other options?* she couldn't help wondering.

And Carmen couldn't stop herself from staring at them a little. Rumpled though he was, the father had a certain dignity you rarely saw in parents of young children. He wore dark twill pants and a faded jean jacket over a gray T-shirt. Carmen had noticed as she'd padded around the aisles that everybody's shoes had come off by this point, but his hadn't. He wore pointed brown leather shoes. They were well worn but elegant. The kind that well-dressed businessmen wore.

She could tell he wasn't Puerto Rican. She assumed he was Mexican, for some reason, but he was rather tall for a Mexican. She wished he would say something, so she would be able to guess from his accent. She hadn't been paying attention before, and now she felt immensely curious.

He had straight, longish, slightly feathery black hair. She thought of Ralph Macchio in the original *Karate Kid,* and then she felt the need to suppress a giggle. She'd had a huge crush on Ralph Macchio. The next thing she thought of was Jones and his shaved head.

The father looked over at her, seeming to sense she was looking at them. She smiled, a peace offering of sorts for all the mean looks and cursing during her phone-withdrawal phase. His face altered slightly, but she didn't think you could call it smiling.

In her mind she begged the little boy to say something to his father, and at last he did. He told his father he had to go to the bathroom. She couldn't tell anything from the boy's accent, so she waited eagerly for the father's response, but the father was remarkably economical with words, she'd noticed. He simply nodded. He was like the Latin version of Paul. But when he stood up he did something quite surprising. He turned directly to Carmen.

"Excuse me. You could—could you . . . take for me . . . the baby?" His English faltered appealingly and she realized he had absolutely no idea she was a Spanish speaker.

She was too surprised to do anything but accept the baby. He figured she was a woman, maybe a mother herself. He figured she'd know what to do. He didn't realize she was an actress.

"We come back soon," he told her, leading the wriggling, dancing boy to the bathroom at the front of the car.

So Carmen held the baby. She was anxious at first. She tried to think back to her early days with Ryan. But truth be told, she'd been eighteen at the time, and hadn't exactly gone out of her way to hold him. Tibby, his godmother, had probably held him three times for every one time Carmen had.

Carmen tried to bring the baby into her body a little, not hold her out as if she were a disease. She rested the baby's considerable diaper on her lap. The baby stared at her with her giant eyes. She didn't express a point of view, she just stared.

"Hi, sweet pea," Carmen said. She smiled, and to her gratification, the baby smiled back. She bounced her a few times. The baby smiled bigger. Carmen had to wonder: Who else in the world would make friends with you so quickly?

"Hey, poopie," Carmen said in a cooing voice.

The baby took this as a compliment and smiled more. She tried to grab Carmen's face in her hand, but Carmen pulled back.

Carmen was just explaining to the baby about hair, when the father and brother returned.

The father gave Carmen a real smile this time. He took the baby from her gratefully, but the baby appeared not to want to go. She leaned and reached for Carmen as she got pulled away. She started to make the barking sound.

Carmen felt as flattered as she had ever been in her life. More flattered than when Bobbi Brown told her she had good bones. "It's okay, I can hold her for a bit longer," Carmen offered. It wasn't like she had a lot of other things to do.

"You . . . no mind?" the father asked.

"No, not at all," Carmen said. She took the baby and bounced her a bit more. She arranged the baby's dress and diaper and smoothed her hair. "You are a very pretty girl," Carmen told her. She turned to the father. "What's her name?"

"Clara," he said.

"Oh. That's beautiful," Carmen replied.

As she talked to the baby, she wondered why she wasn't talking to them in Spanish. And moreover, why the father didn't know she was Latin. Although her hair was highlighted and her accent was as polished as that of any New York actress, she still expected people to know what she was. Wasn't it obvious?

When she was with Jones, she felt it was obvious. *Here he is with his Latin girlfriend,* she would think. *Jones is cool, he's going to marry his Puerto Rican girlfriend,* she would imagine his friends and colleagues thinking. And for his benefit, she tried to tamp it down. She didn't gab and hoot with her mother in Spanish the way she used to. She kept her hair ironed and small. She kept her grandmother and various aunts and uncles and cousins at arm's length to keep him feeling comfortable, to keep the Puerto Ricans picturesque.

She remembered her agent and her manager saying on so many occasions: *Now, we don't want to pigeonhole you. You can play anything. Let's not go the Latin route. That can be limiting.* She remembered her publicist turning down a feature in *Latina* magazine. *Let's see what else we get. It could rule out other things,* she'd explained.

And now she wondered, what had happened to her? What would Big Carmen think? Had she tamped herself down so far, she wasn't even who she was anymore?

Clara pulled her hair gleefully and Carmen spent a while trying to extract each strand from Clara's sticky fist. When Clara started to turn up the volume, the father offered a bottle to Carmen, and Carmen gratefully took it. She settled Clara into her lap and tried to figure out how to best administer a bottle. Clara seemed to know what to do, but she allowed Carmen to feel competent nonetheless. She offered Carmen a couple of smiles around the nipple of the bottle. You could see the smile in Clara's eyes most markedly, and Carmen found it pretty sweet, the baby's basic desire to connect. *Do we all start out like that?* she wondered.

Carmen reclined her chair and relaxed into the sucking sounds.

Clara's body got heavy and the bottle lolled to the side. She twitched a few times, and Carmen realized she had fallen asleep. Gently she took the bottle and put it on the empty seat beside her. She tucked the stray parts of Clara in, and covered them both with her blanket. Carmen turned her head to look out the window, at spring rushing on.

She thought of many things. Mainly she thought of Pennsylvania, and April 2, and the things she most regretted. But Clara was asleep on her chest. Clara trusted her enough to cede consciousness right on top of Carmen's heart. However terrible Carmen was, she took solace from that.

"Doxie, it's Lena," Lena said into her cellphone.

"Lena, where are you?"

"I'm at the airport."

"Where are you going? Oh, my dear." She stopped and made a funny noise. *"Are you going?"*

"I'm going."

"It's not the time yet, is it?"

"I don't want to wait anymore. I can't. I'm going to find him in London."

"You're flying to London?"

"I sold a painting to my mother's friend. It goes with her couch."

"You sound like a different girl, my dear one."

Lena's fingers were shaking when she made the next call. Even in her rush of impulse this was hard.

She went immediately to Carmen's voice mail without a single ring. She hadn't expected that from Carmen, who manned her phone more devotedly than anyone she knew.

Lena didn't know what to do. She finally had something to say, but no Carmen to say it to. The thing she needed to say was not the kind of thing you left on a voice mail message, but she couldn't help it.

"Carmen, it's Lena. I found something out. Tibby didn't kill herself." She heard a sob escape her throat. "She didn't want to die. There was something wrong with her. She knew she was going to die, but not because she wanted to. I don't know what really happened or how you explain it, but there was something she said in her letter that made me know, *know*, it is true."

Lena realized she was crying openly as she talked, right in the middle of gate D7. "She's still gone, I know, and maybe it doesn't change anything." She wiped her nose with her hand. "But it changes everything."

Somewhere between Gastonia, North Carolina, and Spartanburg, South Carolina, Carmen gave Clara back to her father, and her big brother wandered over. She could tell he'd been jealous for a couple of hours that the dumb baby had made a friend and he hadn't. She could read him like a book, and it made her wonder how far she had progressed in her life that she was perfectly in sync with the emotions of a three-year-old.

He introduced himself as Pablo on the way to the dinette. He put up his hand to hold hers as naturally as he walked. It didn't mean anything to him, but it meant something to her.

She looked down at his up-reaching arm and she could remember, almost in her muscles, the holding-hands era of her life. Reaching up to hold her mother's hand. Her teacher's. She could picture herself with Bee holding hands, Bee always yanking her around the yard, but holding on to her nonetheless. She could feel the sensation of holding Tibby's hand, which was small and squirmy. And Lena you were usually dragging. Lena was slow and distractible when it came time to get anywhere, including the ice cream truck. But they held hands anyway, sometimes three or four of them in a chain, even when it tied them down. Why was that? And when did it stop? First grade, maybe? At some point it had seemed babyish. She had probably been the last one to stop.

Pablo begged for a Snickers bar and Carmen was about to get him two, but then she stopped at the memory of how it had been with her around his age when she had a bellyful of candy. Halloweens, Christmases, and Easters were a catalog of frantic behavior followed by tears. She could picture herself crying over her pink Easter basket every single time.

She sat him on the counter and studied the menu. "Have you ever had apples and cheese?" she whispered to him in Spanish, as if it were an international secret.

He shook his head, interested.

"Separately they are good, but together, in one bite, they are so good they shouldn't be allowed."

This, he liked.

"Do you want me to show you?" She looked around, as though concerned somebody might catch them.

His eyebrows were raised. He nodded.

She bought two apples and a pack of cheese and crackers and grabbed a plastic knife. They settled at a table together, him standing on the seat across from her, bent over the table to watch her every move. She cut the apple into small, neat pieces. She saw him eyeing them hungrily.

"Okay, but you can't eat any yet, because that would just be apple," she instructed him in Spanish. She cut the orange cheddar cheese into squares. "Do what I do," she told him. She stacked a piece of cheese on a piece of apple, and he did the same. She held it up to her mouth. "Are you ready?"

He was smiling excitedly. Kids were such suckers for a little bit of ceremony. She remembered that about herself too. She'd get taken in by anything.

"Okay." She popped hers into her mouth and he did the same. He was so excited, she wasn't sure he was tasting anything. He was riveted on her reaction. She closed her eyes and nodded, savoring it. He did the same.

"Good, huh?" she asked in English

"Goooooooood."

They ate about ten more each, stacking them in different ways, into sandwiches, into towers. He wanted to bring the last bits back to his father. "Is it allowed?" he asked her in Spanish.

"Sí," she said.

His father ate them gratefully, and with a lot of instruction from Pablo. He seemed to understand it was a bite worthy of an international secret.

Carmen sat back down and watched Pablo telling his father about the whole episode, getting it all out of order. And the father listened with admirable patience. He took it in without demanding that the facts add up. Carmen's mother had been like that, when Carmen was little.

She wondered about Pablo's father. He was probably not much older than she was—maybe in his early thirties—but he seemed like an adult. It seemed liked he had crossed a chasm that she hadn't.

Jones was almost forty. Had he crossed that chasm? She thought not. Maybe it was fatherhood. Maybe it was becoming a parent, which Jones had vowed not to do.

Carmen sat back and looked out the window. Occasionally she stole glances at the little family across the aisle.

Clara napped and Pablo sat peacefully on the floor, playing for at least an hour with his father's shoelaces. Carmen felt proud that she hadn't just bought him the two Snickers bars.

There was something pretty different between the last time Lena had come to number twenty-eight Eaton Square and this time. The difference was that this time she was crazy.

This time she wasn't freaked out or crushed when the fiancée/girlfriend Harriet answered the door. Lena had Bapi's lion cuff links in the front pocket of her jeans and she was ready for anything. Kostos could have slammed the door in her face three times in a row, and she still would have rung again and said her piece. She'd come more than halfway; she would be damned if she didn't do her part. *At least I tried,* she could say.

Harriet looked different this time. She was wearing jeans and flat shoes and she looked like a normal person. Not a totally normal person—she had twice as much makeup on as Lena had worn to her senior prom—but closer.

Harriet looked at Lena with vague recognition. Lena knew she looked different this time too. She was also dressed in jeans. Her hair was pulled back, her shirt was black, she felt like an adult. Last time she had worn fear. And this time she was crazy.

"Is Kostos home?" she asked politely.

There was nothing friendly about Harriet. "Did you come here before?"

No fear. "Yes. A couple months ago."

The shape of Harriet's eyes was changing and she seemed to be growing larger in stature. "What is your name?"

Lena cleared her throat. "Lena Kaligaris."

"Why did you come here?"

"To find Kostos."

"He's not here." Harriet took a step forward, but Lena didn't step back.

"Do you know when he'll be back?"

Harriet looked like she was debating between shutting the door in Lena's face and replying to the question. There was something in Harriet's expression Lena recognized as curiosity. The sick kind of curiosity you hated yourself for having. "I have no idea when·he'll be back here. Possibly never."

"This isn't his house?"

"It's his house, but he doesn't live in it any longer. He moved out. I thought you of all people would know that."

Lena wouldn't shrink. She would stay right here. "I didn't know that."

"Aren't you the girl he wrote all the letters to, Lena Kaligaris? I'm fairly certain you are. You're the one who made the drawings he had all over his fucking desk and stuck to his mirror. That would be you, wouldn't it?"

"That would likely be me," Lena said, unintimidated, without sarcasm. Who really knew? Maybe Kostos had other pen pals. She'd had worse disappointments.

Harriet gave a mirthless laugh. "He said they were 'friendly' letters. Funny. You don't stay up until two or three every morning writing 'friendly' letters. I thought he'd run off to you a month ago."

Lena looked down and shook her head. "He didn't."

"Well, good luck finding him. Give him my regards. He's a strange man, you know. He's never really with you. My grandmother warned me about shagging a man who doesn't want to marry you at all, and I should have listened. But I landed quite a good house, didn't I?"

"You have been my friend,"
        replied Charlotte.
"That in itself
        is a tremendous thing."

—E. B. White

It wasn't her farm in rural Pennsylvania.

Except for being an old acquaintance, bystander, and unofficial babysitter, Bridget had no claim on it. But after thirty-two hours of cross-planetary travel with a sweaty toddler sticking to her body, after nearly five months—arguably two-plus years—in complete limbo, she stepped across the willow-shaded front yard and felt as if she were walking home.

She hadn't known she liked old farmhouses on twenty-seven acres of lawns and fields and forests, with converted barns, guest cottages, root cellars, and icehouses. She had never longed for any of those things. But as she swooped around the place with Bailey on her hip, she discovered that perhaps, in some way, she did.

Maybe because the whole thing was blooming before her eyes on the most perfect early spring day that had ever been. Maybe because it was the place that Tibby had found and planned to call home. Maybe because of the little soul making headway in her uterus, who was becoming an oddly joyful source of companionship to her.

"We could have animals here," Bridget told Bailey, peering into the dark stalls on the lower story of the barn. "It's like *Charlotte's Web*. We could get pigs and sheep and donkeys. And horses." She was a little suspicious of herself as far as what she meant by "we."

"And get . . ." Bailey paused to put her words in order. "A 'pider."

"I bet we've already *got* spiders here," Bridget said, pointing out the spangly webs at the corners of the stalls as though they'd won the lottery twice. She carried Bailey across the shady central yard, around which the clapboard buildings were clustered.

"We could put a vegetable garden right there. We could grow tomatoes and strawberries and pumpkins."

"Bannas?"

"Not necessarily bananas, but we could buy those."

Brian was in the mostly empty kitchen, trying to scrape together a snack for Bailey. Bridget put Bailey down on the counter.

"Did you buy this?" she asked Brian.

"This house? This farm, you mean?"

"Yes."

"Yes."

"This whole thing?"

"Tibby fell in love with it in the pictures."

"Wow." It wasn't that it was so fancy. Bridget knew it hadn't cost millions of dollars or anything, but still.

"And since I got the programming finished, we won't have to sell it." His face looked a little bit lighter than it had.

"Good news," she said. She had the sense that Brian was trying to thank her, and she felt thanked.

She'd always known he was exceedingly smart with computers. She'd heard a couple of rumors that his company was getting off the ground, but she hadn't paid attention to them. "What kind of program is it?" She didn't know why she hadn't thought to ask before.

"A game. A simulation game." Brian dug in his pocket and handed her some keys. "I haven't been inside the icehouse yet. I've only seen pictures. You want to tell me what you think?"

She left Bailey and ventured across the grass. The icehouse was the last of the structures, sitting at the edge of the woods about twenty yards from the main house. As she got close, she discovered there was a little stream running along the far side of it.

It was a miniature house, white clapboard like the farmhouse, and sort of vertical. She got ready with the keys, but she found the door unlocked, so she pushed it open.

She stood in the doorway, astonished and slightly puzzled. She felt like she'd seen it before, or maybe dreamed it. The ground floor was two simple square rooms, one big and one small. The big one had an open kitchen on one side of it, and the small room glowed with the light of a clerestory. The upstairs was a loft reached by a ladder. Standing below, she could see it was high and white and open, with sloping walls and a skylight. You could see through it to green branches and pieces of sky overhead.

She climbed up the ladder and then back down. She wandered into the smaller room on the first floor and discovered another door. She opened it and gazed through. There was a tiny rustic screen porch sticking into the woods and cantilevered over the stream. She stepped onto it in a state of near-disbelief. She'd never imagined that any enclosed space could be so appealing. There was an old iron daybed against one wall. If you went to the edge and looked down, the water was rushing right under your feet. She couldn't quite get over it, the smell of the woods, the sound of the stream, the quality of the light. It was almost painfully perfect.

Feeling slightly dazed, she walked back to the kitchen of the farmhouse and handed Brian the keys. He didn't take them.

"How is it?" he asked.

"It is perfect," she said, a little breathlessly.

"That's what Tibby thought you would say."

When the train stopped in Toccoa, just past the Georgia state line, they lost Coach Attendant Kevin and got Coach Attendant Lee. Coach Attendant Lee had a paramilitary flavor about him, Carmen decided; he immediately started asking everybody for their IDs.

Carmen produced her driver's license, which was in fact still valid. Lee stared at it and her ticket for a long time. He turned his eyes on her as though she had something to hide. *I'll let you go this time,* his eyes seemed to be saying as he moved across the aisle.

Carmen listened only vaguely at first as the father of the family across the aisle tried to follow the words of the fast-talking Lee. He went into his wallet and found his driver's license. He went into his suitcase to retrieve his passport. Carmen could see that it wasn't a U.S. passport, but she wasn't sure what it was.

Lee started to get crabby as the father had to search for the tickets, at last finding them in Pablo's coloring book. Coach Attendant Lee was not charmed by the decorations Pablo had added to the tickets. His voice kept getting louder.

"What you don't seem to understand Mr. . . ." Lee brought the license up to his face. "Mr. *Moyo,* is that I need to see the papers for these children."

Carmen sat up. Lee was talking so loudly now, the entire car could hear.

The father, understandably, was looking flustered. He presented the tickets again. "See . . . for the . . . boy," he said. He didn't have a proper ticket for Clara, but had some sort of baby voucher. "The baby . . . small."

"I *see* the tickets. I don't *need* to see the tickets again!"

The father looked at him in bewilderment.

"Do you understand a word I am saying to you? Mr. Moyo? I need to see the papers for the children. Are these your children?"

Lee was talking so fast and so loudly, Carmen could see and understand that the father's shaky hold on English was failing him. She felt her heart and her head beginning to throb. She was thankful that both children were sleeping.

"Excuse me?" the father said tentatively.

"Are these your *children*?"

The father's face was frozen for a moment. "Yes. My children," he said finally.

"Thank you," Lee said with a sneer. "Now, what you need to do is prove to me that these are your children and that you are traveling with them legally. And if you can't do that, I am going to need you to get off this train."

The father shook his head. "I am sorry?"

"I am going to need you to *get off this train.*"

Carmen couldn't take it anymore. She got to her feet. "Excuse me," she said. "Mr. uh . . . Lee." She wanted to call him motherfucker, but she resisted. "It seems to me that you don't speak Spanish very well, and Mr. Moyo's English is not quite up to your hounding, so maybe I can help," she went on in a quiet, smooth, and friendly voice. "Why don't you tell me exactly what you need from Mr. Moyo."

Coach Attendant Lee glared at her. He couldn't seem to decide to what extent she was insulting him. "I am doing my *job*, miss," he spat. "And I need to see ID for the kids."

The father was turning from one to the other of them.

Carmen gave the father a look that did not include Lee, and tried to offer a comforting smile. "This man is an asshole," she said to him in quick Spanish, "but he will not leave you alone until you show him some kind of identification for the children. Do you have something? Passports? Birth certificates?" she asked sympathetically.

The father looked at her in surprise. "Oh, is that what he wants?" he replied in Spanish. "Of course. I'm sorry. I should have understood. I have the birth certificates in my suitcase."

Carmen helped him hold things from the suitcase so he could get to them quickly. He produced two birth certificates for Coach Attendant Lee, who looked at them grudgingly. "If you're gonna be in this country, you ought to speak English," he muttered as he passed into the next car.

Carmen stood there shaking her head. The father let out his breath. He put out his hand to Carmen. "Roberto," he said.

"Carmen," she replied as she shook it.

She went back and sat in her seat and looked out the window. When she glanced across the aisle, she saw that Roberto was looking at her. "Thank you, Carmen," he said to her, serious in his tone.

"You're very welcome," she said, serious in return.

When she closed her eyes she kept seeing the way he looked at her. There was something in it that stirred her, not uncomfortably, but in a way she needed to grasp. What was it? Something that reached down to a deep, almost forgotten part of her, and she needed to figure out what it was.

She watched the trees dashing by mile after mile, and suddenly a wide lake opening up in front of her eyes and then closing again. And at last she figured it out. Or at least she figured out some aspect of it: Roberto looked at her like she was an adult. For a moment he'd brought her across the chasm to stand with him on the other side. He looked at her with respect.

That was what it was. And the effect of it on her was incalculable.

Lena's adrenaline wasn't quite as helpful in mapping out step two of her plan. Here she'd overcome a lifetime of reticence and arrived in London with lion cuff links, armed with a bolt of thunder, and now she had nowhere to fling it.

Might Kostos be at work? Could she possibly find him there? She pictured herself arriving at his fortress of finance and the moment of their reunion taking place in the hallway in front of five secretaries. My, that would be awkward.

It was six in the evening on a Monday night. It was possible. She knew the name of his firm because he'd once sent her a letter in an envelope from his office. So she got the number through an automated operator and called it.

"May I speak with Kostos Dounas, please?" she asked after she'd been transferred from the main reception desk.

It must have been his secretary. "I'm sorry. He's not here."

Lena felt her thunderbolt weaken a little. "Will he be in tomorrow?"

The silence felt uncomfortable. "No, I don't believe so. I believe he's traveling outside of the country."

"Do you know when he'll be back?"

"No, I'm afraid I don't."

"Well, can I ask if—"

"I'm afraid I can't give out any further information."

Could he be in Greece? That was her next possibility. She still had the phone number of his house there, so she called it.

After a vast number of rings, one less hopeful than the last, the phone was answered by a woman's gruff voice. She knew the voice.

"Is this . . . Aleta?" Lena asked in Greek.

"Yes, who is this?"

"It's Lena Kaligaris. A friend of Kostos's. Is he there?"

"No, he's not here. I talked to him two days ago. He said he was traveling somewhere. He didn't know when he was coming back."

"Oh. He didn't say where he was going?"

"No, he didn't say."

And you cannot go on
                    indefinitely being
                just an ordinary,
            decent egg.
We must be hatched or go bad.

            —C. S. Lewis

Carmen gave Clara her afternoon bottle and, at Pablo's extreme urging, let her try some bits of apple and cheese. Clara wanted to grab them more than eat them, and spit half of them out, but Pablo was undeterred.

"Good, huh?" he said to his sister in English. It was funny how he seemed to have faith in Clara's ability to appreciate what he appreciated. It occurred to Carmen that Pablo had been where Clara was rather recently, so he took her more seriously and didn't doubt, as the rest of them probably did, that she was an actual person.

She tried to teach Pablo go fish while Roberto carried Clara up and down the aisles of the train cars. Then they played war, which was somewhat more successful. Pablo got it wrong half the time, but he was viciously competitive. She had to keep herself from laughing at the snarly face he made every time he thought he'd won her card.

Roberto brought them back wraps and sandwiches and sodas for dinner, and Carmen gobbled hers down. She realized that it was the first time in years she hadn't calculated the calories of something before she stuck it in her mouth. She hadn't drunk a soda that wasn't diet since she was about ten.

The idea that she had an audition seemed hundreds of miles away, and in fact it was. She didn't want the train to go any faster than it was going.

She discovered that Roberto was originally from Chile, but had crept progressively northward throughout his life. He'd lived in Colombia and Costa Rica, briefly, gone to university in Mexico and stayed there until he'd met his wife four years ago, and moved to Texas to be with her.

Carmen chewed her Caesar salad wrap and wondered about his wife. What must she be like? It seemed to Carmen like an extremely exalted position, to be Roberto's wife and the mother of these children. Carmen pictured a Supreme Court justice with the body of Salma Hayek.

She hadn't seen Roberto with a phone. He must have one. Had his wife called him? Had he called her? Maybe when he was walking around the train. Or maybe they weren't the kind of couple who talked all the time. Not like her and Jones.

Carmen wondered how many times Jones had tried to call and text her in the last two days. What must he be thinking? She should find a way to call him, she thought. And yet, when she pictured Jones, he seemed a thousand miles away. As in fact he was. Planes just seemed to skip you around without really taking you anywhere different. The distances felt real when you were on a train.

She watched the sun go down with Clara on her lap. She kissed Clara's head a few dozen times, and hoped Clara's mother wouldn't mind. She chanted and sang every rhyme and song she could remember her mother singing to her. Most were in Spanish, and when Carmen forgot stretches of words she'd fill in nonsense words. She got busted by Mr. Law-and-Order Pablo a couple of times, who couldn't tell her the right words though he knew she'd gone far off the script.

Eventually the train turned dark and peaceful. Carmen wasn't sure how she would live without the sound of the clonking and rushing under her feet. It was as though she'd developed an external circulatory system with a protective heartbeat of its own.

Roberto put the baby to sleep in her car seat on the floor in front of their row. He lay Pablo out over the two seats and tucked him in with a blanket.

Carmen watched him in admiration. Roberto was really adept at this stuff. Most fathers she observed did these things a little awkwardly and almost for show, as though waiting for the mom to take over before they messed it up too badly. Her stepfather, David, was a bit like that. But Roberto looked as though he'd done every one of these maneuvers hundreds of times. Maybe he was just naturally graceful that way.

He stood in the aisle for a moment, once they were settled, then turned to Carmen. "Could I sit with you for a while?" he asked.

"Of course," she said. She shoved her purse out of the way. She thought of her horror in the first hour of the trip that someone might sit next to her. Now she couldn't imagine wanting anything more.

"Wait," he said, before he sat down. "I'll be right back."

When he returned he was carrying two bottles of Heineken and a brownie. He settled in and she put down her tray to hold the bottles. He split the brownie and she sipped her beer and enjoyed the coziness of it all.

"So tell me about you," he started in Spanish. "Where are you from and why do you speak Spanish like a native?"

She felt happy to talk. She told him about her mom moving from Puerto Rico when she was a teenager and her mom's family. She told him about growing up outside D.C., in Bethesda.

She told him about the Septembers, but she told him with partial amnesia. She couldn't make any sort of picture without them, so she stuck to the happy parts for now. Not entirely happy parts. She told him about her parents' divorce, her dad moving away. Usually when she told that story, she told it like it had happened to somebody else, but this time she knew it had happened to her. Maybe because it had moved down a notch in the hierarchy of her tragedies. She'd take that one if it meant she could hold off the bigger ones.

She told him about her later childhood, her awkward phases, the first summer of the Traveling Pants, and finally the last. She surprised herself by how open she was. The rock through the window, her dad's wedding, the first summer of David, her mom's wedding. High school graduation, the birth of Ryan, the first year at Williams, the first fateful trip to Greece. She decided to stop there.

Roberto listened intently. If he thought any of it was less than consequential he made no sign of it. He had a natural sympathy about him. His face seemed to react to each turn in the plot.

When she stopped talking she saw that her bottle was empty and so was his. The brownie was long gone. She squeezed by him to go to the dinette and buy the next round. When she came back his face was still thoughtful.

She squeezed by him again and handed him his beer. "Now you," she said. "Will you tell me about you?"

He obliged. He told her about his early memories of the tiny town in the mountains where he'd been born. He was the youngest of four, the only boy.

Carmen cut in briefly to say that she too was a youngest child, and immediately realized that in every factual sense she was lying. But Roberto didn't hold her to it.

He explained that his parents had been hippies. They'd both been raised by educated families in Santiago, but soon after they got married decided that his father should be a farmer and his mother should be a poet, and they should live off the fruit of the land and their good minds. After a few very lean years, they finally accepted the fact that they were city folk. His father didn't know how to be a farmer and his mother didn't especially know how to be a poet. They went back to Santiago and eventually his father got a job in manufacturing in Bogotá. They didn't starve after that, but nobody was terribly happy either, he told her.

He took up his parents' discarded dreams, as children will do, he said. He wanted to be a poet. He got involved in politics, somewhat disastrously. He spent two weeks in jail and then dropped out of the whole scene. He moved to Costa Rica and learned how to surf. He got good at it, he said, which she took to mean he probably became world champion. He taught surfing to rich tourists at a fancy resort and discovered he was growing stupid. He moved to Mexico City and enrolled at the Universidad Nacional Autónoma. He studied economics and literature, got a degree, and then an advanced degree. That was where he met his wife, Teresa.

At this point his face changed. His story ended somewhat abruptly, as maybe hers had done. He looked out the window at the nearly full moon, and she looked at the side of his face, wondering. She felt she would have known if he wanted her to ask him a question, and he didn't.

She drew her feet up under her. She heard the conductor announce a station stop in Tuscaloosa, Alabama. She thought of Bee and her grandmother Greta, who lived not so far from here. She wondered where Bee was, and she missed her as she hadn't let herself do since the day in Greece when their world had ended.

After a long silence, Roberto started up his story again in a slightly different-sounding voice. She found herself wanting to touch him. Not in any sexual or inappropriate way. She wanted to make contact with him, offer him her support for she didn't know what. For the tense of a verb.

Teresa was Mexican American from Texas. She was a literature student and a ceramicist.

Was, Carmen heard, *was.*

They got married in El Paso. He looked for a job. They lived with her parents. They had Pablo. Roberto told these parts with strangely little affect. He had wanted to move back to Mexico, where he could teach at the university, but she had thought he should become a citizen first, which he did. He had managed a carpet store. They'd had Clara.

He stopped again. She put her hand on his. There was something coming and she was scared of it. "You don't need to tell me any more," she said. She felt the ache in her throat, the tears rising, and she didn't even know for what. They had moved past the happy parts. She knew where it was going.

What kind of night was this, where they needed to say everything? They'd be in New Orleans in the morning, and it felt like the last night on earth. The miles were grinding away. It felt like they needed to say it all to each other before they said goodbye. Their paths crossed for this one stretch of hours and then fate would send them hurtling apart again. It was only this chance to say it all, to win a stranger's empathy, to earn a stranger's absolution.

"When Clara was six weeks old, we went to Mexico City so she could meet her grandparents. Teresa went out to dinner with friends." He stopped. She could hear his breathing, no longer smooth. "She came home late. She was struck by a car on the Paseo de la Reforma."

Carmen was squeezing his hand with both of hers, probably too hard. If he was brave enough to say it, then God, she would be brave enough to listen. She found it hard to look at his face. She knew the ending.

Why would a man travel thousands of miles on a train with two small children if he had a wife? He wouldn't. His wife didn't call him on his cellphone because she wasn't there. Roberto made the gestures of parenthood like he'd done them thousands of times because he *had* done them thousands of times. There was no faking, no show, no stalling for the mom to swoop in, no mom.

He put his chin to his chest. She held his hand. He got up and walked out of the train car. She watched his back, the shape of his shoulders, the particular rhythm of his walk.

How truly strange it was that after twenty-four hours she knew him better than she knew three and a half years' worth of Jones. She not only knew more about Roberto; she knew him. He'd shown her his seams, as Jones had never done. Maybe Jones didn't have any.

When Roberto returned a few minutes later, it was with two more beers and a face he'd put back close to normal. He sat down next to her. He handed her a bottle and then lifted his to clink against hers. *To what?* she thought. *To saying everything.*

It was the stab of a lion cuff link in her thigh as she folded her knees onto the uncomfortable chair in the British Airways terminal that made Lena think of it. Who knew why? She didn't let herself wait. She found the much-neglected name on her contact list and called it.

For once there was an answer. "Hello?"

"Ef?"

"Lena?"

"Yes, it's me."

"Hey," Effie said. She sounded subdued and uncharacteristically guarded, but what did Lena expect?

"I'm sorry, Effie. I really am. I treated you badly. I'm sorry it's taken me so long to say that."

Effie didn't say anything at first. Lena could hear her breathing. "Not everything was your fault." Effie's voice was shaky when she finally spoke. "You weren't wrong about everything. I made mistakes too."

"My mistakes were much worse, Ef. You came to help me. You brought all that stuff. You were really trying and I wasn't. I wasn't even giving you a chance."

"No, you weren't."

"I wasn't."

Effie paused and Lena heard her sister blowing her nose. "That's why I kept the extra two hundred bucks Mom and Dad gave me and bought a sweet pair of cowboy boots with it."

"You didn't." Lena laughed and Effie blew her nose again.

"I'll share them with you."

"You know they won't fit."

"I bought them big. I thought of that."

"Aw, really? That's nice, Ef."

"Hey, Len."

"Uh-huh."

"I'm sorry about the Traveling Pants. I really am."

"I know. It's okay." For the first time Lena meant it when she said it. She knew that what had happened to Tibby wasn't the pants' fault. In fact, she realized she was grateful that their pants were out in the blue, keeping Tibby company.

They said a tearful goodbye, and Lena looked out over the hated terminal with an unexpected feeling of well-being. One thing you could say about Effie, you never felt alone when she was at the other end of your phone. She'd claimed she didn't matter enough to help Lena, but she certainly had.

After the third beer, it was Carmen's turn again. She had more to tell, and Roberto seemed to know it. He waited for her.

She started with the first couple of years after college, moving to New York. She led him through her succession of painful jobs: hostess, coat-check girl, waitress, telemarketer, food stylist. She told him the longest it had taken her to get fired (seven months) and the shortest (an hour and a half). She recounted the happiest times, the almost two years she'd roomed with Tibby and Bee in the hilariously crappy walk-up on Avenue C and East Eleventh Street, when Lena had slept on their floor four nights out of seven.

She felt the need to try to represent that old time, that old self. "You see, I used to be sort of . . . bigger."

"You mean fatter?" he asked, like that wasn't so hard to believe.

"No. Well, probably. But I mean I was just . . . more *there*."

She told him about her first bit parts: saying one word in the *Sex and the City* movie that got edited out, saying seven words in an episode of *CSI* before she got whacked, getting a commercial for a prescription medicine for female hair loss that paid her rent for two years. She told him about everyone moving apart. She told him about meeting Jones and, soon after, landing her role on *Criminal Court*.

She paused and looked out the window. She wondered what time it was. She doubted this was the kind of night when you ever went to bed.

She told him about Lydia getting sick and then seeming to get better and getting sick again. And then she came to the part where Tibby disappeared. The part where Tibby moved again, just like always, but this time somewhere much farther away. It wasn't Australia that was the problem, it was that she fell out of touch in a different way and it just went on and on. There was some confusion among them. Who had talked to Tibby last? Somebody must be talking to her. There were three emails in a year and they didn't even sound like Tibby.

"We told ourselves it was okay. I don't know why, but we thought she would get home and be our regular Tibby again. I don't think we could process the truth of it, that she had really pulled away from us. We just waited for her to come back." Carmen put a hand to her cheek.

And then came the tickets to Greece. The elation. Getting to the airport on the island. The three of them together, jumping out of their skins to see Tibby again. So much excitement, so much joy. A new life was starting. She could just feel it. And then. And then.

Carmen put her arms around her knees. She rested her cheek on top of her knee.

And then the call. And then the police. And then the denial, and the confusion, and finally the calls to Tibby's parents. Nobody knew how to reach Brian anymore. And then the silence. And the discovery of the things she'd left for them. The terrible knowledge, the incomplete but also inescapable knowledge that it wasn't all an accident. And then. And then. And then. It was a new life indeed.

She finally lifted her head to look at him. She saw that her sadness had gotten all over his face. She saw it more clearly than if she'd looked in a mirror. He put his large hands on either side of her head and pulled her into his chest. He held her tightly and it all came loose.

She passed through Hattiesburg, Mississippi, and over the Louisiana state line with her face in his chest and his arms around her. It was a mysterious thing. She clung to him as though she hadn't first seen him two nights before, but had known him and needed him and depended on him the whole time, from the very beginning.

It was the great peculiarity of her life. The people she loved, really loved, had been with her from the start. She hadn't added a person, not one single person, to that group since the day she was born. There was in fact the legendary picture taken a few hours after her birth, she a tiny hunched-over grub held by her mother and father and surrounded by newborn Bridget with Marly, newborn Tibby with Alice, newborn Lena with Ari. Compared to Carmen, a strapping Lena at three weeks old had looked as if she were ready to go to law school. "We had all just been hanging around, waiting for you to be born!" her mother told her the first time she remembered looking at that picture.

And you could have turned off the camera and called it a day right then and there. Carmen's whole life. No need for further documentation.

There was a certain skill some people used when they needed to hunt and gather people to love and to love them. Well, that was not a skill Carmen had developed. Not to say she hadn't worshipped Paul or felt real tenderness for David and Lydia. She'd had a true spark of something with a guy named Win once. But her heart was the most exclusive club in history: you had to know Carmen Lowell on the first day of her life in order to join.

It wasn't that her heart was small. She knew that. It was big. If anything, it loved too violently, too much. But she couldn't expand its membership. If she asked herself honestly, she'd have had to admit she didn't really believe she could. How else could you explain Jones? Thinking she should marry Jones? What in the world kind of idea was that?

Beyond that, by agreeing to marry him she had been ready to blithely forgo a future of having children. She'd blown it off as though it were nothing. And why? Because maybe she didn't believe she could love them either. Her heart was complete, thank you very much; signed, sealed, and closed to all new business. Why would it be any different with a baby?

And then Carmen thought of Tibby. She thought of that sick physical ache caused by the loss of her, of her heart being torn open—just lying there wrecked and open, so that no amount of talking on her phone, texting Jones, planning her wedding, or buying expensive dresses was going to close it. And maybe closing it wasn't the idea.

Through one eye she saw the first shades of the sun peering up. Here was this strange man all around her, sifting into her very pores, and she wondered if maybe tragedy was what it took to make your heart capable of admitting a new member.

Behold
I do not give lectures
            or a little charity,
When I give
            I give myself.

—Walt Whitman

Because the moving truck wasn't coming until the following day, and the only new furniture that had been delivered so far was a few mattresses, Bridget, Bailey, and Brian went to a pizza place in town for dinner.

Bailey ate three bites of pizza and a slice of pepperoni and fell asleep on Bridget's lap. This left her and Brian with a lot of pizza and a lot of silence between them.

Bridget felt stirred up. Maybe about the farm, about the ice-house, where Brian had told her she should put her stuff. About Tibby's mysterious plans. About the things over time that had made less and less sense. It was cruel, perhaps, to ambush Brian over pizza and his sleeping daughter's head, but she couldn't keep the questions back anymore.

She was a little surprised by the one that came out first. "Why didn't Tibby tell us she was pregnant? Why didn't she tell us when Bailey was born?"

Brian gave her a look that was hard to decipher. Almost as if she were playing him, demanding he tell her things she should already know. "Because that was when she found out she was sick."

"Sick." The word seemed to spin like a coin on the table before it settled. She felt like she could see it sitting there heavily, motionless. She didn't know what to make of it. She felt a strong intuition to go carefully. She cleared her throat. "What do you mean, sick?"

There was his grief-stricken impatience again. "I mean sick. Sick with Huntington's. That's when we found out."

Bridget took a breath. She looked down at Bailey's peaceful face and looked up again. She felt as if she were walking into a very cold, very rough ocean. She put her hair behind her ears. "What is Huntington's?"

Brian sort of squinted at her. He must have known she wasn't asking anything rhetorically. They stared at each other in a strange kind of standoff. Neither of them touched anything or chewed or moved.

"It's a degenerative disease," he finally said, as though it were obvious and she should know. "It's what she died of."

It would have been impossible to follow all the different thoughts to all the places they went. Her breath started feeling shallow. She could only hope to take one thought to one place at a time.

"Is that why you moved to Australia?"

Brian pushed his plate away. "We went to Australia for my job in October. We thought we'd be there for three months and come back home. In November we found out she was pregnant and started doing the tests." His hand was shaking when he picked up his beer. "The diagnosis was confirmed before Christmas. The only positive news was that the baby didn't carry the gene for it. I couldn't think of having a baby then, but Tibby wouldn't think of not having it, no matter what it did to her. But she was scared to come back to the States after that. None of it seemed real over there, but you three and her folks and home were real. She agonized over how to tell you, what to say. She couldn't tell you three or her mom about the baby without telling about the illness. She couldn't do either on the phone, she said. It had to be in person. She wanted you to meet the baby in person, and yet she was scared for you to see what was happening to her. I think a part of her wanted you to remember her the old way."

Bridget clutched her trembling hands. The trembling spread down to her feet and up to her shoulders and jaw, and she clenched her teeth to keep them from chattering.

"Then it took some time to get doctors and treatment set up here in the U.S. It took a while for us to find a place to settle here."

"She knew she was going to die," Bridget said slowly.

"But she didn't think it would be so soon. Not in the middle of your trip in Greece. You must know that. I was worried about her, but she was convinced she was strong enough to make the trip. She didn't think it would be then. After Greece, after she told you all, she was flying back home to D.C. to tell her family. Bailey and I were going to meet her there. She wanted us to get married in front of all of you. We'd bought this house. We thought she would see it, at least. She was going to go into hospice after that. She was going downhill. We knew it would happen. We didn't think it could happen so fast." When he stopped talking he undid his fists. Bridget could see the nail marks dug into his hands.

Bridget took his hands.

He took his hands away. "You can't imagine the time she spent making the plans and writing you the letters. I figured you knew all this." He took a swig of beer. He let out a long breath. He seemed to will the tears back in. The standoff was starting again and she couldn't do it. She couldn't keep her face still. She couldn't keep breathing right. She barely understood anything. She didn't feel like telling him how far awry Tibby's plans had gone, that they hadn't even seen her alive.

He glared at her, like he didn't want to suffer with her anymore. She didn't know anything worth sharing. He could do it better alone. "What did you *think* happened?"

She thought of all the things she had thought, and all the thoughts that those thoughts engendered. It was hard to unwind them all, to unthink them.

Tibby hadn't gone into the Caldera to end her life. Maybe she'd gone in to relive their magical swim in Ammoudi, ten years before. Maybe she'd wanted to experience that feeling, that loveliness once more. Tibby was sick and probably weaker than she knew, but she didn't mean to die.

She looked up at Brian, finding it hard to pull his face into focus. She wasn't going to tell him what they had thought. What they assumed. What they all thought they knew and suffered but wouldn't say. She felt her chin trembling and pressed her lips together. "We didn't know."

———

The final chapter of Roberto's story unwound as the children slept and the sun eased its way up out of Lake Pontchartrain. There were still the final swells, the codas to sing, before you could call it done.

He'd gotten a job managing a garage in Queens. They were living with his uncle, his mother's brother, who was old, and Roberto was taking English classes at night. He couldn't afford a place for them. He couldn't afford child care. Teresa's sister lived with her husband in Metairie and had offered to take the children until September so he'd have five months to save enough money to get on his feet.

"That's where you're taking them?" She was slowly absorbing the horror that he felt.

"I think it's the worst part of all of this."

She tried to think it through. How far a world this was from worrying about stiffing the Shaws at a benefit pre-party. This was a world that needed a few grown-ups around.

They were quiet for a while. They waited for the train to finish the long crossing of the lake and for the children to wake up. There was no night to cover them and make a space for them anymore. They might as well hasten on to the conclusion.

"And so what happened to Jones?" Roberto asked her finally.

"Oh, I'm supposed to marry him next month."

Roberto looked surprised. "You are?"

"Yeah." She shrugged. "I'm not really going to, though."

"No?"

"No."

"Does he know that?"

"Not yet. I guess I should tell him." She picked at the rough skin around her thumbnail. In the scheme of things, calling off the wedding didn't seem so desperately important. "Honestly, I don't think he'll mind that much."

Carmen was supposed to absorb the city of New Orleans at warp speed. She was supposed to talk the talk, walk the walk, eat the food (but nothing too fattening!), see some hurricane damage, and visit at least one graveyard, according to the strict orders of her manager. And she had a script to read while she was at it.

The problem was, she couldn't say goodbye to them. She held Clara with one arm and dragged her roller bag with the other while Pablo held on to her free pinky, and Roberto carried two giant bags, one large bag, a diaper bag, and a car seat through the train station to the RTA bus depot.

How was Roberto going to do this alone? Carmen knew he'd managed to do it for the last eight months alone, but now she was there to worry about every tiny juncture—the first bus, the second, the aluminum race car that was bound to fall out of Pablo's pocket, Clara's bottle! As though they could not make it another step without her. Or perhaps it was she who couldn't without them.

They finally straggled their way to the bus depot. It was time for Carmen to leave. She couldn't leave them, but what else could she do? She couldn't exactly get on the bus and go to Metairie with them. She imagined introducing herself to Teresa's sister, giving a big wave. "I'm just the lady they met on the train."

She'd already given Roberto her cellphone number (should she ever get the thing going again), her address in New York ("though I probably won't be there much longer"), even the number of the hotel in New Orleans. He'd given her his cellphone number too. She didn't know why. There wasn't much point to any of it. It was just another way of not saying goodbye for a little longer. He had a life to get on with. So did she.

"Hold on to your car," she told Pablo. "Her diaper feels heavy," she said to Roberto. "Do you think you have enough formula to get you all the way there?" She realized she was starting to cry as she said these things.

The bus came. She held on to Roberto for too long. She was going to make them miss their bus. She put her face in his collar so the kids wouldn't see her tears. She was ashamed of herself, making it a sloppy goodbye.

Roberto kissed her forehead, he kissed her cheek. His one big hand was pressed to her back and the other one covered her ear. Now he was worried about her along with everything else. That was not what she wanted.

It was an act of will to pull herself together when she kissed Pablo and Clara the last time. An actress at her finest. *I am not falling to pieces as I sniff your head. I am not losing my shit as I do this.*

She stood calmly as she waved goodbye to them and they waved back through the window of the bus. They were too far away to see her shaking, weren't they? She tried to look composed. And then the bus turned the corner.

And she dissolved.

WTF? was the thought running through her head as she sat down in the middle of the sidewalk and cried. *What has become of me?*

She dragged herself to the cabstand. She cried all the way to the Ritz-Carlton hotel. She left her suitcase in the lobby but didn't go up to her room. She walked to the riverfront. She walked back and forth, she couldn't keep track of how many times.

Oh, there was local flavor aplenty. There was a riverboat, and there were people shouting and milling about and selling things. She was supposed to be taking in the sights, she knew, but she could only think about the toy car inching out of the pocket of a little boy she would probably never see again.

Bridget slept on the bare mattress on the icehouse floor for a long night and most of a day. Sometimes she felt that her sleeping mind did better work than her waking mind.

She had millions of dreams, it seemed to her, all starting and stopping and twisting together. There was her grandfather, and Billy from her old soccer team in Burgess, Alabama. There was her old friend Diana who lived in a fancy suburb of New York City now with her husband and two kids. She dreamed of Carmen's kitchen in the old apartment in Bethesda and the shoes she wore to senior prom. She dreamed of getting stung by a bee. She dreamed of the lake at the old soccer camp where she and Eric took out a canoe. That had been in Pennsylvania too. She dreamed of swimming in the turquoise Baja Sea with Eric when she was still fifteen and all she wanted in the world was to make him love her.

She dreamed of the time in Rehobeth Beach before they left for college, when she and Carmen, Tibby, and Lena had found one another at the edge of the ocean in the middle of the night and clustered and talked until morning. In her dream there was a fire in the middle of their circle, both illuminating and changing their faces.

When she finally opened her eyes, Bailey was staring at her, her face about two inches away. "Hi, baby," Bridget said groggily.

"Hi, Bee."

She sat up and Bailey climbed onto her mattress with her. Tibby's little girl. There was no way she could leave this child.

She looked at the yellow light coming down through the skylight. She had no idea what time it was. "What's up? Did your crib come?"

"Your crib come!" Bailey said.

"Can I see?"

Bailey climbed off the mattress and Bridget followed her to the main house. She kept looking back over her shoulder to make sure Bridget was right there.

For the first time, Bridget wished she had not thrown her phone into the ocean. Carmen was Carmen, Lena was Lena, she was herself, and the past had slipped back into place behind them. They hadn't failed Tibby. They were infinitely diminished without her, but they were who they thought they were. She missed them. She needed to tell them what she knew. She needed to tell them that Bailey was in the world, brightening it by the hour. God, she missed them, how they once were.

It was not only the crib that had arrived. After the moving truck had fully disgorged its contents, a truck from Pottery Barn arrived carrying three sofas of different sizes, a half-dozen upholstered chairs, dining tables and chairs, bureaus, bed frames, night tables. A different truck brought a bunch of carpets and lamps. She and Bailey sat on the grass cheering like spectators at a soccer game, watching it happen.

She watched Brian directing it all, impressed. She was great at moving and leaving, but not that great at buying things, let alone putting them where they belonged.

Some furniture began to pile up on the grass outside of the icehouse. "Do you mind?" he asked. "I'd thought I'd cover the basics."

"It's your house," Bridget said.

"No, it's yours."

"Brian, it's not."

"Tibby thought it was."

She looked at him for resentment, but there wasn't any. While she'd slept he'd forgiven her for her ignorance. "So can they move the stuff in?"

"Of course," she said.

She and Bailey watched the men with the wide belts carry in a kitchen table, a desk, a small sofa, various chairs, a bureau, two table lamps and a floor lamp, even a headboard and frame for the bed. Once everything was in, she and Bailey climbed around on it all and played house. It seemed like great fun to both of them.

Bridget thought back to the four-poster bed Eric had bought on the last day that had caused her such trauma. She couldn't understand it. That person felt like a stranger to her now. She watched Bailey jumping on the high, springy bed, and she couldn't begin to understand.

Carmen stayed out until dark, just wandering. She was doing a poor job of taking in the external sights, maybe, but she was doing an extensive job of taking in her internal ones. After years of not thinking more than three thoughts in a row, that seemed more important.

Finally she stopped at an Apple store and watched with ambivalence as they got her phone, Tibby's phone, working again. Particularly when the little icons flashed on, informing her she had twenty-seven phone messages, nineteen texts, and ninety-nine new emails. She felt a pang, a moment of grateful love, for the mysterious and often busted version of Tibby's phone.

She didn't check any of them. She just stuck the phone in her back pocket and kept walking. She imagined the train ride in the alternate universe where the phone had worked, where she'd called people and blabbed and answered 145 messages, all while casting nasty looks at the crying baby and the overwhelmed father across the aisle. Carmen felt like a lotus-eater who'd finally woken, looking back over long narcotic dreams.

There was a message light blinking on the phone in her hotel room when she eventually got there. Manager? Agent? Publicist?

Mother? Fiancé? She threw herself facedown on the bed and just thought for a while. She was sure getting a lot more attached to the inside of her head.

And then it was time to get up and face the music. With trepidation she hit the message button and listened.

"I just wanted you to know that the formula held out, the Matchbox car was not lost, the diaper was only pee, and we made it safely to Metairie." There was a noise Roberto made that she couldn't decipher, like a cough. "Thank you, lovely Carmen . . . for everything."

I like my body
when it is with your body.
It is so
      quite new a thing.
Muscles better
      and nerves more.

—e. e. cummings

Brian joined Bridget on the screened porch of her little house after he put Bailey to bed. He sat on one of the new kitchen chairs he'd brought out and she sat on the creaky iron daybed. They listened to the stream under the floor.

As the light was fading, the rain started. You could hear it drumming against the skylight and see it tapping the surface of the stream. It turned the trees into liquid green. It gave the air on the porch a texture and a taste. This little house was sunny, all right, but it was never more beautiful than in the rain.

"I know it might not feel like it," Brian said, "but we are rejoining the world here."

"Are we?"

"Yeah."

"It doesn't feel like it."

"It will."

"When?"

"Couple of days."

"Really. How?"

"You wait. You'll see."

"Okay."

"Enjoy the quiet while you have it." Brian sounded like he was talking to himself.

"Okay."

He gave her a hug before he started back to the main house. "Oh, one other thing." He pulled his phone out of his pocket. "You want to borrow this?"

"Your phone?" He tossed it and she caught it. "Why?"

"In case you want to call anybody."

Bridget sat on the porch with the phone for a long time, but she didn't call anybody. She dragged the new floor lamp onto the porch with her, glad the cord reached far enough, and turned it on. She sat cross-legged on the daybed and finally opened Tibby's other letter. She was still two days early, but she wasn't afraid of it in the same way anymore.

> *Dear Bee,*
>
> *I put an address at the bottom of this page, and I want you to go there. It's kind of demanding of me, I know, and you don't have to if you don't want. It sounds crazy, because I haven't even been to the place myself, but I feel like you belong there. I have this fantasy that you'll see it and you'll want to stay. You laugh, my persistently moving friend, but there's a little house on the property that is meant for you. Seriously. As soon as you see it, you'll know what I mean.*
>
> *There are a couple of important things waiting for you there, if you decide to go. One of them is my daughter. She'll be two in June. That's a big one to drop on you, I know. I may have already told you about her in Greece. The second is Brian. He's been through a lot.*
>
> *When I try to fall asleep at night, and I'm full of thoughts and fears for the people I love most, I have this recurring image of you holding my daughter's hand. My fantasy is that all three of you will help grow her up, but it's you I seem to picture in the nitty-gritty*

of it. Who knows why—maybe it's just an odd fancy of mine. I know kids aren't your thing. And yet I cling to the thought that you will teach her the way you are— your independence, your toughness, your joy. I'd love it if she got an ounce of your bravery, Bee. I really would. Maybe that's the root of my wish. I want you to give her things I couldn't, no matter how long I lived. I feel like she could give you something too, though I can't quite grasp what it would be. I don't know. Forgive the meanderings of your old pal.

One other thing I wanted to say. As I think of you— and I do more often than you could imagine—I think of your many beautiful traits, but also your fitfulness. I've watched you go through dozens of jobs, apartments, phones, plants, and obsessions. You would think that such a voracious girl as yourself would have gone through dozens of boyfriends, dozens of lovers, but it occurred to me the other day that you haven't. You've only had one. You told me once that Eric was your touchstone, and I've thought of it many times.

It's natural to overlook and even sacrifice the things that belong to us most easily, most gracefully. So here's me asking you to please not make that mistake.

Really, Carmen couldn't say exactly what happened at the audition—er, meeting. She couldn't honestly say if it was a complete failure or a weird kind of success.

She knew she walked into the meeting room in a snazzy mansion in the Garden District. She recognized Grantley Arden from his picture. There were several producers and a couple of executives, about half of whom she'd met at various industry functions, usually on the arm of Jones, who would wear socks with sandals before he'd forget any of their names. Carmen couldn't remember one of them. Arden was wearing a baseball cap and jeans while the rest wore suits. There were airy clasps and kisses all around.

She vaguely recalled sitting down. She didn't have the script, so somebody handed her one. She'd made a mad dash through it that morning but hadn't learned any of the lines.

The producers talked for a while about the concept of the film, the vision and so forth. There was a lot of hyperbole thrown around—"stunning," "groundbreaking," "astonishing"—but none of it really sank in. Nobody expected it to, she realized.

Then they asked her to read a character, the floozy named Fiona. Carmen surprised herself by not skittering right over the top of the lines with all the obvious moves, as she expected to do, but walking down into them.

Fiona was a mess, really. Carmen knew she was supposed to do it funny, but as she read the lines, one struck her as more tragic than the next. When she looked up, there were tears in her eyes. She was very emotional lately.

There was a bit of silence. "Carmen, can you come over here for a minute?" Arden asked her. He drew her into the corner and walked her close, almost like they were in a huddle.

"Honey, I can see your veins," Arden said in a low voice.

"You can?"

"Yes, I think all of them."

Carmen's hands felt a certain fluttering responsibility, but how could you cover up every vein?

"I'm sorry," she said. She was sure it was a breech to show up with all your veins sticking out to the "most important meeting of your life."

"No, don't be sorry."

"Why not?" Even as she said it, she felt that what few veins perhaps weren't showing before were probably popping out now.

"Because that's how it is. Unfortunately, this role is comedy. The rest of the big roles are cast. I brought you here for comedy, but the comedy I'm getting from you could tear us all to pieces. This particular audience is not ready for it, I regret to say."

"Okay," she said. "I have no idea what you are talking about."

"I know," he said. "That's all right."

"So I guess I go, then."

"Yeah. I'll call you when I'm back in New York."

She gave him a steady, honest look. "Why?" She was not in the mood for bullshit, it turned out.

"Because I've got to do *something* with you," he said. He gave her a kiss, not a fake air one but a real hard one on the side of her head, and sent her on her way. "Make sure Wanda has your cell."

"I don't have a cell," she lied.

He stood in the hallway and watched her go. "Don't try to cover them up," he called after her as she walked to the elevator. "What a waste that would be."

Carmen knew, walking down the street away from the snazzy mansion, that she probably shouldn't be relieved. Her reps would be crushed. Jones would blow a gasket. But she wasn't planning to marry Jones.

She now knew what the most important meeting of your life probably felt like, and it wasn't this.

The sessions with Arden and the rest of them were supposed to go on and on for days; they were supposed to want to get her on film, and she was not supposed to leave New Orleans without a contract. Oops. She'd been in there for less than fifteen minutes and now she was being sent home.

Home. That was tricky. Where was home? Where was she going?

And then she knew where she needed to go—to Pennsylvania, on April 2—and she felt not scared but hopeful.

London was the place you got stranded, Lena decided. Heathrow airport was the place where you slept by the window and brushed your teeth in the restroom and felt like a complete asshole.

She couldn't just go back after all this, could she? It was now Thursday, and April 2, the appointed day, was Sunday. Did that mean Kostos was going to Pennsylvania? He wouldn't have left so early, though. He was traveling somewhere else, entirely unrelated. Maybe that was it.

By Friday morning she felt lost and sad. It was tiring, carrying a thunderbolt around this long. Sometime between the time she cried in the magazine shop and the time she threw up her lunch in the restroom, her cellphone rang.

"Hello?"

"Is this Lena?"

"Yes." All the blood in her body seemed to drain to her feet. "Who is this?"

"It's Kostos. I'm standing outside your apartment building. I've been ringing your bell for hours. Where are you?"

She closed her eyes and put the phone down for a moment while her whole body shook, trying to stave off spasms of laughing and tears.

"I'm in London, looking for you."

He was stunned to silence. "Why? Why London? Why aren't you here? We're supposed to meet in the States!"

It was a raw sound she made. Maybe like laughing. He spoke of their meeting as if there had never been a question of his intent.

"Because I couldn't wait," she said. "I wanted to come more than halfway."

Kostos was quiet for a second. His voice was full when he spoke again. "Oh, Lena. I couldn't wait either." He laughed. "I wanted to go all the way."

She was still shaking. "I want to too." Her face was burning hot. She was laughing and shaking too much to talk.

"I want to see you so badly. I can't wait anymore."

She let out a little sobbish noise, much more like crying. She couldn't make up her mind. She couldn't say a single word.

"Lena, do you want to stay still and I'll get on the next plane and come to you? Or do you want to come to me?"

Lena sucked back tears, and though her voice was a mess she answered with confidence. "You stay. I'll come to you."

Bridget used Brian's phone to call Eric just after midnight, nine o'clock his time. She felt semi-delirious when he answered.

"It's Bee," she said sheepishly, eagerly.

"Where are you?"

She was so glad to hear his voice. "I'm in Pennsylvania. Bucks

County, south of a town in New Jersey called Belvidere," she said. "I have so much to tell you." A sob escaped her chest unexpectedly.

"Are you okay?"

"I'm okay. Do you think you could come here?"

"To Pennsylvania?"

"If you fly to New York, it's only an hour and twenty minutes by car."

"When?"

She realized she was being absurdly presumptuous. She had no business asking him for anything. He was the one who'd been left, and her misery didn't make it any nicer for him.

She tried to calm herself down and step into his shoes. "I know you have work. You can't get carried away. When do you think you can come?"

"I can get carried away," he said. "When do you want me to come?"

"Now? Tomorrow?"

"Are you sure you're okay?"

"Yes. I have something important to tell you."

Eric was quiet. She couldn't blame him. This wasn't the same as her coming back. She'd never made it easy on him, not from the very beginning. "Bridget, is this something I'm going to like?"

She closed her eyes. "I really hope so."

Eric called from the rental car to say he was an hour away, and Bridget couldn't stand waiting. For the entire hour, she stood in the middle of the road, watching for a car she would not even recognize. She hated waiting.

Her heart surged when she finally saw his face through the windshield. When he slowed way down to turn she screamed moronically and jumped on the hood of the car. He laughed and drove the last twenty-five feet with her sitting on the hood. It was a testament to his love that he always let her happiness sweep him along and make him happy.

The moment he got out of the car she mowed him down. She clobbered him on the grass and rolled him around. This was perhaps the downside of a tall girlfriend. He laughed as she kissed him all over the face. She stuck her hands under his shirt. His joy was unstinting, even after all this.

At last she let him sit up. Eventually she even let him stand and look around. "This place is beautiful. Where are we?"

"This is the farm Brian and Tibby bought before she died." She shook her head, letting some of the sadness in, keeping most of it out for now. "I have so much to tell you."

"Please tell me."

She led him toward the icehouse. She would have wanted to introduce him to Bailey first, but Bailey was napping, so she led him directly through the tiny house to her porch. This was where she thought such a talk should take place.

They sat down on the creaky daybed. "I will tell you everything, and it will take a while. But first I have to tell you one thing that won't."

"Okay." He looked a little nervous and unbelievably dear to her. She'd thought she knew how much she missed him starting after she'd hung up the phone last night, but looking at him now, she realized she'd missed him even more than that.

"Okay." She was nervous too. "Okay, the thing is . . ."

He looked terrified. She prayed he wouldn't look more terrified after she finally got the news out. She touched the ends of her hair, wishing it weren't in disastrous condition. She squeezed her eyes shut. She swallowed down a vast amount of saliva. "I am, we are, having a baby."

"What?" For a moment his face was unreadable, and then it all started to open up. *"What?"*

"I'm pregnant. Around twenty weeks, I think. More, even. It must have happened the night before I went to Greece." She was talking quickly.

He seemed to be following her lips as though he were hard of hearing and not quite getting all of it. "You are pregnant?"

"If I stand, you can sort of see it." She demonstrated and put his hand to her belly.

He seemed to regard her belly and his hand as though they were both deeply unfamiliar.

"That ring I had on my cervix must have worn out and I forgot to get a new one. That's what the nurse thought happened."

"The nurse?"

"At Planned Parenthood. In Sacramento. That's where I found out."

Eric nodded slowly. He was staring not at her stomach, but at her face.

"I'm sorry I didn't tell you before this. I really am. I should have, but I couldn't. I was scared and I didn't know what to do." She felt teary and suddenly unsure of him. "Even now it's not too late to . . . not do it," she said quickly. No, that wasn't true. It was far too late for her not to do it. "Or I guess I should say, I won't put any pressure on you to be part of it if you don't feel— I mean, I would understand if you aren't ready for something like this—"

The way he watched her face, he knew her. He knew this hadn't been easy. She realized he was being careful. So careful he barely swallowed, barely moved. He was easier with his feelings, but he was like any other person in not wanting to see them get destroyed. "How do you feel about it?" he asked soberly.

"I feel like we are its parents."

"And is this something you are sure you want?"

Tears had been building up and she let them fall. "Yes. It really is." She couldn't remember not wanting it. The person who hadn't wanted it was a stranger. "I've had a while to think about this, and I admit I didn't take to it right away. But I know, *I know* it's what I want." She wiped her eyes and gathered her hair in a bunch. "The question is, is this something you want?"

He moved toward her on the creaky daybed. He put his arms around her waist and pulled her onto his lap. He pressed her hard against his chest. He put his face in her neck.

"This is something I want," he said, and she could hear the emotion in his voice. "This is something I've always wanted."

When Lena stepped off the plane from London in JFK airport in New York City, the first face she saw was his. He'd somehow managed to talk, bribe, or wrestle his way all the way up to the gate to wait for her.

She saw Kostos walking toward her in long slow-motion strides, his gray tweed coat flapping open. His eyes were steady on her face. He wasn't smiling, but he didn't look sorry. He looked serious, like a serious man would look doing a serious thing.

Here we go. She walked toward him and he toward her, as far as he could come, into the throng of the departing passengers and past the gate attendant, who seemed to be annoyed with him and calling out to him. But he didn't say anything back or even turn his head. He kept his eyes on her and she didn't look away. She didn't feel self-conscious or nervous. She didn't need to smile or ask silently for reassurance. She was sure.

She didn't see any of the people around her as she went. She saw the determination in his face and she felt it too. She found herself thinking, *Well, this is it,* and knew she was walking into the rest of her life without another pause or question or even a glance to either side. *I choose you,* she thought. *Come what may, you are what I choose.*

She didn't stop until he was right in front of her. They just stood there staring at each other for a moment. She wasn't sure what happened after that. He put his arms around her, she put hers around him, she was up off her feet and he was squeezing her against him as hard as he could have without knocking the wind out of her.

People streamed around them and the gate attendant continued carping at them and he put her back on her feet and they kissed like they had been waiting to do that and only that for a dozen years.

At some time after the people were gone and the gate attendant had given up and moved to straightening the desk, they broke apart and looked at each other again.

He took her hand and they started walking toward the baggage claim. They didn't say anything to each other. They swung their held hands like little kids, like they believed anything could happen, like they might take off soaring into the air. All the things you wanted to happen could happen. Why not?

She looked over at him and he was smiling. How she loved the British Airways terminal.

"Hey," he said. "It's someday." He said the last word in Greek.

Country roads,

    take me home.

—John Denver

Carmen crept along the bewildering roads in a rented Ford Focus certain she was lost. She'd flown from New Orleans to New York the night before last and stayed long enough to meet Jones at their loft and tell him she didn't want to get married. "Not now, or not ever?" he'd asked.

"Not ever," she'd said as gently as she could manage. She wasn't sure if he was more disappointed by that or by the earlier revelation that she'd come home from New Orleans four days prematurely and without a contract.

He wasn't so bitter, really, except when he told her he was keeping the loft. He seemed to think she was going to fight him over it, but she said fine. She hadn't wanted to stay in it anyway. She had never loved it the way he had, and even the third of the rent she paid was honestly more than she could afford.

He sat on the bed for the first hour and watched her pack. He told her she was making a big mistake, and she nodded even though she knew she wasn't. He told her single girls over thirty in New York City never found husbands, even if they were beautiful, and she nodded, though she found it frankly insulting. He told her magnanimously that he wouldn't let this tarnish any working relationship they might have, and she nodded even though she didn't believe him.

She packed one big suitcase to last a couple of weeks and

arranged to have the rest of her stuff boxed up and sent to her mom and David's house. There was nothing keeping her in New York until August, when her show resumed, and that was assuming she got picked up again.

She spent the night in a comfortably untrendy hotel in Midtown and rented the car in the morning. It was a strange feeling, driving out of town with her suitcase in the back. She had no apartment, no fiancé, and no idea where she was going. Really no idea. She'd veered off the map, which was supposed to take her to an unknown place in rural Pennsylvania.

Tibby's note had said she wanted Carmen to meet someone. What was that about? Who could Tibby want her to meet at this point? She hoped it wasn't some kind of blind-date situation. That would be seriously uncomfortable. Granted, Tibby hadn't liked Jones any better than Lena or Bee had liked him, but still.

Damn. She pulled over and studied the map. Why was she trying to get to Belvidere, Pennsylvania? Why was being on the right road to get there any less lost than being on the wrong road to get there?

But she turned herself around and persevered anyway. The evidence gave her no reason to believe she even knew who Tibby had been during the last two years, but she still trusted her. She couldn't help it. And if nothing else, the landscape was quite beautiful, with forests and farms and valleys glowing with the yellow-green of early spring.

A little past noon she turned into a driveway. She saw the street number on the white fence post. She eased up the lane very slowly, taking in the pretty clapboard farmhouse, the shaded yard, and the handful of buildings surrounding it, including a classic red barn.

She stopped the car and peered over the wheel. She was debating whether to walk up to the farmhouse and knock on the door, when the very door swung open and a tall, thin man with a baby in his arms walked out of it. Her brain was trying to process the identity of these people, when she turned her head and a figure came running out of the barn and suddenly became Bridget. In a dreamlike way, Carmen turned her head again and watched the man with the baby become Brian. She was too surprised to get out of the car until Bridget flung open her door and pulled her out.

It was a completely strange place and yet here was the first familiar thing she'd felt in months. Bee put her arms around Carmen and held her for a long time, so artlessly it felt like nothing had changed. For all the stumbling and dreading Carmen had done over the first words, there was nothing she needed to say.

"Where are we?" she asked.

Brian was standing a few feet from her when Bridget pulled away. Carmen went to embrace him, but stopped and stared at the little girl in his arms for a long moment. She had the strangest feeling. She knew this face, but she hadn't seen it in a long time.

"This is Bailey," Brian said.

Tibby had a baby. Carmen was too awed to speak.

"There's so much to tell you," Bridget said excitedly.

It was like a dream you might have after death in which lost people came back to life, your friends loved you again no matter what you had done, and your failures were unaccountably forgiven.

Bridget grabbed Carmen's hand, as naturally and tenderly as the old Bee would have, and pulled her toward a yellow cottage just beyond the house.

"Brian says Lena should be coming today too."

Lena was a person who understood happiness through sadness, and because of it, the happiness that unfolded that day was robust.

The discovery of Bailey, a little girl plucked out of her memory, was all the more extraordinary because of her mother's loss. *You gave us a way to keep loving you, Tib. You must know this child will never be without mothers.* Bailey's face was so evocative and so beautiful, Lena had to turn her head away.

Soon after she and Kostos had arrived, Lena had taken a few moments sitting on the grass with Bridget and Carmen to confirm what she already knew from Tibby's last letter. Painful as the facts of it were, they made sense to her. Each one took its sensible place in the tragedy, and the joy of their reunion was all the lovelier in light of its sadness.

And then there was Kostos. Out of the soil of more than a dozen years of disappointment, joy bloomed in every single thing she and

Kostos did together, in every dumb thing. Sitting next to him in the car on the drive up, buying him a cup of coffee at the gas station (learning how he liked it for a thousand future times), sharing a Milky Way, getting lost on the back roads, her spilling her water bottle on her lap, him mopping at her skirt with two napkins.

There was sexiness in everything that passed between them: her putting change in his hand for the toll, him pushing her hair aside to see the map better. Every time he looked at her. Every time she looked at him.

And then there was that particular look they gave each other when they saw the queen-size bed made up and waiting in the magnificent barn loft intended for them. Every year of not having each other added something to that look.

How could they possibly wait? Kostos spun her into the bathroom and clutched her for a heated moment before they heard Bailey's feet slapping across the wooden floor.

Tibby had given them the child's dream of love, having all your needs met without having to ask, without even knowing what they were.

Lena recognized in each moment of that day, maybe in her happiness more than anyone's, the hand of an artist. Tibby had spent the last fifteen years learning to write a script, and this was her gift to them, her masterpiece.

As Lena walked across the farmyard with Kostos to join the group for a spaghetti dinner in the big house, she looked up at the stars and gave Tibby thanks. She didn't have to throw her thoughts far to know they reached her.

What was the best part? That was what Carmen asked herself as she lay on the yielding mattress that smelled like new, in a bedroom of the pristine cottage Brian insisted, crazily enough, belonged to her.

The best part was seeing Bee and Lena and knowing they were going to be okay. It was meeting Bailey for the first time, understanding without needing anyone to say it who she was. It was watching Lena and Kostos walking toward her holding hands. It was Lena's happiness. It was Bee's pregnancy and witnessing her and Eric's obvious joy in it.

The saddest part, undoubtedly, was learning the truth about Tibby. The saddest thing was learning what she'd gone through. But maybe it was finally the happiest thing too, knowing she'd loved them all along, that they hadn't failed her, knowing their time wasn't over, that they'd lived the life they thought they had.

But as Carmen lay there, letting the thoughts breed and grow in her head, she pushed her fear aside and allowed the two things, the sadness and happiness, to mix. Tibby's suffering had been outside of their friendship, outside of their control. It didn't represent a failure of their bond. But Tibby had kept it from them, and that represented a different kind of failure. She hadn't let them in at that darkest juncture in her life. They couldn't have prevented any of it, but they could have given her comfort and they hadn't. Why hadn't they? Why hadn't she let them?

Because we aren't built for leaving, Carmen realized. Tibby hadn't known how to leave them. There was no precedent. Maybe she hadn't thought they could handle it. *Maybe we couldn't.*

Carmen remembered the dream Tibby had once had that her great-grandma Felicia had gotten their Traveling Pants taxidermied as a graduation present. And she remembered Tibby describing her horror in the dream. *But they have to be able to move!* she'd screamed. Carmen wondered if they had forgotten that somewhere along the way. You had to let them move. Maybe you even had to let them go.

There were daffodils in a glass on the bedside table, and a few well-made pieces of furniture throughout the three small bedrooms of the house and the downstairs rooms. "You can add the rest yourself," Brian told her. "I just wanted you to have a few of the basics, you know, to get you started."

Carmen had looked at him in puzzlement and disbelief.

"I mean, you don't have to add anything," he'd added quickly. "It's up to you. You can do whatever you like with it. It's a place that will be here for you whenever you want it."

It was hard to fathom that this was her little place, mind-blowing to think of all that Tibby must have considered. Tibby had tried her best to make it easier on them.

Carmen felt the tears slide onto the pillow as she lay in this bed with the window open and the chirping coming from both grass and trees, with Bridget and Eric in the little house across the yard, and Lena and Kostos in the barn, and Brian and Bailey in the house next door. What a joyful context. How different from the Vietnamese restaurant, newspaper stand, and lighting store she was used to.

She remembered so well Tibby's distress the summer they left for college, troubling over the notion of home. What would hold them together? Where would it ever be again?

Carmen did feel strangely, for the first time in her adult life, like she was home.

Could I revive within me
Her symphony and song,
To such a deep delight
'twould win me
That with music loud
and long
I would build that dome
in air.

—Samuel Coleridge

Epilogue

You'll be happy to know, we did conduct the last pants ritual that Tibby had assembled for us in Greece but that we never got to have. I, Carmen, the last to arrive, was the one to suggest it. It seemed like the right thing to do, and I have always been a sucker for a ceremony.

On a much bleaker day in early November, Lena had carried the suitcase from Santorini to her parents' house in Bethesda. Just a couple of days earlier, she'd asked her mom to ship it up to the farm.

We snuck away from the group, which had now grown to include Tibby's parents and Nicky and Katherine staying in the farmhouse with Brian and Bailey. We decided to hold our ceremony in the loft of the barn, because with its shiny wooden floors and tall open space, it reminded us the most of Gilda's, the aerobics studio where our mothers met and where the old ritual had always taken place. The absence of the pants, the incorporeal presence of Tibby, didn't make it any less effective.

We stinted on no part of it. Not the candles nor the Pop-Tarts nor the Cheetos nor the tears. Bridget sang her lungs out along with Gloria Estefan. Tibby would have laughed over that. We held hands. Teenage Tibby tended to balk at that, but I knew she would want it now.

Looking around at the hopefulness in my friends' faces, I couldn't help staring behind me into the cave where we'd dwelt for the last five months, really the last two years. In my mind's eye, I tried to see these faces as they had been the first time we opened this suitcase. But then, why do that to yourself?

How did Tibby achieve these transformations? I don't know. There have always been mysteries in our friendship.

Where will we go from here? I don't know that either. Tibby's parents and sister and brother are supposed to leave on Sunday, but I'm not sure about the rest of us. I've got a little house to furnish. I've got a small girl to love. New York is close enough to drop in for an audition once or twice a week if I need to. I've got a heart that appears to have broken open. I feel hopeful where I am.

Eric is talking about switching to a New York firm, commuting three days a week so Bee can raise animals, make a vegetable garden, and grow her baby alongside Bailey in a place where she's happy.

Bridget looks older and obviously a bit rounder, but I've never seen her lovelier. Lena bought a pair of scissors and expertly cut off the matted ends of Bee's hair. Bee let me wash her hair in the sink with my most outrageously expensive shampoo and sat cross-legged and talking on my bed for hours while I combed it out.

Kostos is on leave from work. Though they won't stay here forever, I don't see him and Lena going anywhere anytime soon. "Already we're living together," Kostos said with a knowing laugh to Lena over breakfast this morning. "What would our grandparents say?"

Two days ago he disappeared in the afternoon and returned with a full-size easel for Lena, which he proudly set up for her by the northern windows in a wash of artist's light.

And in the middle of us is Bailey, joy of our hearts. It seems to me we all arrived here lost and lonely, needing something we couldn't name, pent up with love. Tibby named it. She must have known how much we had to give.

A long time ago Tibby had a friend named Bailey, for whom little Bailey is named. The first Bailey died tragically young, and her death struck Tibby hard. But I once heard Tibby say that before Bailey died she'd left Tibby everything she needed to live a happy life, if only Tibby was wise enough to take it.

And now we are the ones wisely taking what Tibby left for us. I guess you could say Tibby's magic is deep and lasting. I don't know when any of us will go.

But I know this. We're ready to move forward again in our way. Together or apart, no matter how far apart, we live in one another. We go on together.

Acknowledgments

I would like to thank Jennifer Hershey, first and foremost. I would also like to thank Jennifer Rudolph Walsh, Gina Centrello, Beverly Horowitz, Leslie Morgenstein, Josh Bank, and Jodi Anderson.

With love, I acknowledge my parents, Jane and Bill Brashares, my husband, Jacob Collins, and my children, Sam, Nate, Susannah, and the little one soon to be born.

About the Author

A lover of summer, pants, and travel, ANN BRASHARES lives in New York City with her husband and their three children. Her Sisterhood novels—*The Sisterhood of the Traveling Pants; The Second Summer of the Sisterhood; Girls in Pants: The Third Summer of the Sisterhood;* and *Forever in Blue: The Fourth Summer of the Sisterhood*—comprise an internationally bestselling, award-winning series that inspired two major motion pictures and reached #1 on the *New York Times* bestseller list. Her new stand-alone novel is *My Name Is Memory*.

About the Type

This book was set in Sabon, a typeface designed by the well-known German typographer Jan Tschichold (1902–1974). Sabon's design is based upon the original letter forms of Claude Garamond and was created specifically to be used for three sources: foundry type for hand composition, Linotype, and Monotype. Tschichold named his typeface for the famous Frankfurt typefounder Jacques Sabon, who died in 1580.